Giff backed her up against the door,

his solid hips blocking her.

He'd caught a glimpse of tinted windows, could hear the low hum of the powerful engine over the drum of his own pulse. "They're still there, maybe watching. Kiss me back."

In the glow of the light left burning over the back door, Roxie watched his head bend to her and his lips part as they settled on hers. He was more gentle this time, but not much. In moments, he made it impossible for her to think about the danger they might be in.

This was just for show, she told herself. He was kissing her so that Sam or whoever was in the car would leave, thinking they'd interrupted two lovers. Giff Jacobs or Jake Garrison—or whoever he was—was a man she didn't know and certainly didn't want to.

Only her heart wouldn't listen.

Dear Reader,

The year may be winding to a close, but here at Intimate Moments the excitement hasn't waned. We've got some of your favorite authors—several of them award-winners—for you this month, as well as another of the talented newcomers we've been bringing your way in recent months.

Marie Ferrarella offers *Callaghan's Way*, featuring American Hero Kirk Callaghan. Back in town after a long absence, he runs smack into childhood friend Rachel Reed—and her irresistible young son. In *A Soldier's Heart*, Kathleen Korbel proves once again why she's known as one of the genre's most powerful writers. There's just no way to read one of her books without identifying completely with her perfectly drawn characters.

Round out the month with *Scarlet Whispers*, by Diana Whitney, a tale of small-town secrets and steamy passions; *Fugitive Father*, by Carla Cassidy, a top-notch secret-baby story; and Pat Warren's *Only the Lonely*, featuring Giff Jacobs's quest for revenge and the woman who crosses his path at just the wrong—or is it the right?—time. Finally, there's that new author I promised you. Her name is Elizabeth Sinclair, and in *Jenny's Castle* she makes a debut I think you'll really enjoy.

And don't forget to come back next month, when we'll be bringing you more of the terrific love stories you've come to expect from Silhouette Intimate Moments.

Enjoy!

Leslie Wainger
Senior Editor and Editorial Coordinator

Please address questions and book requests to:
Silhouette Reader Service
U.S.: 3010 Walden Ave., P.O. Box 1325, Buffalo, NY 14269
Canadian: P.O. Box 609, Fort Erie, Ont. L2A 5X3

ONLY THE LONELY

Pat Warren

Published by Silhouette Books
America's Publisher of Contemporary Romance

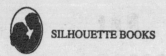 SILHOUETTE BOOKS

ISBN 0-373-07605-3

ONLY THE LONELY

This edition published by arrangement with Harlequin Enterprises B. V.

® and TM are trademarks of Harlequin Enterprises B. V., used under
license. Trademarks indicated with ® are registered in the United States
Patent and Trademark Office, the Canadian Trade Marks Office and in
other countries.

Printed in U.S.A.

PAT WARREN,

mother of four, lives in Arizona with her travel-agent husband and a lazy white cat. She's a former newspaper columnist whose lifetime dream was to become a novelist. A strong romantic streak, a sense of humor and a keen interest in developing relationships led her to try romance novels, with which she feels very much at home.

To Jane Kidder,
whose terrific sense of humor
is exceeded only by her
wonderful talent

Chapter 1

He looked dangerous, Roxie thought. The subject of her reflections was the tall man following Trevor Ames, her restaurant's manager, into her office.

"Miss Lowell," Trevor said in his proper British accent, "this is Giff Jacobs, the gentleman who's applied for the bartender position." The look Trevor gave her as he set the application form on her desk told her he thought the man was anything but a gentleman. He swung about to face the other man. "Miss Lowell is in charge of the hiring for the Eagle's Nest," he explained, his gray eyes cool.

As Trevor withdrew, Roxie reached out her hand to Giff, having been taught by her father that often much could be learned from a handshake. Giff Jacobs stared at her hand as if surprised by the gesture, then enclosed it in his own. His fingers were long, calloused and very strong, as if he used them a lot and worked them hard. Not the usual bartender's hands, she thought as he gripped her fingers and held on a fraction longer than she thought necessary. "Have a seat, please."

Giff settled his rangy frame into the chair opposite her desk and decided there was a hell of a difference shaking hands with a woman than with a man. Her skin was soft, cool, her bone structure almost delicate. Of course, the fact that he hadn't touched a woman in over three years might have added to his unnerving reaction to a simple handshake.

Then he took a deep breath and found her scent even more disturbing. That was one of the things he'd missed most, the way a woman smelled. At first, he'd lain on his bunk nights, trying to conjure up the remembered fragrances. But he'd soon learned that that was a short route to madness. So he'd schooled himself to stop recalling, stop thinking too much, stop feeling altogether.

However, in the first minute of being enclosed in the small office with this woman, the sight and scent of her was leading him down a path he no longer wanted to walk. She was a looker, as Luther would have said, with her huge brown eyes and long blond hair pulled back and tucked into a gold clip at her nape. She wore a plain white blouse and, as he'd noticed when he'd walked in and she'd stood up briefly, a slim black skirt. A simple working-woman outfit that she somehow managed to make appear enticingly feminine. Or was it his own abstinence that made it seem so? Giff was willing to bet that her legs were slender, shapely and long enough to make a strong man weak.

Any man but him. This man wasn't in the market.

Roxie noticed that despite his casual slouch, there was an alertness about Giff Jacobs, as if he was ready to leap up at a moment's notice. He wasn't handsome, not by any conventional yardstick. Oh, he was broad-shouldered and slim-hipped, but there it ended. His black hair was cut poorly and quite short. His face was lean, angular and very tan. His mouth was nicely shaped, but he looked as if he didn't know how to smile . . . or had forgotten how. His eyes, a piercing, unfriendly blue, had a haunted quality.

Those same eyes were quietly assessing her with an unmistakable intelligence, as well. Roxie had the feeling she'd been judged and found wanting in some way. She cleared her throat and picked up her pen. She always thought better with something in her hands.

"Trevor tells me you mix drinks better than anyone he's interviewed," she began. "Where'd you learn?"

Giff glanced at the application, wondering why she hadn't bothered to read it, then back at her face. He liked her voice, though he was trying not to. He didn't want to like anything about her. She was a means to an end, he reminded himself. "I worked my way through college, first as a waiter, then as a bartender. I enjoy it."

His voice was deep and smoky, as if rusty from not being used much. She found that odd since most bartenders tended to be chatty. She skimmed the form in front of her and learned he was thirty-four which meant he'd been out of college for about twelve years. A man with a degree who preferred bartending to a more conventional profession. She had a feeling there were a few things he'd left off of his application.

"Ever since your school days, you've worked at Tony's Bar and Grille in Tucson?" she asked.

Giff crossed his long legs. "You can call Tony if you like and check me out. I wrote down the number."

"Thank you. I will."

She was the careful type, and Giff didn't blame her. But Tony would cover for him. He did enjoy bartending, but not enough to make it his life's work. He'd found his real vocation when he'd attended the police academy after college, then joined the Tucson Police Department. He'd worked his way up to the rank of detective before the incident that had changed his life had occurred.

Incident. A hell of a word for something that had stolen three years of his life, his pride and his self-esteem.

He appeared to be answering direct questions when, in fact, he was actually being evasive, Roxie concluded. Where had he learned to be so cagey? His black shirt and tan slacks looked new, but not of good quality. Perhaps he'd fallen on hard times. Everyone had their problems, their secrets. She had a few of her own. One thing was obvious: with this man behind the bar, there'd be less chance of any rough stuff, such as the fight that had broken out last week between two men over a woman.

Basically, the Eagle's Nest was an upscale restaurant in a quiet section of Scottsdale, a business that had been in her family for years. But times had changed and their once-sedate clientele had evolved into an eclectic mix. It wouldn't hurt to have someone on hand who most people would think twice about going up against.

Still, before offering him the job, she wanted to know more about Giff Jacobs. "What made you move up from Tucson?"

He shrugged. "I hear that change is good for the soul."

A nice, evasive answer. "Do you have family here?"

"No." He could see she wasn't convinced she should hire him. He couldn't blame her. He was obviously not the sort who usually applied for work in the Eagle's Nest. Not if that snooty manager was any indication. He needed this job, not for the money, but for personal reasons. But he wouldn't beg. If she turned him down, he'd find another way of getting what he wanted.

He shifted his eyes from her, letting her look over his application, and glanced around her compact office. Nicely paneled walls, oak desk and filing cabinet, computer, fax machine. Very efficient, not conspicuously feminine, yet he could spot the warmth of a woman's touch everywhere. The photo of an older couple in a silver frame on her desk. The three yellow roses in a slender vase. The roadrunner glass-catcher hanging on her window as the warm October Arizona sun shone in.

And plants everywhere—a ficus in the corner, African violets on the wide windowsill, a Wandering Jew trailing down from atop the bookcase.

"You like working in a greenhouse?"

She answered without looking up from the form she was studying. "I like living things."

Giff wondered what her partner's office looked like.

"You've listed no home address or phone number," she said.

"I intend to look for a place nearby. I prefer to live close to where I work." He liked to walk, to be out in the open air. After the way he'd lived for three years, he craved light and space. He was glad the bar at the Eagle's Nest had a skylight and several arched windows that looked out on a fenced cactus garden.

Shifting his weight, he wished she'd make up her mind about hiring him.

Roxie lay down her pen and leaned forward. "You're not what I expected when Trevor first told me about you." Of course, Trevor, a man in his late fifties who'd never married, sometimes reminded her of someone's maiden aunt with his fussy ways. From Trevor's unflattering description, she'd expected a rough-and-tumble character straight out of a B-western. Instead, she was facing Eliot Ness who seemed reluctant to reveal more than his name, rank and serial number.

"You're not exactly what I expected, either," he said almost lazily, his eyes roaming down to her breasts and back up again. "Most women who run bars aren't quite so...refined."

Temper flashed in her eyes, then abated. She supposed he meant that as a compliment, but she needed to straighten him out, anyhow. "The Eagle's Nest isn't a bar. It's a very reputable eating establishment that happens to have a bar."

"Don't take offense. I've met some fine people in bars, and some not so nice people who've never been in one."

He had a point. "The bartender's job involves shift work. Right now, we'd want you on nights. Six in the evening until two, then cleanup and lockup."

"I don't have a problem with that."

"There is one thing. If you have a problem working for a woman, I need to know now."

"I thought you had a partner."

Apparently, he'd heard the rumors, probably from his previous employer. The restaurant-bar business had its gossip mills like every other line of work. "Sam Farrell isn't a partner. He's the new owner. When Sam took over the Eagle's Nest, I agreed to stay on and manage the personnel as well as oversee the catering operation. For a while." A stipulation that galled Roxie to the bone, yet she'd had no choice but to agree to Sam's demand. But she didn't have to like it—or him.

Giff noticed that she had a guarded look the moment they'd begun talking about Sam Farrell. So they weren't partners, at least not in the restaurant. Were they partners outside the business?

"You'd answer only to me. Some men have trouble working for a woman. Do you?"

He wasn't crazy about the idea, but it wasn't for reasons she might think. It was more because things might get a little hairy and he wouldn't want her to get hurt. She seemed bright enough, but how innocent was she? Giff knew from firsthand experience that it didn't take much to convince even a seemingly loyal woman to take the easy way out if it meant she'd be improving her life. He'd learned his lessons about women the hard way. If Roxie Lowell was involved up to her pretty eyebrows, he'd take her down without a moment's hesitation.

"I'm not sexist, if that's what you mean," he said.

"Good, then we'll get along."

"Of course, I'd have to be dead not to notice you're a female, but if it doesn't bother you, it won't bother me."

She raised an eyebrow slowly. After years in a tough business, Roxie knew how to ward off an unwanted advance or discourage suggestive remarks. What he'd just said didn't fit into either category, yet it disturbed her.

Giff saw the sudden new concern on her face and sat up straighter. "Listen, I'm a good bartender. I don't drink, and I don't skim the profits. Why don't you hire me on a trial basis? You won't be sorry."

Her eyes darkened as she took his measure. "We have mostly female waitresses and kitchen help. How do I know you won't bother them?"

He was getting annoyed and trying not to show it. "You don't. You'll have to take my word for it. I have no interest in women."

At that, she raised both eyebrows and stared at him.

He cleared his throat. "Let me rephrase that. If I want a woman, I'll find one, but she won't be someone from here."

"Good. I fired the last headwaiter who felt otherwise." To give herself a moment, she picked up his application again, and pretended to look it over more thoroughly.

Roxie Lowell knew the restaurant business. She'd started working in the family restaurant while still in high school, learning all facets of it from the ground up. She'd taken time out only for college and a brief, disastrous marriage and divorce, then had gone right back to the long hours and unrelenting demands. Not long ago, she'd realized she was burned-out and had decided to make a change.

That's when circumstances beyond her control had forced her to keep at it a while longer. Her one consolation was that she felt she was good at what she did, especially in judging the character of the people she hired. She was certain there was more to Giff Jacobs than his vague résumé revealed. But Roxie believed in going with her instincts and, although there wasn't a shred of warmth emanating from him, her gut reaction was to give him a chance to prove himself.

She looked up to find his cool blue gaze studying her. "Trevor's already explained the pay scale, which I assume is satisfactory to you. He'll also give you a key. Maybe today you ought to come in an hour early so Ronnie, the day bartender, can show you the ropes." She gave him a smile. "Welcome aboard."

His hard mouth didn't return her smile, but the coolness had left his eyes. "I'm hired?"

"Yes. Isn't that what you wanted?"

"Yeah." He ran his long fingers over his short hair in a gesture that was so natural it was probably a lifetime habit. "About your partner. I mean, the new owner. How much will I have to do with him?" He couched his question in nonchalance, but he very much wanted to know.

Giff knew more about Sam Farrell than Roxie would guess, though he'd seen him only briefly well over three years ago. He'd spent those years thinking about the day he'd find Sam, and now that he had, he could be patient. One of the first things he wanted to know was if Sam was using Roxie Lowell or if she was involved with him, romantically or financially.

"Sam handles the ordering of food, liquor and supplies, and oversees the restaurant as an on-premises host." The latter was something that annoyed her greatly since that had always been her father's role. But then, a great deal about Sam annoyed her. "As I said earlier, you'd answer only to me. You should have very little to do with him." She stood, but didn't offer her hand again.

"Thanks." Giff rose and checked his watch. A little after noon. He'd have just enough time to find a place to stay before his night shift began. He didn't need much. He'd made do for quite a while in a room smaller than Roxie's office.

As he turned to the door, he heard the sound of off-key whistling and a quick knock. The door opened.

"Roxie, got a minute?" Sam Farrell asked, then noticed that she wasn't alone. "Oh, sorry."

Roxie stepped around her desk. "Come in and meet Giff Jacobs, our new bartender. Giff, this is Sam Farrell."

Farrell had a slim, wiry build and was a good six inches shorter than Giff's own six feet. His dark, curly hair touched his collar, and his eyes behind wire-rimmed glasses were almost black. Apparently, he thought himself a natty dresser in his pin-striped suit and bow tie. But the most important thing Giff noticed was that Sam's face reflected not a hint of recognition.

Sam reached out his hand. "Glad to have you with us. I've been filling in at the bar, and I don't know a gin fizz from a wine spritzer."

Giff shook the owner's hand, aware that though Sam wasn't large, there was strength there.

"Giff starts tonight, so you're off the hook. What was it you wanted?" Roxie said.

"Have you got next week's waitress schedule finished yet?" Sam asked. "Trevor's run into a problem."

Roxie reached for a sheet on her desk and handed it to him. "Here you go."

Sam took the schedule, his tan fingers stroking hers as if by accident. He smiled at her. "Thanks. See you both later."

She hadn't returned the light caress, but she hadn't brushed him off, either, Giff noted. If they were just business associates, and only recent ones at that, would she have allowed the gesture?

Roxie, suddenly able to observe Giff more closely, noticed that he had a scar on the left side of his chin that added to his dangerous look. She also saw how he watched Sam's departure with what seemed like more than casual interest. "Do you know Sam?"

Giff swung back, his face expressionless. "No, we've never met," he answered honestly. "Tell me something. Why'd you hire me without checking my references?"

"I'm going to call as soon as you leave. If you don't check out, you won't start."

She wasn't as trusting or as naive as he'd thought. Then, because he'd made a bet with himself, he dropped his gaze and found her legs as incredibly long as he'd imagined. And gorgeous. Not that he cared, one way or the other. He glanced up and saw her questioning look.

"Is something the matter?" Roxie asked, unnerved at being given the once-over by those hot, hungry eyes.

He allowed himself the faintest of smiles. "Not a thing. I'll be back around five."

One large suitcase and two boxes. That was all he had to haul out of his ancient Bug and carry up two flights of stairs to the furnished loft apartment he'd rented three blocks from the Eagle's Nest on a side street with the whimsical name of Via de Amigo. Giff hoped the name would turn out to be prophetic. Though he wasn't out to make friends, he certainly didn't need any more enemies.

"Can I give you a hand, son?" Clarence Dowd asked as Giff walked up the porch stairs carrying the second load.

"Thanks, but I can manage, Clarence."

The landlord was a white-haired retiree somewhere in his seventies whose wife had died last year and who, Giff mused, looked like the grandfather he wished he'd had. Clarence spent most of his time puttering around his large backyard rock garden and the rest sitting on his enclosed porch talking to his green parakeet named Bette Davis. "On account of her big eyes, don't you know?" Clarence had explained. Giff decided that Clarence seemed the sort who'd mind his own business, which is why he'd moved in upstairs.

Inside his new apartment, he set the box down on the kitchen counter and looked around. Leaded glass windows cranked open onto a huge palm tree that swayed in a light breeze. The house was old but well built, the apartment small but compact. The furniture was best described as early marriage, a hodgepodge of colors and woods and fabrics. Giff couldn't have cared less. It was spotlessly clean, airy and comfortable.

And it was private.

Lord, how he'd longed for that. That had been one of the hardest things to give up, to get used to. People always there, in your space, in your face. The noises, the lights, the intrusions. He shuddered, then clicked off the memories. There was no point in dwelling on the past.

There *was* a point in finding the person who'd ruined his life.

Methodically, he put away his few things, then quickly made a list of what else he'd need. Sheets, towels, a few kitchen items. His new job included dinner, so he wouldn't need many groceries, which was good since money was in short supply. Finishing, he reached for the phone, still in place from the former tenant.

He had an important call to make now that he was settled. Someone he had to look up, to meet with. He hated needing anyone's help, but he'd come to realize he did. With a little assistance, he'd even the score. Then he'd probably spend the rest of his life paying back the people who'd helped him. There were only a couple, but he would owe them plenty.

It would take him years, but it would be worth it.

In her office, Roxie thoughtfully hung up the phone. Tony Garrison, the owner of Tony's Bar and Grille in Tucson, had answered all her questions and recommended Giff Jacobs highly. When she'd asked how long he'd known Giff, Tony had laughed and said it seemed like forever. It appeared that they were good friends, so it would follow that the man would give Giff a glowing recommendation. Still, he'd substantiated everything Giff had put on his application.

Why, then, did she have an uneasy feeling that both men were leaving something unsaid?

Setting Giff's file aside, she decided she'd let him start tonight, but she'd keep an eye on him. Perhaps she was being overly cautious. Picking up her catering order, she left her office and headed for the kitchen.

"I was just about to look for you," Trevor said as she entered. He held up a copy of the order. "Is this number of guests a three or a five? We can't make it out."

Roxie leaned down and checked. "It's a five. There'll be forty-*five* people at the Scottsdale writers' banquet tonight." It was a group that the Eagle's Nest had catered to for several years, covering their monthly meetings held in a nearby rented hall as well as occasional larger functions such as the one this evening.

Patrick, the head chef, glanced over. "I thought so, but I wasn't sure." He pointed to the crême caramels clustered in two large stainless-steel containers. "All set to go. The rest is already packed."

"Great, Patrick. Let's go over the entire menu, just to be sure." She bent to her list and went over each item with him. Satisfied, she nodded her approval. "Wonderful job, as always. The dinner's scheduled for six so you can start loading the truck any time." Leaving the kitchen, she noticed that Trevor had waited for her. "Do you need me for something?"

"Not really." Trevor tugged on the ends of his neat, black vest. "I guess you hired that bartender."

Roxie stopped in the hallway leading to the offices. "Yes. He said he'd be back around five so Ronnie can show him the ropes. Would you give him a key, please?"

"Certainly," Trevor answered, but not before a look of resigned distaste fleetingly crossed his face.

"You don't approve?" she asked, wondering just why she should care. Trevor Ames had been with the Eagle's Nest from the first day her parents had reopened the restaurant at its new location after a fire had burned down the original. That had been seventeen years ago when Roxie had been twelve. She honestly liked Trevor, but she could count the number of people he approved of on the fingers of one hand.

Trevor ran manicured fingers over his thinning, sandy hair, pausing as if debating whether to speak out. "He's a ruffian, Roxie. I don't believe your father would have hired him."

Roxie sighed, hating the reminder. "Perhaps not, but my father's dead, Trevor." And, though she couldn't bring herself to blame Henry Lowell, she had to admit he had left her with a terrible mess. "I'm doing the best I can, and I believe Giff Jacobs will work out."

Trevor looked contrite. "It wasn't a criticism, but rather concern. He's . . . well, he's not *our kind of people.*"

She nearly groaned aloud. "Lord, Trevor, I don't even know what that means. We're hiring him to tend bar, not to lead us in prayer. We need someone who can handle things if someone gets drunk or disorderly, like that incident we had recently."

"I suppose you're right." Trevor's eyes softened. "I just don't want you to have more problems."

Roxie knew he didn't have full knowledge of her problems, but it was sweet of him to worry about her. With no family of his own, she supposed Trevor had transferred his need to stew over someone to the Lowells. She touched his arm lightly. "Thank you, but you worry too much."

Once he'd gotten started, Trevor found it difficult to stop. "I'd like to see you happy, and I know you're not. You work too hard, and you're much too thin."

"She is not," Sam said as he stepped out of his office, obviously having overheard. His eyes roamed the length of her, admiring the pale peach-colored suit she wore. "She looks wonderful."

Roxie made it a point to go home for a couple of hours every afternoon, to change clothes and freshen up before returning for the dinner crowd. She wasn't quite sure why, but compliments from Sam always made her uneasy. Maybe because they overstepped the bounds of the awkward business relationship they had. More than once in their three-month alliance, Sam had broadly hinted that he'd like to spend time with her away from the restaurant.

But she had no interest in a personal relationship with Sam Farrell.

"Of course she looks wonderful," Trevor said, saving Roxie from having to respond to Sam. "But I stand by my earlier statement. She works too many hours."

"I like to keep busy," Roxie explained vaguely.

Trevor straightened his tie. "Yes, well, I, too, must get to work." Moving past her, he made his way to the dining room.

Sam removed his glasses and placed them in his breast pocket. "So you hired the so-called ruffian."

Roxie shook her head. "Not you, too?"

Sam laughed. "I think he's just what we need. I don't want to see another brawl in this place. Bad for business."

"Exactly. Glad you agree." She moved as if to pass him, but he caught her hand.

"You do work too hard. Why don't we skip out tonight, have dinner somewhere quiet, just the two of us?"

Roxie felt herself stiffen. She wasn't by nature a rude person, but it was difficult enough working with Sam under the circumstances. A cool friendliness was all she was willing to give. "Look, Sam, we've been over this. I don't get involved with people at work."

Sam's dark eyes narrowed. "I'm not exactly the hired help. I own the place, remember?"

Roxie pulled her hand free. "Oh, I remember, all right." She still couldn't believe he did, couldn't believe what her father had done. Of course, Henry Lowell hadn't known he'd have a fatal heart attack at fifty-five. "You'll have to excuse me. I have work to do."

Turning, she walked to her own office and closed the door.

Chapter 2

Giff walked along the winding path that bordered the small man-made lake that was the focal point of Hayden Road Park. The October temperature was in the eighties, drawing out the tenants from the several apartment buildings nearby. He passed two small children launching a sailboat under the watchful eye of their mother, while farther along, an old man sat on the grassy bank fishing. Scooting out of the way of a bicyclist, he rounded the bend and saw the man he'd come to meet seated on a park bench.

Detective Neil Kingston had moved from Tucson to Scottsdale and joined its police department right after Giff had been ousted. Giff and Neil had grown up together and become cops the same year. Giff had been best man at Neil's wedding. Other than Giff's brother, Neil had been the only one who'd stuck by him through all his troubles, who hadn't turned against him.

Neil saw him approach and removed his ever-present pipe from his mouth as he waved him over. Average was the word for Neil's looks, which was only one reason he was such a good undercover cop. Of medium height with brown hair and eyes, and no distinguishing features, Neil blended well into any crowd. Unless you were discerning enough to look beneath the surface and notice the predatory alertness that characterized men of his breed. Men like Giff himself.

Giff sat down and dredged up what passed for a smile these days, then slowly stretched out his hand.

Neil gripped Giff's hand in a firm shake. "Long time no see, pal. You sure look different without your beard. You're also a little leaner, a lot tanner."

"Three years working outside will do that to a man," Giff answered. "I needed to make a change. Different name, different look." He propped his left ankle on his right knee and looked Neil over. His friend was considerably grayer, though they were both in their mid-thirties. Men in Neil's line of work often aged early. He wore a sports coat over jeans and his running shoes were a bit scuffed. He was a sight for sore eyes and probably the only friend Giff had left, outside of his brother. "I wasn't sure you'd want to meet with me."

Neil angled his body around. "Why's that?"

Giff shrugged, feigning a nonchalance he was far from feeling. "I was down in Tucson. Found out that Phil quit the force and no one's seen him in over a year."

"So you figured I'd run out on you, too?"

Giff gazed out at three white ducks way out in the water. "When you've been through what I have, it's damn hard to know who your friends are." He hadn't kept in touch, hadn't felt like writing. Now he wondered if that had been a mistake. A lot can change in three years.

Neil pocketed his unlit pipe. "Then let me lay it out for you. We go back a long way, but that's not all of it. I happen to believe you were set up, and I'm willing to help you any way I can. You can trust me."

Letting out a jagged breath, Giff nodded. If Neil hadn't come through, he didn't know what he would have done. He didn't have a lot of options.

"So what else did you learn in Tucson?" Neil asked.

"Tony told me he'd heard that Sam Farrell bought into the Eagle's Nest a couple of months ago after keeping a low profile for some time. Turns out he owns it. Previous owner died, but his daughter's staying on, helping Sam run the place."

"You think he's going to set up the same operation he was part of in Tucson?"

"That'd be my guess. I got a job there bartending. I start tonight."

"You saw Sam, and he didn't recognize you?" Neil raised his hand, answering his own question. "I'm not surprised. I'm not sure I could have picked you out of a crowd."

"At the most, he caught a very fast glimpse of me that night. There were pictures in the paper, but clean-shaven makes a big difference. I'm sure he didn't make me."

Neil frowned. "You'd better keep your nose clean. He may only be the front man, but he's no Sunday school teacher."

A muscle twitched in Giff's jaw as he remembered. "I want the top man, the one who shot me. And I want the one who set me up, the SOB who ruined my life."

"I suppose it's stupid of me to ask, but we haven't exactly kept in touch so I wouldn't know... Did you look up Carla when you were in Tucson?"

Giff struggled to keep from balling his hands into fists. "She cut during the trial. I have no idea where she is."

"So what's your plan, or do you have one?"

"I wanted the job so I could watch Sam. I want to see who his friends are, how the business is run, if it's clean."

"What about the girl, the former owner's daughter?"

"I don't know yet. I just met her. If she's involved, we take her, too."

Giff had been hard before, Neil thought, but now he was hard, mean and bitter. A lethal combination. He would bear keeping an eye on. "What can I do to help?"

"First, run a check on Sam Farrell, see if he's been in any trouble since . . . since our last encounter. I want to know if he's had so much as a parking ticket. Then, nose around and try to find out how much he invested in the Eagle's Nest and where the money came from. And if he's got any silent partners. I can't figure why he'd want to buy into the place when he wouldn't have had to. Last time, he just got a job there and used the restaurant as a base of operation. And why the Eagle's Nest? Were they in trouble financially?"

Neil made notes in a small notebook he always carried. "Could be the former owner was shady, or maybe the daughter."

"Yeah, right. His name was Henry Lowell and the daughter's name is Roxie. There's a hard-nosed manager named Trevor Ames. Probably too uptight to be involved, but you ought to check him out, too. I don't like surprises."

"Got it. Anything else?"

"I rented a place a couple of blocks from the restaurant." He handed Neil a slip of paper. "Here's the address and phone number. I got an answering machine today so you can leave a message. And I'll check in with you when I can."

Neil put away his notebook and stood. "Give me a couple of days."

Giff got to his feet, realizing he'd been pretty self-involved. "How's your family?"

"Lisa's still teaching school, and the boys are fine." Neil put his pipe back between his lips.

Giff nodded, started to walk away, then turned back. "Neil?" He waited until his friend met his gaze. "Thanks." The word covered far more than today's offer of help.

Neil knew it. "I'll be in touch."

The crowd was kind of thin for a Thursday night, Giff thought as he stood behind the bar dunking a beer mug in soapy water, shoving it through the brushes, then rinsing it.

At nine o'clock, there were only a dozen people, most of them nursing their drinks, in a room that easily held forty including bar seats. However, the dining room served meals until ten, and perhaps some folks would wander in for after-dinner drinks.

The room itself was interesting, the walls paneled in rough planking and a huge eagle with about an eight-foot wingspan positioned above the bar. The center section of the roof was skylight from which hung heavy fishnetting. Strategically placed within its folds were pots holding a variety of cactus plants from prickly pear to small barrels, adding to the desert atmosphere. Giff liked the ambiance and wondered if Roxie had had a hand in the decorating.

The two waitresses were typical of most bars. Tammy was working her way through college, still in her second year at twenty-three. Ginny was a single parent supporting a twelve-year-old she'd labeled incorrigible. She'd confided to Giff that the boy needed a strong father figure and she needed a husband so she could quit working and be home with him. He wished her luck.

He saw Roxie enter through the arched doorway and stop at a booth to chat with an older couple who appeared to be either friends or regulars, judging by the warmth of her welcome. Giff had to admit that she had a really nice smile. He wondered if there was one special someone who waited for that smile. It had been a long while since he'd conjectured about a woman, but he did so now, for more reasons than the obvious.

She'd changed into a silk suit that made her look even more feminine. Her hair was loose, worn to a length just below her shoulders, with feathery bangs drifting onto her forehead. As she stood talking, she twisted a silver ring worn on her right hand that looked to have engravings. He wondered who'd given it to her. He watched her turn from the booth and stroll toward his end of the bar, looking as fresh as if she hadn't already put in a very long day. Her walk was unconsciously sensual, but it had him tightening nonetheless.

"How are you making out?" Roxie asked, noticing that the bar looked well tended and clean.

"Just fine. Not real busy."

"It'll pick up after the diners clear out."

Idly, he polished a glass. "I'm surprised your bar's open till two every night. Most places attached to restaurants close when they do."

A frown skittered across her face. That innovation had been Sam's idea, and Roxie still didn't like it. After eleven, when they were left with a mostly serious drinking group, was when trouble was apt to flair up. If they hadn't needed the money, she would have objected more strenuously. "We're trying out the new hours. The bar gets pretty crowded, especially on Friday and Saturday nights."

He hadn't missed the frown and wondered at its source. "Can I make you something to drink?"

"No, thanks." Turning, she surveyed the room in time to see Sam briskly heading her way, that irritating whistle preceding him. Automatically, she braced herself.

Stopping only to give a quick pat on the back to two men seated at a small table, Sam reached her side and slipped an arm around her waist, turning his back to Giff. "My offer still holds," he said, his voice low and intimate.

She couldn't pull away without her efforts to extricate herself from Sam being obvious to several patrons as well as Giff, who was watching with veiled interest. However, her eyes on Sam's were frosty. "As I said before, I'm busy. But thanks, anyway."

"A rain check?"

It was all she could do not to slap him for this public persistence. "Of course," she said, even managing a smile.

"Great. Listen, I've run into a couple of friends just finishing dinner. I'd rather have gone out with you, but they've asked me to their place for a while."

Stepping aside, she felt relief. "By all means, please, go."

Sam seemed unaware of her eagerness to have him leave. "I'll ask Trevor to lock up."

"Don't bother. I'll stay and show Giff the procedure."

Sam raised a questioning eyebrow at her.

"So he'll be able to close up on nights when we're not available."

Sam's eyes slid to Giff who was busily filling an order for Tammy. "Right. See you tomorrow." He left, though his step wasn't as bouncy as when he'd come in.

Maybe tomorrow, Roxie thought as she walked toward her office, she'd tell Sam once and for all that there was nothing between them and never would be, that she'd appreciate it if he'd back off. He was definitely getting on her nerves.

Handing the bar bill to Tammy, Giff frowned as he watched Roxie leave the room. He hadn't been able to overhear what they'd said, but he'd sensed some tension between her and Sam. Again, the man had casually slipped his arm around her and she hadn't moved away, as if the gesture was mutually desirable. Giff felt oddly disappointed that she was apparently involved with Sam, then steeled himself to remember why he was here.

If she was dumb enough to fall for that crook, she deserved whatever happened. She'd appeared honest and straightforward at first meeting. But hadn't he learned some time ago that women could fake outward appearances far better than men? And the women who'd taught him hadn't had loyalty as their strong suit, either.

He wished he could leave the bar unobtrusively and stroll over to the restaurant side to see who Sam was apparently rushing off to meet. But he couldn't risk being that obvious his first night on.

Ginny interrupted his musings to give him an order. Measuring liquor into the blender, Giff wondered how deeply Roxie was mixed up with Sam, if she knew anything about the man's past. And he wondered if she'd switch sides if the wind shifted. He'd known plenty who had.

His mind drifted to Carla. Carla with that ebony hair and those eyes so dark a brown they were almost black. She was just a little thing, but she'd surged with life, with fire. He'd made it to age thirty without making a fool of himself over a woman. Then he'd fallen so damn hard, so damn fast. And, for a while there, she'd acted as if he'd hung the moon. Until the day it really mattered. Then, she'd taken a hike.

"Hey, sweetie," Ginny said, leaning onto the service bar, "you daydreaming over there?"

With a start, Giff finished the order and handed her the drinks. "Sorry."

He was over her, Giff reminded himself as he wiped off the bar. Over Carla and through with women. He didn't want anyone in his life who would reawaken long-dead feelings. He needed his thoughts utterly focused on his mission.

"The only lights we leave on inside are the perimeter lamps in the restaurant, the one behind the bar and this overhead light in the back hallway." Roxie stopped at the rear entrance and turned to Giff. "Any questions?"

He pointed to the end of the hall. "Where does that door lead?"

"To our storeroom. All nonperishable food is delivered there, plus supplies and liquor. Sam and I are the only ones who have a key. If you need something, you'll have to get one of us to unlock the door."

"You don't have a built-in burglar alarm system?" He was surprised since most bars did.

Roxie let out a frustrated sigh as she led the way back into the bar area where they'd left fresh cups of coffee. "My father hadn't believed it necessary and, frankly, right now, we can't afford it." Sam didn't think alarms were necessary since they had good door locks. Why should she care? she asked herself. One day soon, she'd no longer have to worry about the Eagle's Nest.

She seemed annoyed, Giff thought, and worried. Alone with her, he decided to probe a little. He took a sip of his coffee as she slid into a booth. "How did your father die, Roxie?"

Lowering her eyes, she stared into her cup. "A massive heart attack. In my memory, he hadn't been sick a day in his life." She couldn't help adding that last comment since she could still hardly believe he'd been taken so suddenly.

"That must have been hard to handle. Are you his only child?"

Roxie nodded. "His death devastated my mother. She'd worked alongside Dad for so many years. I thought she was going to curl up and die, too."

"Does she live with you now?"

"No. She's with her sister, my Aunt Marian, in Florida. Marian's a widow, too." She'd had to get her mother away from the memories. And from the bill collectors.

In the muted light from the bar, her face looked sad. But Giff hardened his heart as he sat down opposite her. He couldn't afford to be soft toward this woman who worked closely with Sam. "So Sam Farrell happened along and offered you a buy-out?"

Her laugh had a sharp edge. "Not exactly. I had put up the restaurant for sale, through brokers and through ads." After the funeral, after she'd discovered how heavily mortgaged the place was and how little insurance her father had. "Sam answered one of my ads." He was the only one who had. Times were tough and investors few.

Only he hadn't called to offer her a buy-out.

"Sam seems like a pretty friendly guy." He watched her face closely, saw her try to keep her reaction guarded.

"The customers like him." The reticent man she'd interviewed this morning had turned into a chatterbox. Why all the questions? she wondered. Could he be "casing the joint," or had she been watching too much television? "You seem really curious about Sam. Are you sure you don't know him?"

It was his turn to look disinterested, but he was better at it than she. "As I said, we hadn't met until today. I noticed that Trevor seems to admire him."

"Yes, he does." Which she still couldn't figure out.

Giff drained his cup and zeroed in. "And you? Do you admire Sam Farrell?"

Admire wouldn't be a word she'd choose to describe her thoughts about Sam. But she didn't feel she should reveal too much to this relative stranger. "Why should how I feel about Sam matter to you?"

He shrugged. "It just seems as if you two are more than just friends." He watched heat flash in her eyes. "Are you?"

"I don't believe that's any of your business." Rising, Roxie placed her cup on the bar. "We'd better leave."

Giff followed her out the back door, feeling sure he was right, wishing he weren't. And telling himself he didn't care.

"If you're sure you can handle things," Trevor said, his voice conveying that he had serious doubts.

Giff glanced at him over his shoulder as he stocked the bar refrigerator with beer. "Yeah, no problem. I'll close up as soon as I'm finished here. It was so busy tonight, I got a little behind. I don't want to leave the place a mess for Ronnie." He bent to his task.

"Good night, then." Trevor left by the back way.

Listening, Giff heard the door lock click as he wiped his hands on a bar towel. He'd thought the finicky man would never leave. Quickly, he finished straightening the bar area, in case Trevor popped back in to check on him. He'd been working at the Eagle's Nest a week now, and this was the first night he'd been left to lock up alone.

After ten minutes, he was fairly certain Trevor wasn't coming back. He made short work of turning off the restaurant and bar lights, then moved into the back hallway. Walking to the storeroom, he removed his wallet, found the small tool he needed and stooped down to the lock. In moments, he was inside.

Cautiously, he left the door slightly ajar and, instead of turning on the overhead light, he extracted a flashlight from his back pocket. He aimed the powerful beam all around. He was in a windowless room with deep shelves built along all four sides stacked high with labeled cardboard cartons. More free-standing stainless steel shelves were back-to-back in the center of the room, also filled with a variety of cartons. There was a wall phone near the door and next to it hung a clipboard with pages of inventory attached. It looked to be a standard restaurant supply room.

Giff knew how Sam Farrell worked, knew what he was looking for. Shipments of cocaine, originating in Colombia or Guatemala, were moved up through Mexico and smuggled over the border. Arizona was a natural destination to store the stuff until Sam and the men he worked for could funnel the bundles to their distributors, probably all over the States. They used a restaurant as a front for the operation since supplies were constantly being delivered to eateries.

Twice, they'd had a lead on Sam in Tucson. They'd watched the first place—a Mexican fast-food joint called El Poco Polla—for months and finally got wind of a big delivery. Giff and Phil had been partners, staking out the place for hours. But Sam must have been warned, because the stuff never showed and Sam suddenly dropped out of sight.

It had been many months before he'd reappeared, working at a place called La Casa Vieja on the south side of Tucson. Again, they'd set up their team, tracking deliveries, watching from a surveillance van. It wouldn't have served their purpose to get Sam or the delivery guys. They wanted the man behind the smuggling operation, the kingpin.

Then had come the fateful night, the one their most reliable snitch had said would hold the mother of all deliveries, the time when the big guy was supposed to show. Only something had gone wrong. Terribly wrong.

Shaking his head to rid himself of the hateful memories, Giff stealthily moved along a row of cartons, checking each in the glow of his flashlight. Supply boxes were usually marked with the name of the manufacturer, the product code number and sometimes the date. He was searching for an unmarked box or one out of sync with the rest, with numbers out of sequence.

On the next to last shelf, he found one with no label, date or code. Before going any further, he stopped for a moment, listening carefully, but heard no sound. Then, sticking the flashlight under his arm, he dug his Swiss army knife from his pocket and silently sliced open the box top.

Large cans labeled Tomato Juice filled the box. Giff picked one up and shook it. Definitely liquid inside. He checked a few more and decided they really contained tomato juice. Unlikely that a smuggler would take a chance on ruining expensive cocaine by dunking the bag inside anything liquid, then sealing the can, boxing and shipping it. Too risky.

He replaced the box, shoving it to the back of a shelf behind an unopened carton. At the door, he listened again. Satisfied he was still alone, he left the storeroom, engaging the lock.

Nothing this time, but that didn't mean Sam was playing it legit. Giff was convinced that leopards never changed their spots. He'd wait and see. After all, he was a patient man. He'd had to learn to be.

Quickly, he went outside to the deserted parking lot and locked that door, then set out to walk the few blocks to his apartment. It was a beautiful, clear, star-filled night and he breathed in the clean air.

As soon as he'd cleared the lot, he was strolling down a residential street. Although it was past two in the morning, some houses still had lights shining through their windows. A lot of people had trouble sleeping. Giff could relate.

He'd never needed much sleep, which had served him well on the many stakeouts he'd been involved in, as well as the frequent middle-of-the-night calls he'd gotten when he'd had to move into action on one of the cases he and Phil were following. They'd worked well together.

What the hell had happened to make Phil turn against him?

Giff heard the echo of his footsteps on the concrete and decided that the subject of Phil was one he couldn't allow himself to dwell on. The list was getting longer.

Tonight hadn't borne fruit, but he hadn't really expected it to at first try. He'd keep checking the storeroom and keep an eye on Sam. And the lovely lady who worked with him or for him or whatever. Roxie Lowell puzzled him. It looked as if she'd come from money, yet the restaurant was run as if they had to pinch pennies. He'd heard her say she had a condo nearby. He'd have to look up her address and drive by, see what kind of place she lived in. Maybe that would tell him a little about who and what she was.

Not because he was personally interested. Women only clouded a man's mind, especially a man with a goal. But he needed to know if he had two people to watch carefully, or one. She and Sam seemed a shade too friendly for business associates of a short acquaintance. And, though Giff didn't consider himself a great judge of women, Sam didn't seem her type.

Carla hadn't been his type, either. His brother had certainly told him that often enough. But he hadn't listened and lived to regret it. Who the hell ever listened to advice when it came to wanting someone so badly your hands shook when the person walked in the room?

Annoyed with the direction of his thoughts, Giff turned in to the driveway of his new home and walked to the back stairs. On his way up, he saw that Clarence was dozing in his easy chair on the enclosed porch, the television on. A plaid cloth was draped over Bette Davis's cage.

Unlocking his own door, Giff looked around, checking the place with eyes that missed nothing. Lifetime habits were hard to break. His caution had saved his life more than once. And, although it was unlikely anyone other than his brother and Neil knew where he was now living, he nonetheless examined each room and closet before locking the door.

It was a flimsy lock, he noted, not for the first time. Tomorrow, he'd get a dead bolt and install it. Feeling safe was vital to him. He poured a tall glass of milk, dipped his head back and drank thirstily. Without turning on a light, he walked into the bedroom, stripped down to his briefs and opened the window.

A warm October breeze rustled the high palm outside, a soothing sound. Someone had mown the lawn this evening, making the air heavy with the pungent smell of cut grass. He inhaled deeply. Crickets in the backyard chirped their endless song. Giff tossed back the coverlet and lay down on the bed.

He was comfortably tired, but not sleepy. He propped his hands under his head and drew in another deep breath.

God, it felt so good to be free.

Ankles crossed, Giff leaned back against the counter behind the bar and sipped a foamy root beer. Monday nights were slow in the restaurant and even slower in the bar. He wondered how Roxie would take to his suggestion that staying open every night except Sunday was costing more than it was bringing in. Maybe he should talk to Sam, get friendlier, win his confidence. He'd have to do something soon since he hadn't been able to catch him acting like anything other than a concerned suburban businessman. For two weeks now, Giff had checked the storeroom nearly every night, and still found nothing. Impatience gnawed at him.

Sam had steered clear of him, too, treating Giff as if he were merely a fixture behind the bar and not much else. He rarely spoke to him, unless they passed in the hallway coming and going, and then only a quick word or two. Which was fine with Giff, except it wasn't achieving his purpose.

Maybe if he pushed a little, Sam might let something slip, make a minor mistake. Unlikely, but worth a try.

It wouldn't be tonight, though, as Sam never came in on Mondays. Trevor was handling the dining room, which was almost ready to close since it was nearing ten. Only one waitress was working the barroom, and she didn't have much to do. A young couple sat at a small table by the window, deep in conversation, an older man nursed a beer at the far end of the bar and three businessmen types were rowdily downing their third round of Manhattans at a circular booth.

Ginny cleared off a recently vacated table across the room. She was pushing thirty-five and was quite friendly, which earned her good tips. She was attractive, Giff mused as he sipped, in an obvious kind of way. Her uniform shorts showed a lot of long leg, and the black blouse was buttoned tight across full breasts. But she wore too much makeup and her smile was a bit too desperate. Another lost soul looking for a fresh start.

His eyes shifted to the archway as Roxie entered, and Giff was shocked at his body's unmistakable response. He narrowed his eyes, annoyed that he'd begun to look forward to seeing her, watching for her to walk in, following her quiet movements as she greeted people she knew and smiled a welcome at newcomers. The fact that he was eager as a damn puppy for a glimpse of her worried him.

And frightened him. He couldn't afford to be dragged off his path by hormones that he'd struggled for over three long years to keep in check. Of course, that was probably why the mere sight of her sent him into overload, because of his long period of celibacy.

However, under the best of circumstances, Roxie was the wrong woman to want. First, he still didn't know if she was involved with Sam, romantically or illegally. Second, she was out of his league. He'd been by her home, an expensive condo in an area of Scottsdale known as McCormick Park. In their conversations, he'd learned she was educated, well traveled, a woman born with the proverbial silver spoon in her mouth. The fact that she now worked long hours for reasons he had yet to determine didn't change any of her past.

And he'd grown up and worked on the mean streets.

He watched her sit down with the young couple, both people smiling at her warmly. She was wearing slim dark gray slacks and an oversize silk blouse a shade lighter. As was her habit, she wore her hair down in the evening. Giff swallowed around a dry throat as Ginny came up to the bar.

"Another round for the boys in the booth," Ginny said as she reached for fresh cocktail napkins.

Giff hesitated. Most bars established rules regarding serving drinks to already intoxicated people, or heading in that direction, not only to safeguard the customers but to protect themselves from being responsible for an accident due to drunk driving. Roxie had told him that the Eagle's Nest had a policy of serving not more than three drinks an hour to each customer, which was fairly lenient. It appeared that the three men were out-of-towners, very likely staying at a nearby hotel on a business trip. They'd come in from the dining room just about an hour ago and had probably already had drinks before dinner. He had no idea if they had a rental car or would be taking a cab back to their hotel. It didn't really matter, since the house policy was clear.

"Tell them we can't serve them any more just now, Ginny. They've already passed the legal limit. Offer them coffee on the house."

Ginny sighed, knowing the news was not going to be well received, which might blow her tip. "Look, they're just having a good time."

Giff shook his head. "Sorry. Tell them about house policy."

She walked back to the booth as Giff watched. He saw that the men weren't happy, swearing colorfully about the dumb policy, claiming they weren't anywhere near drunk and that they'd be taking a cab and not driving, anyhow. They all but begged her to make an exception. Ginny glanced back at Giff's unsmiling face, then turned back and shook her head.

Picking up a towel, Giff moved down the bar polishing the surface, keeping his eye on the booth. He noticed peripherally that Roxie was also watching.

The taller man on the end became loud and obnoxious. "What the hell kind of a place is this, little lady?" he asked Ginny. "Can't a man relax with his friends?" He slipped an arm around her waist, then moved lower to pat her bottom. "Why don't you sit down with us for a while, honey? I'd rather have you than another drink, anyhow."

Ginny scooted out of his hold. "I'm sorry, sir. We're not permitted to sit with the customers."

The man scowled across the table at his friends, his voice getting thunderous. "This is one damn unfriendly place, boys. Who the hell owns this joint, anyway?"

Roxie had moved unobtrusively alongside Ginny. "I do," she said softly. "Is something the matter?"

He looked up at her, his eyes not quite focused. "Hell, yes. Why can't we get a drink? Isn't this a bar?"

"I'm sorry, sir," Roxie went on, motioning Ginny out of the way. Of all nights not to have Sam around. However, she was keenly aware that Giff was watching closely. "Bar owners have to abide by the law." She sent what she hoped was a persuasive smile at the other two, both looking equally as far-gone as their friend. "Why don't you call it a night and I'll phone for a cab?"

The tall man slapped the table with his open hand. "Don't want a damn cab. I want a drink."

"Come on, Norm," the shorter man next to him said. "Let's get out of here."

"Yeah," the third man agreed as he threw some bills on the table, "we got an early plane to catch."

But Norm wasn't giving up. He grabbed Roxie with a beefy arm and pulled her down onto his knee. "Why don't you join the party, sweetheart, and let us buy you a drink?"

Giff was out from behind the bar and beside her faster than she'd have thought humanly possible. Touching her arm, he pulled her free of the man's hold and placed her behind him, out of harm's way. "Gentlemen, your evening just ended. Ginny, call that cab."

Norm was just drunk enough to have discarded his good sense. Still, he rose to his full height quite steadily, considering his condition. "I don't like to be told what to do," he snarled at Giff, his large hands forming fists.

The man was several inches shorter than Giff, but he outweighed Giff by at least thirty pounds. However, Giff was all lean muscle and had no doubt he could easily take him. But a bar brawl was not on his agenda. He glanced at the other two and saw they were willing to be reasonable. "Why don't you take your friend and wait out front for the cab?"

"I guess you don't hear so good," Norm said just before he raised his fist, swinging up toward Giff's face.

Giff blocked the man's arm easily and braced himself. But not before Norm's other fist grazed the left side of his mouth. Giff thought it best to put an end to it. With a smooth punch, he cuffed the big man on his chin and watched him crumble and slip to the floor.

"Damn," his friend said as he scooted out of the booth. "Now look what you've done. You had no call to hit him."

Trevor picked that moment to come bustling into the bar. "What's going on here?" His pale gray eyes took in the situation. "I'm calling the police."

"No!" Giff's voice was commanding. "These gentlemen were about to leave, right?" he said, looking at the men in the booth.

"Apparently not," Trevor went on when no one moved. "I believe the police will persuade them otherwise." He started toward the phone.

"Trevor, don't." Giff's voice was hard, unyielding.

The short man scooted out of the booth. "Hey, we don't want no trouble. Alec, let's get Norm outside." He looked up at Giff. "Don't call the cops. Just a cab. Okay?"

"A cab's on its way," Ginny said.

Giff saw that Norm was coming around, rubbing his chin, then sitting up. He bent to help the man's friends get Norm out the back door, thinking the fresh air would clear his head enough so he could walk to the front and wait for the taxi.

"That was handled badly," Trevor said to Roxie, his lips a thin, disapproving line. "Giff had no business overruling me. The police should be informed when bar patrons get out of hand. Your father—"

"Isn't here." Roxie frowned at him, irritated with Trevor's constant references to the way her father had run the place. "It was handled just fine, and exactly as my father would have wanted it. We don't want the police to be called every time there's a problem, not if we can take care of the situation ourselves. Do you want the Eagle's Nest to get a reputation as a restaurant where brawls take place weekly?"

Grudgingly, he acknowledged the validity of her comment.

Roxie pushed back her hair with both hands. She had a few questions for Giff herself, but not till they were alone. The man who'd been drinking at the bar had left at the first sign of the scuffle, and she saw that the young couple who lived on her block were rising and paying their tab. "Is the restaurant empty?" she asked Trevor.

"Yes. I was about to close up."

"Please do. I'm going to close the bar, as well. It's silly to stay open on Monday nights for a few stray customers."

Trevor straightened his perfect tie. "I'm not certain Sam will agree."

"I'll handle Sam." Turning from him, she said good-night to her neighbors, then walked over to where Ginny stood by the bar. "Are you all right?"

The waitress nodded. "That Giff sure throws a mean punch."

Roxie thought so, too. "Let's call it a night, Gin. Tally up and go on home."

Pleased with the ten-dollar tip the men had left her, Ginny was ready to end her workday. Giff walked back in as she finished settling up her tabs. "Thanks for taking care of them, Giff. It's nice having you around."

"Anytime." As she left the room, he turned to Roxie. "I put all three into a cab."

He was wearing black slacks and a white shirt with the sleeves rolled up on his tan arms. His hair was growing out and looked much better than when she'd first met him two weeks ago. He wasn't disheveled or winded from his en-counter, but he had a small cut at the left-hand corner of his mouth and those intense blue eyes were wary. "Thank you. I decided to close up early. Monday nights are too slow to remain open till two."

"I agree."

"Come into my office. I have a first-aid kit. Let me put something on that cut."

Giff touched the spot gingerly. "It's fine. You don't have to bother."

She frowned impatiently at him. "Will you stop being so damn macho and come with me?"

Surprised, he followed her, fighting a smile. It seemed the cool blonde had some fire in her, after all.

Seated on the chair opposite her desk, he watched her take a cotton swab and dip one end in some pink antiseptic. Turning to him, she bent down and carefully touched it to the cut. He didn't flinch; he'd endured a whole lot worse. What he did do was breathe in her scent, something floral, something expensive, and wished he hadn't. When she stepped back, he was grateful.

Until he looked up and saw she'd leaned against her desk and was studying him with those huge brown eyes. "Thanks," he muttered.

Roxie crossed her arms over her chest. "Why were you so insistent we not call the police tonight?"

He shrugged, trying to look casual. "Wasn't necessary. We handled the guy. Why get him in trouble? He'd just had too much to drink. By the time the cab arrived, he looked as if he wished he'd stopped with one. He's going to feel like hell in the morning."

She regarded him thoughtfully, then went with her instinct. "It seemed more than that, more as if *you* didn't want the police to show up."

He thought he'd bluff it out. "Must be your imagination."

Roxie reached for his hand, turned it over, studying the calluses, the small scars, the obvious results of physical labor. "This isn't the hand of a bartender." She let go of him and waited.

She was too damn smart, Giff decided. If he lied and she found out, he'd lose his best chance to watch Sam. Maybe, if he told her just enough to satisfy her curiosity, she'd back off. He shifted in his chair and dropped his gaze, choosing his words carefully. "I left out a couple of things on my application. I used to be a bartender, but not for a while. I just got out of prison. I'm on parole and it wouldn't look good to be involved in a barroom fight."

The image came to her unbidden, this obviously proud man behind bars, trying not to let his confinement break his spirit. She struggled not to let the picture soften her too much until she knew more. "I see... Then Tony down in Tucson lied to me. And so did you." She felt a heavy disappointment at that, even as she understood his reason for not telling her the truth about his past. "I don't like liars."

Giff let out a rush of air. "Neither do I, ordinarily." Reaching into his pocket, he removed his key ring and slipped off the one to the Eagle's Nest. He'd have to find another way to track Sam's activities. He held the key out to her.

Instead of taking it, she studied his eyes. Some instinct told her she still wasn't getting the whole story. "Give me a reason not to let you go."

This time, he could answer sincerely. "I didn't do anything against the law. It involved drugs, and I was set up." He gave a short, bitter laugh. "Every guy at the state pen has the same story. It's your call."

"Why did Tony lie for you?"

This he hated to reveal, but Giff knew that if she checked around enough, she'd find out sooner or later. "He's my brother. He put up the money for my defense, but it wasn't enough. I owe him a lot."

Years of experience in the restaurant business, hiring many, firing some, had honed her intuition, and she still felt she hadn't been wrong about hiring Giff. Yet his evasiveness puzzled her. "Why didn't you go to work at Tony's after you got out? Why here?"

He kept his features even, hoping she couldn't see past his masked expression. "I need to start over, where no one knows me. A new life." Which was certainly true, but not until he cleared his name could he truly be free. "Can you understand that?"

Roxie could, and wished she were free to do the same. Somewhere else, in some other town, in some other business. Away from the memories, the worries. "Yes, I think so." She relaxed fractionally. "Put away your keys."

She'd surprised him again, not an easy thing to do. Slowly, he got to his feet and stood mere inches from her. "Just like that, you'll take me on blind faith?"

Roxie was leaning against the desk, not standing to her full five foot seven, and he seemed to tower over her. Oddly, though, despite what she'd just learned about him, she wasn't afraid of Giff Jacobs, and wondered why. She looked up and tried to pretend his nearness wasn't affecting her.

"Not exactly. I have my reasons." One day perhaps, she'd tell him. Right now, she didn't know him well enough.

Gratitude didn't come easily to Giff. And being this close to her was muddling his mind. "Whatever the reasons, thanks." He took a step back, wondering if she'd accepted his story to throw him off-balance, wondering if she'd run to Sam and tell him everything. "I think everyone's gone. I'll lock up and walk you to your car."

"That won't be necessary. I leave on my own many nights. Besides, it's not even eleven."

At the door, he swung back to her. "It doesn't get any darker. Believe me, it's a big, ugly world out there."

Maybe she should believe him. She'd be willing to bet he'd seen a great deal while he'd been locked up. And maybe before. "All right. I'll meet you at the back door."

Giff left, having glimpsed the sudden vulnerability in her eyes. Damn, but he wished he could get a handle on whether or not he could trust Roxie.

Three nights went by before Giff had a chance to check the storeroom again. He'd patiently waited until everyone had left, giving the excuse of having to stay behind to finish cleaning up. Alone at last, he picked the lock and was beaming his flashlight along the boxes at the back wall when suddenly the overhead light flashed on. Swiveling about, he turned toward the door.

"Hold it right there," Roxie said.

Giff stared in shocked surprise. In her hand, she held a Smith & Wesson .38 snub-nosed Special.

Chapter 3

"Do you know how to work that thing?" Giff asked, wondering if she'd doubled back after having left over an hour ago, or if she'd only pretended to leave and been hiding out somewhere.

"You'd better believe I do. My father got this for me quite a while ago." She held the gun steady, her eyes on his. "Would you care to explain what you're doing in here, after hours and without permission?"

Although he decided it would be unwise to look amused, he couldn't resist trying for a little levity. "I don't suppose you'd believe that the bar's out of scotch and I came in here, looking to restock?"

A look of impatience crossed her face. "Is this a game to you? Because I think you should know, this is loaded and I'm not playing. I want an answer, and I want it now."

Lowering his flashlight slowly, Giff nodded. "All right, only... could you put that thing away? I hope you don't think I'm a threat to you."

In the bright light, she searched his face and hoped she wasn't making a terrible misjudgment. "Let's go into my office. And this better be good." Roxie still held the gun as he preceded her into the hallway. She snapped off the light, locked the storeroom and followed him to her office, seating herself behind her desk. She waited until he draped his long frame into the chair opposite. "Start talking."

As Giff saw it, he had little choice but to take a chance on her. If he didn't and she decided to call the police, he'd be in parole violation, and back in prison. If she was in with Sam and he was waiting in his office to come nail Giff, it'd be all over with soon, anyhow. If she knew nothing, maybe he could salvage things.

"I didn't tell you everything. Maybe when I do, you'll understand." He saw she was listening intently. "I was an undercover cop, a detective in the Narcotics Division, Tucson Police Department. My partner, Phil Weston, and I had been working on a big drug bust for months. The smugglers were bringing cocaine over from Mexico using various restaurants for fronts, stashing the bags in supply boxes and leaving them in the storerooms until their connections picked them up. From there, they'd be shipped all over and sold on the street."

"How long ago?"

He crossed his legs. "Three and a half years."

She knew a source, could check his story easily tomorrow. "Go on."

"We had a reliable snitch who'd given us a name. The guy was fronting for the big boys, and we were watching his every move, hoping to draw out the kingpin. We were on a stakeout late at night when things came to a head. The pickup van showed up, and we thought we had our man. But things started to go wrong."

"How wrong?"

Remembering, Giff kept his eyes on his hand as it restlessly traced the seam of his slacks. "Bad. Three guys in ski masks. All hell broke loose when we stormed in. Phil got hit in the leg, and I got it in the back. But before I passed out, I saw one of them. He'd pulled off his mask to check me out, but he wasn't the one who'd shot me from behind."

"So you saw at least one face. Do you know his name?"

He looked up. "Yeah. Sam Farrell." He watched her turn as white as the papers neatly stacked on her desk. There was a long pause.

"You're certain it was Sam?"

"Absolutely." The news seemed to shock her. Nobody could be that good an actress, could they? He watched her face and saw that her quick mind had moved to the next step.

"So you came here because of Sam, because you think he's using the Eagle's Nest for...for a drug drop-off spot?" Roxie felt as if the rug had been neatly pulled out from under her. For the first time, she was glad her father wasn't alive to face this. "Is that why you were searching the storeroom?"

Giff nodded.

"Did you find anything?"

"No. But I can't believe he's gone legit."

She hadn't liked Sam from the beginning, hadn't liked the smarmy way he'd pushed himself into what had once been a family business. And she hated the way he kept trying to insinuate his way into her personal life. But she hadn't even considered the possibility that he was dishonest, much less involved in a drug-smuggling operation. Dear God. Roxie rubbed her forehead where a full-blown headache had suddenly appeared. "Have you any proof of all this?"

"My brother, Tony, knows everything. And an undercover cop here in Scottsdale. You can check my story with them."

"What about your former partner, Phil something?"

Giff shifted in his chair, the anger rising though he tried to push it back. "I don't know where he is. He quit the force some time back. He skipped out during my trial."

She frowned, puzzled. "Trial?"

"Yeah. I woke up in a prison hospital the next morning. A bag of cocaine had been planted on me. Not too many people believed I was set up. In undercover work, you make some enemies. And cops aren't paid very well, there were those who thought I was in on it, on the take. One of them was the judge."

"That's why you were in prison." She shook her head. "What a mess. I imagine you're here because you want to clear your name, to get Sam."

"Does that bother you?"

She looked at him oddly. "Why would it?" She stared for a long moment. When he didn't answer, she realized what he was thinking. "Do you believe *I* have something to do with this? You've got to be crazy. My grandfather started the original Eagle's Nest half a century ago. I'd never do anything to dishonor my family's reputation."

Giff leaned forward, trying to look past her righteous indignation. "I've watched him with you. He wants you."

She was well aware of that, but it took two. "Well, I don't want him." She tried to control a shudder, unable to imagine wanting Sam Farrell. But something else was bothering her. "How is it that Sam doesn't recognize you? If you saw him that night, didn't he see you?"

"Yeah, but a different me. I had a full mustache and beard back then. And I was using my real name."

"Which is?"

"Jake Garrison. Gifford is my mother's maiden name."

Of course. His brother was Tony Garrison, the one who owned the bar in Tucson. The pieces were falling into place. Still, tomorrow, she'd check out what he'd said. Wearily, she glanced at her watch and stood. She'd gotten more than she'd bargained for tonight. It would take her a while to digest it all. "It's nearly three in the morning. We'd better go."

He got to his feet as she came around the desk. He had to ask so he could gauge her future behavior. "Do you believe me?"

Inexplicably, she did. But she also saw doubt in his eyes. "Yes. Do you believe I'm not involved with whatever Sam may be up to?"

He wanted to. For the sake of his plan, he had to trust her. "Yes. But tell me, what made you come back tonight?"

Roxie angled her head thoughtfully. "I'm not sure. A feeling I had that something was amiss. I can't explain it."

Giff could buy that. A gut feeling had saved his life more than once. He waited while she put her piece back into her large shoulder bag and locked her office door. "Do you always carry a gun?"

"I have a permit for it, if that's what you're asking." Roxie started walking toward the back. She followed him out into the parking lot, locked that door and was about to tell him that her earlier vague suspicion had had her leaving her Mustang on the side street, when she heard a car approaching.

Suddenly, rough hands grabbed her shoulders and yanked her around. She barely had time for a small cry of surprise when Giff's mouth crushed down on hers and his strong arms pulled her close.

Stunned, Roxie tried to move her head while her hands trapped between them closed around fistfuls of his shirt. She might as well have been a gnat struggling against an elephant. His arms bound her to him like steel vises as one of his hands cupped the back of her neck to further ensure her captivity. She made a sound of protest and shuffled her feet, trying to free a leg so she could kick him a good one.

Giff's mouth inched back a fraction. "Stop fighting me. A gray car just turned into the lot and stopped. Sam drives a gray Chrysler."

Her heart was still hammering, from the surprise assault, from the dizzying kiss and something new: fear, after what she'd learned just minutes ago about Sam. Why would Sam be returning to the Eagle's Nest in the middle of the night?

Giff backed her up against the door, his solid hips blocking her. He'd caught a glimpse of tinted windows, could hear the low hum of the powerful engine over the drum of his own pulse. "They're still there, maybe watching. Kiss me back."

In the glow of the light left burning over the back door, Roxie watched his head bend to her and his lips part as they settled on hers. He was more gentle this time, but not much. In moments, he made it impossible for her to think about the danger they might be in as his hands slipped down her back and molded her body to his. Instantly, she felt his heat suffuse her and wondered if the greater danger was here in her arms.

This was just for show, she told herself. He was kissing her so that Sam or whoever was in the car would leave, thinking they'd interrupted two lovers. Giff Jacobs or Jake Garrison was a man she didn't know and certainly didn't want.

Only her lonely heart wouldn't listen.

Greedy. His mouth was greedy, drinking from her, devouring her, filling her with an incredible need. Roxie heard warning bells, but chose to ignore them. She was sure she hadn't given her arms permission to sidle up to circle his neck, yet there they were, her fingers moving into his hair, drawing him nearer. Swamped by a hot wave of desire, she clung to him.

Giff found himself trembling, and cursed the weakness. He should have known better than to touch her, to light the fire that had been smoldering inside him since he'd first looked into those wide brown eyes. She'd fooled him, though. He'd thought her cool blond perfection cloaked a dispassionate nature. But from the moment his mouth took hers, she'd erupted like a long-dormant volcano.

Giff heard a throaty moan come from her and felt the effect of her reaction pound through his blood. He should pull back now, before she took him under for the third time, before she made him forget everything and everyone else. But her flesh beneath his hands felt silky soft, her lips under his tasted wonderful, and it had been so long. So very long.

Roxie felt him change the angle of the kiss and take her deeper, knowing it would have been a perfect opportunity to let her go, to check the parking lot to see if the car had gone. Yet he didn't and she was glad, for she was loathe to lose these mindless sensations rushing through her system. He was so strong, so solid, so eager—as shamelessly eager as she.

She felt the hot flame of desire deep inside leap to life, and she wrapped herself around him. The real or imagined threat of danger dimmed alongside the overwhelming onslaught of his lips sliding down to taste the column of her throat. Reawakening feelings shuddered through her as pleasure sighed along her skin. She arched against him, felt him press against her and knew how close he was to losing control.

The gunning of an engine and the squeal of tires broke the spell. Startled, Roxie's nerves twitched and she pulled back as she heard Giff's muttered oath. Over his shoulder, she could see that the car was gone and they were alone.

"It's okay," she whispered. "You can let me go now."

If only he could, and do so easily. Giff pressed his forehead to hers, breathing hard. "Give me a minute."

She waited, letting her own system settle. She'd been held close enough to become aware of his problem, yet she felt oddly disoriented standing in a deserted parking lot at three a.m. with a man she'd known only a couple of weeks. A man who'd just kissed her senseless. And the knowledge that she certainly hadn't done anything to stop him.

Shakily, Giff took a step backward, then another. He couldn't remember the last time something like this had happened to him. It was the three years of celibacy, he reminded himself. He was, after all, a normal male who'd reacted to holding a beautiful woman.

But why, exactly, had she kissed him back as if there'd be no tomorrow?

Glancing around the parking lot, he frowned. "Where's your car?"

She pointed down the side street. "Over there."

Taking her arm, he walked her to it. "Do you enjoy playing cops and robbers, sneaking around at night, trying to surprise someone who might have broken in, waving your little gun? Do you know how simple it would have been for me to get that away from you?"

Roxie bristled. "I don't think so. I—" She gasped as he whipped her shoulder bag from her, tossed it to the ground and had her arms pinned behind her back with his other hand in less time than it took her to expel her next breath.

"You were saying?"

Her eyes under the streetlight glared at him. "All right. You proved your point."

He let go of her, picked up her bag. "Promise me you won't do any more sleuthing. I assure you, it's not at all like on TV."

He was angry and she didn't think it was directed at her. At her car, she pulled out her keys with unsteady hands. "Look, maybe we should go to the police with this, let them handle Sam."

"They haven't managed in three years to catch him." Giff ran a frustrated hand through his hair. "Sam isn't working alone. I need to find the others, to get them all. These are very dangerous men. If you'd have surprised Sam tonight, his partner probably would have finished you off. He left me to bleed to death on the ground with a planted bag of coke in my pocket. If you caught him at something illegal, he'd probably do the same to you, despite the fact that he wants to get you into his bed."

She believed him, but she also wasn't going to sit back like a good little girl while some man took care of her problem. "I won't go off half-cocked again, but I'm also not going to sit on the sidelines and watch. This is my family's restaurant. You either work *with* me, or I'll go to the police tomorrow with what you've told me and let them handle Sam."

Giff felt like throttling her. Why did she pick tonight to go poking around and mess him up royally? He sighed, realizing she left him no choice. "What exactly do you mean, work with you?"

She stood with one arm on the open car door. "Keep me informed. Let me know what you're planning, what you find out. And the next time you want to check the storeroom, you won't have to pick the lock. We'll use the key, and I'll go in with you." Her eyes challenged him. "So, what do you say? Have we got a deal, partner?"

He found himself grinding his teeth as he stared at her. A coconspirator—one he still didn't trust a hundred percent—wasn't exactly what he'd had in mind.

"I usually work alone."

"Not this time you don't."

He jammed his hands into his pants pockets. Frustration gnawed at him. Just when he'd set things up, she'd stumbled along. If he didn't cooperate, she'd screw everything up. "All right," he mumbled unhappily. He caught her half smile as she got behind the wheel, and stood watching as she drove off.

What in hell had he gotten into now? he asked himself.

The telephone in Roxie's kitchen rang and she snatched the receiver quickly. "Hello?"

"Roxie, it's Doug. I have the information you called about."

"Great." Earlier this morning, she'd phoned her friend, Doug Freeman, a reporter on the *Arizona Daily Star* and asked him to see what he could locate in the newspaper's back files that would verify Giff's story. She'd gone to college with Doug and knew she could trust him. "What did you find out?"

"That aborted drug bust happened three years ago last spring at a restaurant on the south side called La Casa Vieja. Two undercover cops shot, suspects escaped."

"Does it give the names of the officers?"

In Tucson, Doug leaned closer to the viewing machine displaying the microfiche card accessing the correct page. "Detective Phil Weston was shot in the leg and Detective Sergeant Jake Garrison took one low in the back, just missing his kidney." He skimmed ahead, nodding to himself. "I remember this now. Garrison had a bag of coke on him, and he went to trial. Lost in court with Weston testifying that he'd thought for some time that his partner was on the take. He got seven years."

Seven? Then why was he out in three? Good behavior? Roxie had trouble picturing the man she knew as Giff Jacobs behaving that well for three months much less three years. "What happens when a cop like that goes to prison, Doug?" she asked.

"They have to separate him from the other prisoners. Chances are, there are men inside that the cop helped put away. His life is in danger daily. The guards don't treat him real well, either, not a cop who is said to have been on the take. Which is pretty ironic considering the number of prison guards whose hands aren't all that clean."

Roxie found herself shuddering involuntarily as she pictured prison life from the little she knew. "So he'd be lucky to get out alive."

"You got that right," Doug answered. "But Garrison's probably used to being on guard. I covered the police beat a while back, including vice and drug enforcement. Undercover's the toughest job there is. Most cops don't want it and can't handle it. One mistake—one jerk blows your cover when you've infiltrated a group or one junkie goes berserk or one informant lies—and it could be your last day on earth." He was thoughtful a moment as he read another paragraph. "I can't imagine why Garrison flipped to the other side. He'd chalked up more citations for bravery than anyone else on the force, plus two commendations from the mayor. Must have done it for the money. Cops risk it all and get paid peanuts. Maybe he got tired of seeing the bad guys driving Caddies while he could barely afford some beat-up jalopy.''

Maybe. Or maybe, as Giff claimed, he'd been set up. "With all those citations, why was he found guilty? Surely his record had to have stood for something."

"The thing that hurt most was his partner's testimony. Garrison wasn't the first cop with a chestful of medals to chuck it all. You can take only so much of the seamy side of life and you want to go live on an island somewhere and be left alone."

"Is there a picture of the two detectives in the paper?"

"Yeah. Both have long hair and full beards, but then, that's not unusual. When they're on a job, most undercover guys do everything they can to change their looks. Their own mother wouldn't recognize them until they clean up."

"Is there anything mentioned about the suspects?"

"No names, if that's what you mean. Apparently, the shipments were coming over from Mexico and they were using the restaurant as a front. But the owner wasn't involved and was cleared." Doug leaned back in his chair. "Why are you so interested in this old case, Roxie?"

She had no intention of going into her reasons. "It's a long story."

"Well, I wouldn't waste too much time on Garrison if your paths cross. Guys who work undercover have trouble relating to people. They're a hard, suspicious, pretty arrogant bunch, and they trust no one."

That summed up Giff fairly well. She had trouble thinking of him as Jake Garrison. Still, he'd inspired great loyalty in his brother and stacked up a pile of citations and commendations.

And somewhere along the line, he'd learned to kiss like no man who'd ever touched her before.

Roxie cleared her throat. "Thanks, Doug. I appreciate the information."

"Anytime. You coming down our way one day soon?" Doug was single and a real party animal.

"I don't plan to, but if I do, I'll let you know." Hanging up the phone, Roxie checked her watch. Nearly noon. They'd be in the middle of the lunch rush at the Eagle's Nest. She'd better get going.

It appeared that Giff was telling the truth. But he probably hadn't told her everything. The first chance she got, she'd get that local cop's name that he'd mentioned and check further.

A good kisser or not, she had no intention of being taken down the primrose path.

Giff was growing impatient. It had been a full week since his uneasy alliance with Roxie and each night, after closing, they'd checked the storeroom. Nothing.

By unspoken agreement, they'd avoided each other during working hours so as not to arouse Sam's suspicions. Since Sam hadn't mentioned seeing that passionate embrace in the parking lot to Roxie or him, Giff assumed the driver of the gray car had been someone else, perhaps lost or turning around. Still, he kept his eyes and ears open as he worked the bar.

He'd had a minimal report from Neil about the things he'd asked his friend to check. There was no rap sheet on Sam Farrell, not in Tucson nor anywhere else. And there was no recorded information on how Sam had acquired the Eagle's Nest, just the agreement signed by Henry Lowell's widow transferring her interests to Sam.

Had Roxie been part of the payoff? Giff asked himself as he stood waiting for the last two Monday-night patrons to finish their drinks and leave. Why was she hanging around after the transfer of ownership? Maybe Sam had something on Roxie. If he did, then she had sufficient reason to dislike him. Observing them more closely, he'd noticed that she often stiffened when he so cozily slipped his arm around her. Yet she wouldn't be the first woman who'd warmed a man's bed even hating him.

He didn't want to be thinking along those lines, but with his background, Giff knew his cynicism spilled into everything. On the surface, Roxie Lowell appeared to be a beautiful, confident businesswoman, cool and controlled. But when he'd kissed her that night, he'd discovered a passionate woman beneath the facade.

Not that he'd been searching. Not that he wanted involvement. But he couldn't seem to forget that encounter. There were times when he'd look up and see her watching him, see heat move into her face before she'd look away, and he knew she was remembering, too.

Giff watched Ginny walk over and present the bill to the lingering couple, probably reminding them that they'd be closing soon. It was the one night they wound things up by eleven. Trevor was finishing up in the restaurant and the kitchen staff had already left. Pouring himself a root beer, Giff leaned against the back counter.

There were still too many puzzle pieces missing. What was Sam up to? Why would he want to buy into this place? Had he decided to take a crack at being legit? Giff dismissed that thought immediately. He'd seen other criminals try, but giving in to the lure of those big drug bucks was a hard habit to break. He couldn't imagine Sam being content to gladhand restaurant patrons for the rest of his days. Of course, he may have stashed away a bunch of money and gone into some other sideline.

But what?

Neil hadn't been able to discover if Sam had any silent partners, or where the buy-out money had come from. The Lowells and even Trevor had all checked out clean, at least as far as police records showed. There was something missing, Giff knew. He'd simply have to be more patient.

The last two people left and Ginny went behind the bar to get a drink and to tally her vouchers. Giff saw Roxie appear in the doorway and nod to him. It was their signal that told him she'd wait in her office until he'd finished and everyone else had gone. When all was quiet, they'd check the storeroom.

As he stepped to the sink, he heard glass shattering and turned.

Ginny looked near tears as she gazed at the red wine staining her uniform and at the broken shards all over. She glanced at Giff. "I'm sorry. I'm a mess these days. I can't seem to do anything right."

Giff knew she also worked a day job and felt sorry for her. He bent to scoop up the broken glass. "When we're tired, nothing seems to go right. Don't worry about it."

"If I could just cope with my son, the rest would fall into place." She sniffled into a tissue. "The principal called and wants to see me tomorrow. Jeff's skipping school, hanging around on the streets. I'm so afraid he's going to get in with the wrong crowd."

He knew a little something about how Jeff might be feeling. Twelve was on the brink of manhood, yet still very much a boy. Dropping the broken glass into the waste container, Giff straightened. "How much time do you spend with him, Ginny?"

"Not much. With my having to hold down two jobs and being so tired and all, I hardly ever see him. My mother lives with us, but she can't handle Jeff at all."

With a wet towel, he mopped up the spilled wine on the counter as he spoke. "You may have to give up one of your jobs, Ginny. If you want to save your boy before he's beyond saving, that is. Believe me, I know what I'm talking about. A kid with too much time on his hands and no one special who cares about him, he's ripe for trouble. Jeff could get into petty stealing, drugs, gangs. It's a rough world out there."

Ginny nodded. "I know, but I've been trying to save for his college education and a better car. It's hard."

"I'm sure it is, but what good will a college fund do you if you've lost the kid along the way? He's feeling alone. He needs to know you care."

Her eyes were wide, pleading for understanding. "I *do* care."

"Then let him know he means more to you than a new car. Spend time with him. *Listen* to him." Projecting, Giff suddenly realized. He was projecting this kid into the same life he'd grown up in. He shook his head, annoyed. "Not that it's any of my business."

Ginny lay a hand on his arm. "No, don't say that. I needed to hear it. Thanks, Giff. You make a lot of sense." She placed her bar slips next to the cash register. "I get the feeling you're talking from experience."

He shrugged as he gave the bar a final swipe. "Yeah, there's no better teacher."

"I appreciate it." She grabbed her purse from under the bar and walked around. "See you tomorrow."

As Giff watched her leave, he saw that Roxie was standing in the archway, and he frowned, wondering how much of their conversation she'd overheard. He wasn't pleased that she'd caught him in one of his softer moods.

It took him longer than he'd thought to close out. As he finished, Roxie walked over, sipping a cup of coffee, and settled herself on a bar stool.

She swallowed a yawn, a reminder that this whole situation had been giving her restless nights. "I'm beginning to think we're on a wild-goose chase," she said as Giff turned off all but one light and came out from behind the bar. She'd overheard his advice to Ginny, which Roxie had thought was right on the money, and had been surprised he'd made the effort to counsel her. "Maybe the man you saw wasn't Sam Farrell, after all. Or maybe he's reformed."

The day pigs fly, he thought. "I didn't make a mistake. When you're trying to trap someone, you have to have patience." Something he was a little short on these days, too.

Roxie slid off the bar stool and followed him to the back hallway. As she unlocked the storeroom, she heard the rattle of keys at the outside door. She felt Giff grab her arm and propel her inside, quickly turning the lock.

As noiselessly as possible in the dark interior, Giff guided her to the farthest corner behind the tallest packing crates. "Isn't your car in the back lot?" he whispered into her ear.

"No. On the side street. Who do you suppose—"

He cut her off with a hand over her mouth. "Shh." Cursing the fact that he didn't have a piece, only a small knife, Giff eased her behind him and waited, ears straining.

A man's footsteps, unhurried, confident, striding toward the front. Alert to the slightest sound, Giff listened. All the employees had keys—was it someone who'd forgotten something? Or was it Sam, checking out the whole building before coming to the storeroom? He wished for the latter, wanting to know for sure.

The sounds came closer, then a key turned in the lock, the door opened and the light went on. Giff heard the unmistakable off-key whistling that identified the new arrival almost as surely as the sight of him would have.

By the sound of his slow footsteps, Giff tracked Sam as he made his way along the first row of shelves, then turned and strolled along the second, where he stopped. He could hear a box being lifted and placed on the floor. Fairly certain that Sam's back would be toward them, Giff gambled and peeked around the carton in front of them. Resplendent in a black-and-white tweed jacket and dark slacks, it was Sam Farrell, all right.

Reaching into his pocket, Sam dug out a switchblade and cut open three sides of the carton. Lifting the lid, he grabbed a clear plastic bag filled with a white substance and held it up, inspecting it thoroughly. Not quite satisfied, he removed the twist-tie, stuck in a finger and tasted the powdery contents. Apparently, it was the right stuff, for he put everything back together, shut the box and picked it up.

Giff ducked back and stood very still, aware that behind him Roxie was almost holding her breath. He heard Sam walk to the door and pause there, probably looking around. Then the light went out and a key turned in the lock. The sound of footsteps receded in the direction of the back exit. Cautiously, Giff moved to the door and cocked his head, listening. He heard a slam and more keys clattering.

Nevertheless, he stood perfectly still. Finally, he heard the faint sound of a car starting, then driving away.

"He's gone," Roxie whispered as she came up behind him.

"Shh. Let's wait." Sam hadn't gone undetected this long by being a fool, Giff thought. Giff would rather err on the side of caution. If Sam smelled a rat, he could have set his own trap and be doubling back. He could sense Roxie's impatience, but he waited a full five minutes before carefully leaving the storeroom.

The only window that faced the back was in the kitchen. Giff warned Roxie to stay put while he checked. In the dark, he climbed onto the counter and peered out the high window. Not a sign of a car in the lot, nor of anything out of place. He scrambled down and went to the hallway. She was standing by the door, her eyes huge and round. "Are you all right?"

She ignored his question, not wanting to reveal just how frightened she'd been, huddled in that storeroom. "We need to call the police."

"Not the police in general, but my contact there." Giff opened the back door. "I'll walk you to your car and call him from my place." Taking her arm, he started for the side street.

"No. I'll drive us to my place and you can call from there. I want to hear what he has to say."

He didn't like that plan. "Trust me. I'll call you right after I talk with Neil."

Roxie stopped and swung to face him. He couldn't possibly know how much she hated to hear the phrase *trust me*. It usually meant you shouldn't. "Look, how do I make this clear to you? You're not going ahead without me. We're partners, whether you like it or not."

Clenching his teeth, Giff held out his hand. "Give me the keys. I'll drive."

"You don't know where I live," she said, trying to keep up with his long strides.

"Don't bet on it."

Chapter 4

"I know it's a violation of my parole, but I'm willing to take the risk." Pacing the length of Roxie's living room while speaking into her portable phone, Giff turned and marched back. "Do you think you can get me an unmarked piece?"

Neil's voice was low, reluctant. "Yeah, I'll get it. But I've got to tell you, I'm not in favor of this."

"Yeah, well, there's more than my safety involved here."

Neil hesitated, before saying, "You mean the daughter, Roxie Lowell?"

"Among others," Giff answered noncommittally. "Is there any way you could put a tail on Sam—unofficially, that is?"

"Doubtful. Can't get a man authorized without going to the captain with all of it."

"I don't want you to do that." Giff did another turn of the room, passing Roxie as she sat on the couch listening to his end of the conversation. "I can't figure why he had just one small box. Do you think he's testing the waters?"

"Probably. He's only been at the Eagle's Nest three months."

Giff ran a hand through his hair. "We need to find out if and when a bigger shipment is scheduled. We need to draw out the big guy." Maybe he'd start his own surveillance of Sam on his off-hours. The trouble was, his Bug was too easy to spot. "Have you got any snitches you can trust who might know something?"

"A few. I'll put the word out."

"Okay. Call me as soon as you get that piece."

"Will do. Watch your back, buddy."

"Thanks. Hope I didn't wake Lisa or the boys calling so late."

"No problem. I'll be in touch."

Giff hung up, then walked over to sit down at the opposite end of the couch. He knew Roxie was waiting. He felt better about her since the incident in the storeroom. Trusted her more. She hadn't fallen apart on him. "I guess you heard."

"You asked him to get you a gun?"

"I felt pretty naked in there tonight without one."

Roxie had to admit she'd have felt better if he'd been armed, too. Lord, what was she doing, going along with a defrocked cop out on parole who wanted to get an illegal gun and stalk a man who was a drug smuggler? She who'd rarely done anything more dangerous than cross against the light. With unsteady hands, she removed the gold clip at the base of her neck and shook out her hair, wishing she could return to the carefree days before her father's untimely death. "Do you ever wish you could turn back the clock?"

Giff stretched out his legs and turned from her because the sight of all that golden hair settling around her slender shoulders had his palms itching. "Yeah, I wish that pretty often."

What a stupid thing to ask a man who'd just gotten out of prison, Roxie thought belatedly. "I'm sorry, that was thoughtless of me. I'm sure you have a carload of I-wish-I-hads."

"I guess most everyone past the age of ten has a few." He glanced around the room, liking her choice of colors, a soothing pale peach and shades of green. Like her office, it wasn't overly feminine, yet definitely showed a woman's touch. There was an abundance of plants on shelves, the fireplace ledge, the windowsills. He couldn't see anything that hinted of a man in her life. "This is going to sound like a cliché, but how come a nice girl like you isn't married with a couple of kids, instead of working twelve, fourteen hours a day?"

Leaning her head on the couch back, she turned to face him and looked into those intense blue eyes. She felt her pulse scramble as she realized that she could easily get lost in them. "I was married—once."

"What happened?"

"It didn't work out."

"How long were you married?"

"Six months."

"I guess when you meet someone and they hit you like a ton of bricks, and you're crazy enough to think it'll last forever, it seldom does."

Roxie watched a muscle in his jaw clench. "I guess you've been there."

"Yeah, and I wish I hadn't."

She sighed, wondering why she felt so melancholy tonight. "It didn't happen like that with me. Brad and I grew up together. We liked the same things, had the same friends. I knew him, or thought I did... I wonder if we ever truly know anyone."

She had his curiosity up now. Six months wasn't much of a marriage. "Did he turn into a monster right after the wedding?"

"Not exactly. Brad's father works for the FBI in Phoenix, a desk job. After college, Brad joined him in the office. He told me his work wouldn't be dangerous because he'd be a pencil pusher, as he called it, just like his father.''

"But he changed his mind," Giff guessed.

She nodded, toying with a thick rope of pearls that hung around her neck. "He was invited to the training grounds in Virginia to observe. In no time, he was hooked. He became a special agent, working out in the field, always on secret assignments where I couldn't reach him.''

"And you got fed up with it."

Roxie's laugh was hollow. "No, he got tired of being married. Or so he told me on one of his rare weekends home. He didn't want to be tied down, to be worried about me worrying about him.''

He could see her struggle not to let him see what the rejection had cost her. Giff wasn't a toucher, so the urge to reach out for her hand surprised him. "He's not worth your tears. What he felt for you wasn't real, or he never would have let you go. He's a damn fool, if you ask me.''

Looking away, she blinked quickly. "Oh, I've said the same things to myself often enough. But it's still a little hard on the old self-esteem." Roxie sat up straighter. "How about some coffee or a cold drink?''

"Thanks, but I really should get going and let you get some sleep.''

"What about you?" she asked as he rose. "Have you ever been married?''

Though he wished it hadn't, Carla's image swam into focus, and his mouth became a hard line. "No.''

Roxie picked up her keys and her bag. "Not even any close calls?''

He stopped at the door. Carla hadn't been the marrying kind, she'd told him, even though being with her had put the idea in his head for the first time. But her declaration hadn't stopped him from falling for her far more deeply than was good for him. "I cared about someone once, but we never got around to discussing marriage.''

"You broke up?" she persisted as they walked outside to her Mustang, wondering why she was suddenly so interested.

"Yeah. Three years ago." He reached for the keys. "I'll drive."

Roxie got in beside him. Three years ago. Right around the time of his Tucson court trial. There was a whole lot more to his story than he'd revealed, but she felt he'd already said more than he'd intended.

The short drive to his apartment was silent and Giff was grateful that she left him alone with his troubled thoughts. He pulled into the driveway and stepped out.

Roxie scooted out her side and walked around since the console prevented her from sliding across to the driver's side. "I'll see you tomorrow evening."

He studied her face in the glow of a nearby streetlamp. She was a woman who'd had to be strong and had risen to the occasion more than once. He'd hate to see her hurt. "Listen, Roxie, things might get rough real soon. Neil and I are trying to see if we can learn when they'll be bringing in a large shipment, something we can catch them doing redhanded. From now on, you're out of it. You have to leave it to the professionals."

Stubbornly, she stood her ground. "No, you can't make me back off. If you insist on shutting me out, I'll throw a monkey wrench into your whole scheme."

Exasperated, he glared at her. "Don't you want to catch this guy, to prevent him from flooding the States with that crap, getting kids hooked on it?"

"Yes, I do. I also have personal reasons for wanting to see Sam Farrell out of the Eagle's Nest, and out of my life. But I absolutely insist on being a part of things." She'd spent too many years on the sidelines, letting her father take charge, unaware he'd been so financially troubled. No more.

"Okay, you leave me no choice, but you'll do as I say."

Having won, she could smile. "Yes, sir."

He tossed her the car keys, but she bungled the catch and they landed on the ground. They both bent to retrieve them, missing heads by millimeters. Straightening, blue eyes looked down into suddenly aware brown ones.

Giff reached to brush his fingers along her cheek. "You're very stubborn. And very beautiful."

Roxie felt more than saw him move fractionally closer and thought she knew what was on his mind. Eyes still locked on his, she took a step back. "I keep getting hurt by guys like you, guys who shove and push their way through life, trying to make it a better world, but who can't manage a personal relationship because they're too driven, too dedicated. You were right earlier. Brad didn't care enough, and I cared too much. I'm not going to make that mistake again."

She'd told it like it was, and Giff should have been relieved. Why, then, did he feel a hint of disappointment? he wondered. "Not only beautiful, but smart. Good night, Roxie." Turning, he walked to the back stairs, not looking back.

"Why do you want to see it?" Roxie asked, looking up at Giff who was standing at her desk.

He shrugged, making his request appear mildly important but not vital. "I've been thinking about how and why Sam bought into the Eagle's Nest." He glanced toward the closed door and lowered his voice even more. It was late the following afternoon and Sam was due back any minute for the dinner crowd. "I'd like to see the purchase agreement. Unless you object, for some reason." Neil hadn't been able to find out much. Maybe he could. Trying to come up with a reason for Sam's sudden foray into an ethical business enterprise nagged at him.

Rising, Roxie went toward the safe bolted to the floor in the corner. "I don't object. But I want you to know that our family attorney checked over the agreement and said it was legal and binding."

As she bent to work the tumblers, Giff sat down, not wanting her to think he was interested in learning the combination to the safe. "You said before that Sam showed up in answer to a for-sale ad you'd put in the paper. Did he just walk in, look around and say he'd take it?"

Roxie reached into the safe, extracted a blue packet, then stood. "It wasn't like that. Apparently, he and my father made this agreement three months before Dad's death," she said, indicating the packet. "He said he hadn't known Dad had died until he'd seen my ad. I'd never heard Dad mention Sam nor had I ever seen him before."

"With the restaurant in your family so long, didn't you want to keep the place going after your father's death?" Perhaps he was wrong, but he'd pegged her for a traditionalist.

"With my father gone and my mother so upset, I just wanted out of the business. I wanted to move on to other things, maybe even move away. But unfortunately, I can't. Not yet. The least I can do is give Dad this one year."

It was more complicated than he'd thought. "I don't understand."

Wearily, Roxie sat down at her desk. She hadn't fallen asleep last night until just before the sun had risen. "After Dad died, my mother and I went through all his papers. Neither of us had known about the second mortgage he'd taken out, the insurance loans or all the additional cash he'd borrowed. There were IOU's and promissory notes made out to several personal friends and a few names we didn't recognize."

"I can't believe this place couldn't hold its own."

"It did, for a long time. Poor Dad. You see, his timing was bad. He'd decided to expand the restaurant just about the time the recession hit. If only we'd known what a financial mess he was in, we might have been able to come up with something to help him. I'm sure the strain caused his heart attack."

Giff nodded toward the document she held. "And you found that among his papers?"

"No. I don't know what happened to Dad's copy." She held the blue packet toward him. "Sam showed up with this and my ad about a month after Dad's funeral."

Frowning, Giff opened the packet and read the two sheets quickly. A demand note for two hundred thousand dollars, signed, witnessed, notarized and dated six months ago. "Promissory notes usually aren't notarized unless they're secured by property. How did Sam wind up with the restaurant if the business wasn't put up as collateral for this note?"

Roxie released a frustrated sigh. "We paid off the small loans from the little insurance that remained. But we still had two mortgages on the building and we were going deeper in debt each month. During good times, the property and business combined would be worth over four hundred thousand. But, with the recession, business had fallen off. Between the bank and Sam's note, we owed more than the total worth."

"You keep saying *we*. Was it all in your mother's name and yours?"

She shook her head, thinking that somewhere along the line she must have decided to trust this man. She'd never gone into her financial situation this thoroughly with anyone. "No, it was in my mother's name and Dad's. Mom's health isn't the best. She just wanted to leave. So, to get out from under, she signed the business over to Sam."

There was still something puzzling him. And worrying him. "You said you'd wanted a change, yet here you still are. You're not financially obligated. Why did you stay?"

Roxie toyed with her pen and wondered if this hard man would understand her reason. "There are obligations other than financial that bind us. Sam has a *demand* note. He could have taken my mother to court and demanded payment. Everything she had was mortgaged to the hilt. He agreed to settle for the business, which isn't worth what he's owed, and to continue making payments on the mortgages . . . *If* I would stay on for one year to ease the transition of ownership. I didn't feel his request was out of line, so I agreed.''

Giff wasn't sure whether she was extremely honorable or very naive. "You wouldn't have had to stay on, not really. It's doubtful he'd have won the lawsuit, if he'd have gone that far.''

She looked up at him then, her brown eyes steady and clear. "I felt I did. I still do. I owe Dad a great deal. He...he was a wonderful father. One year isn't too much to ask. I don't like Sam Farrell, nor do I approve of him. But that's beside the point. Of course, if we can prove that he's using the Eagle's Nest for criminal activities, I would reevaluate the situation.''

Giff read over the document again. It didn't take him long to guess what had probably happened. He looked at Roxie, wondering how to tell her, or if. She'd had a lot on her plate over the last six months.

"What is it?" she asked, noticing his serious expression.

"Maybe Sam's been up to more than smuggling drugs." He walked around to her side of the desk, deciding that she'd have to be strong enough to handle the news. "Do you see how this is drawn up, two pages with the body of the note on the first page, spelling out the agreement and the amount, right? The terms of repayment continue on to the second sheet." He flipped to the next page stapled to the first. "At the top, this states that it's page two of two. On this second sheet are all the signatures, and the notarization.''

"Yes, and that's my father's signature, if you're thinking it's a forgery. His handwriting was very distinctive. I'd know it anywhere.''

"It undoubtedly is. However, how hard would it be to remove this staple, redo the first sheet, changing the amount owed, and restaple it to the second one?''

"You mean, this isn't a true document? We don't really owe Sam two hundred thousand?"

"You probably owe him something, whatever amount your father borrowed from him. But isn't it possible that Sam altered that figure, especially since your father's copy is missing?"

How could she have been so naive? Roxie asked herself. "Of course that's possible. But why would he want this business? I mean, making ends meet is still a struggle. If all he wanted was a front to use for his drug operation, he could just as easily have gone to work for a restaurant, as you told me he did in Tucson. There are hundreds in this area."

Giff straightened. "Sure, but what better way to keep the questions to a minimum than to own the place? If someone gets nosy, he fires them."

It still didn't make sense to Roxie. "But why would he want me to stay on for a year?"

Resuming his seat, Giff shrugged again. "I can think of several reasons. You lend legitimacy to the Eagle's Nest. Your family's been here for three generations. He could let you run the place while he sets up the operation. By the time you leave, he'll have everything in place and be accepted as the new owner. If he's careful, he can use it for years. Besides, we don't know what that original note read. For all you know, he could have picked up the place for a song. You said most of the other promissory notes were for minimal amounts. And still another reason—you're awfully easy on the eyes. I still think he wants to get you into his bed. From what I've seen, he's the kind of guy who sees you as a conquest, a challenge."

Roxie rubbed a spot above her left eye, wondering how she'd managed to get into such a mess. "Is there any way we can prove all this?"

Giff leaned forward, glad she was finally believing him. "One way would be to check the books. If your father really received two hundred thousand from Sam six months ago, what did he do with all that money? Why would you still have found two mortgages, insurance loans and an assortment of small notes to friends? Or was he in trouble personally? Was he a gambler? A drinker? Did he have a life on the side neither you or your mother knew of?"

"Heavens, no. My father was such a hardworking man. He was here at the Eagle's Nest every day, usually no later than ten a.m. and he rarely left until we closed at two in the morning. Mom worked alongside him much of the time. Their first vacation in ten years was a cruise I talked them into last year."

"Did you go through the accounting books after his death?"

"Yes, the ones I could find. But several are missing. Dad handled all the bookkeeping. They're probably somewhere, but I haven't been able to find them. Since we balance currently, I haven't really searched very hard."

Giff felt a rush of satisfaction that he'd been on the right track. "I'd be willing to wager that the missing books cover the time period of Sam's loan. Am I right?"

Oh, Lord, it had to be true, she thought, recalling the dates of the missing ledgers. All of it was true. She felt like such a trusting fool. "Yes."

"If it had been a legitimate loan, your father would have entered the two hundred grand, then paid outstanding bills with it. Was that done?"

"Apparently not, since there are still debts unpaid."

Just as Giff had thought. "Since that wasn't done, I'd guess the amount of the loan was much lower. To cover that, Sam got rid of the books."

Sitting back, Roxie jammed her hands into her jacket pockets, feeling the weight of frustration. "But how? How could he have gotten in here and taken out accounting books?"

"Did you take inventory of the books *after* he showed up, or before?"

She saw where he was headed. "After. I hadn't had time before."

"And by then, he was here. Probably had a key, the safe combination. Even if he didn't, I'm sure he'd have found a way to get to the ledgers."

"I suppose so. If you can jimmy a lock, I imagine most criminals can also."

"I'm afraid so."

"Damn!" It was easier to be angry than hurt. "Why doesn't the law require that promissory notes be recorded? That would have prevented this situation."

"It does, *if* property's involved. Sam was too smart for that." He pointed to the agreement. "And, the way he set up that payment schedule, it's no wonder your father went for it. No payments the first year, then minimal quarterly payments the following year, at a low interest rate. That had to look good to a man desperate for money. He probably figured the business would pull out of the slump within a year or so and he'd pay everyone back."

Roxie stared at the document. "Yes, and that's why I found no payments made out to Sam Farrell in any of the books." She tossed aside the papers. "You can't imagine how much of a sap I feel right now for having bought into this so readily."

Giff got up and went to lean against her desk, looking down at her dejected face. The setting sun crept in through the slatted blinds on the window, changing the yellow of her hair to gold. He had an uncharacteristic urge to take her in his arms and tell her not to worry. "Don't blame yourself, Roxie. He's shrewd and very persistent. He's covered himself for nearly every eventuality."

"How convenient for him that my father died when he did." The moment the words were out of her mouth, a dreadful thought occurred to Roxie. "You don't suppose he . . ." It was too horrible to consider.

Last night, as he'd lain awake into the wee hours, the same possibility had occurred to Giff. A man who'd walk away from a wounded cop would certainly have no problem removing a tired old man who was in his way. "It's possible. Just how did your father's heart attack occur?"

"He died here, at the Eagle's Nest." She'd thought it fitting at the time, because the business had been her father's life since his early teens when he'd begun working with his father. "He was often the last to leave. He had the attack in his office, the one Sam now occupies. Apparently, he felt it coming and grabbed the phone, hitting the quick-dial to his house. Mom picked it up, but all she heard was a garbled sound. I think she knew. She called 911 and they found him dead on his office floor, the phone still in his hand. The death certificate reads massive coronary."

"And he hadn't had a heart condition that you knew of?"

"No." Roxie struggled with a sudden rush of emotion. "Oh, God, I can't believe ... how could anyone do such a thing?" she said, jumping to her feet.

Giff took hold of her shoulders and eased her into a clumsy embrace. "We're not sure it happened that way. He'd been worried. Financial problems are a strain on the heart, especially if you're no longer young."

"I know. But if we find that Sam was involved in any way in my father's death, I want to make him pay, Giff." She looked up, pain and regret suddenly etched on her lovely features. "I understand now how badly you want to get him."

She was pretty nearly the only one who did. "We will. Just be patient and let me call the shots, but I promise you, we'll get him." She wasn't crying, just leaning into him for a small measure of comfort. It felt good, Giff thought, holding her close, rubbing her back. Too damn good.

They both heard it at the same time, the off-tune whistling followed by quick footsteps. Before they could move, the door swung open.

"There you both are," Sam said, his dark eyes taking in the scene. "Am I interrupting something?"

Roxie stepped back, finding it difficult to meet Sam's eyes, but not for the reason he might imagine. "Did you want something?"

He checked his watch pointedly. "We're supposed to have a meeting in your office at six—Trevor, you and I, remember? It's six." His eyes shifted to Giff. "Aren't you on duty now?"

Giff's expression was closed. "Thanks for the reminder." He walked out past Sam and headed for the bar.

Sam strolled to the chair opposite Roxie's desk just as Trevor came rushing in and sat down. "You two seem quite cozy," Sam said to Roxie.

She placed a file folder over the document she'd been discussing with Giff, picked up her clipboard, then turned cool eyes on Sam. "Are you ready to go over the food and beverage orders for the week?"

"Yes, indeed," Trevor answered for them. Efficient as always, he handed over his requisition sheets.

Roxie thought the brief meeting would never end. They went over paper supplies, food orders, menus, catering appointments, beverage needs and even discussed a few personnel problems. She tried to keep her mind on the conversation, but her eyes kept straying to Sam and her mind kept replaying the things she'd learned during the last hour. She fervently prayed he couldn't see past her tight expression and she passionately promised herself she'd find a way to put Sam Farrell out of commission.

Finally, they wound down. "I guess that's it, then." She arranged the papers on her desk in neat stacks, wishing they'd both leave her alone. Tension had given her a monumental headache.

"Thank you, Roxie," Trevor said, as he always did before leaving.

Sam rose, but lingered a moment.

Ignoring him, Roxie opened a desk drawer and searched for her bottle of aspirin.

"Is anything the matter, Rox? You seem a little uptight."

How astute of him. "Just a headache." She found the medicine, shook two into her palm and reached for the carafe of water on the credenza behind her. She swallowed the pills quickly and turned to find him still studying her. "I'm fine, really."

Sam's face moved into a smile that didn't reach his eyes. "What you need is more recreation time. How about that rain check? I found this great Mexican place about five miles south of here. Looks like a joint outside, but inside, you'd swear you were in Acapulco. And the food, like heaven."

Be nice, her instincts told her. *Nice, but firm.* "Just like Mom used to make, you mean?" She watched the smile fade and his face harden. Hit a nerve, had she? What kind of an upbringing had he had to warrant such a look? she wondered. "I really don't think this is a good night for Mexican food for me. But you go ahead." The less he hung around, the better she'd feel.

He eased a slim hip onto her desk, shoving papers out of the way as he sat. "How long are you going to keep putting me off, Rox? Am I so hard to take? Or do you have a date with someone else?"

"Sam, I have a bad headache, really." She saw the edge of the blue document sticking out from beneath her clipboard and hoped he wouldn't spot it. He might recognize it and wonder why it was out of the safe and on her desk while Giff had been with her. She nodded toward her leather couch along the back wall. "I think I'll lie down for half an hour and let this aspirin go to work."

Reluctantly accepting still another rejection, Sam got up and smoothed his hands along his paisley suspenders. "Want me to get you a cold cloth? Or I could rub your temples. Someone I know used to rub my temples when I didn't feel good. Works every time."

Roxie couldn't bear the thought of his hands touching her. "I appreciate the offer, but I'll manage." She stared him down, hoping she wouldn't have to be rude in order to get rid of him.

At last, he walked to the door. "I'll make sure you're not disturbed."

Alone, Roxie sank into her chair, propped her elbows on the desk and rubbed her own temples. Maybe a nap wasn't such a bad idea. She simply couldn't keep working such long hours on so little sleep.

The problem was that when she finally lay down, she couldn't turn off her restless mind that kept going over her conversation with Giff, the disturbing things she'd learned. And the disturbing things she'd felt, the way he'd held her, the rock-hard strength of him, the solid comfort of his arms. His touch hadn't been deliberately sensual, yet she'd been stirred by his gentle caresses, had been moving toward arousal. She was attracted to him, she could freely admit. Just as freely as she'd declare he was the wrong man to want.

Lonely. That's what she was and why she was suddenly yearning for a man. For *this* man, she corrected. She hadn't consciously been aware that she was lonely until Giff had shown up. But she was, despite a carload of friends, relatives and business associates. She was deep-down lonely, longing to share herself with a special someone. A man who would not only heat her blood, but capture her imagination, challenge her intellect, involve her heart.

Waiting. It seemed as if she'd spent her whole life waiting, again not consciously. For that special feeling, that punch-in-the-solar-plexus breathless feeling. She'd taken a wrong turn with Brad, only later admitting she'd never felt all she should with him. But when Giff had kissed her, she'd recognized that special feeling instantly.

Wrong. Again she reminded herself that he was the wrong man to want.

It was rare that Trevor lingered after the restaurant closed. But this evening, he walked into the bar and sat down at a corner table to have a cup of coffee with Roxie. He turned his concerned gaze on her and saw the shadows of fatigue beneath her eyes. "You're working too many hours, Roxie, dear," he said kindly.

She smiled at him as she passed the cream. "Thank you for your concern, Trevor, but I'm fine."

"Are you sure? I know we could handle things here if you wanted to take a few days off." She'd scarcely stayed away a full day since her father's death.

"Maybe after the holidays. Are you staying here for Christmas or flying back to England?" She knew he had distant family there.

"He's staying here," Sam said, joining them from behind Roxie. He patted Trevor's shoulder. "We can't get through the season without Trevor."

Surprisingly, Trevor's face flushed with pleasure. "Actually, I'd planned on staying."

How odd that Sam had managed to win Trevor over, Roxie thought, not for the first time. "Well, good. We can certainly use you."

Tammy approached the table. "There's a call for you, Roxie. You can take it on the bar phone over there."

Thanking her, she excused herself and walked to the phone. Sam's eyes followed her, dark and suspicious. "I wonder what she's thinking. She's like a volcano, hot and churning inside, but keeping most people at arm's length."

"Is that how you see her?" Trevor asked. He'd known Roxie for years and didn't think there was a devious bone in her body.

"I walked into her office today and found her in *his* arms." With his chin, he indicated Giff behind the bar pouring a drink.

Trevor's eyebrow rose dramatically. "Hard to believe."

"Yeah, I thought so, too."

"I believe Roxie's got better taste than that. Must have been a momentary lapse. Or perhaps she had something in her eye."

Sam sent him an incredulous look. "Right. And I'm Bugs Bunny." He stood, his eyes narrowing. "Pretty funny, considering she won't even have dinner with me."

"She's tired, that's all." Trevor always defended Roxie. But privately, he hoped Sam was wrong. Giff was uncouth and he made Trevor uncomfortable. The man was so blatantly sexual that Trevor felt certain women could sense it the moment they saw him. Disgusting.

He watched Sam walk away, then finished his coffee and decided it was time to go home. He'd recently purchased a priceless collection of the works of William Shakespeare and he was anxious to examine them closely. Rare books were his main extravagance. Standing, he saw that Roxie was finishing her call, but she probably wouldn't return to sit with him. Long ago, he'd resigned himself to the fact that she looked on him as merely an uncle figure.

A pity, Trevor thought as he left the bar, for he would have been far nicer to her than these intense younger men. He'd also wager she had no idea how well off he was financially. He had a beautiful home on Camelback Mountain, lovely furniture, including some exquisite period pieces, and a sizable investment portfolio.

And wouldn't Roxie and most everyone else he knew be surprised at how he'd accumulated his holdings? No one knew, no one guessed. It was his little secret, he was very good at it and it paid very well. He kept his job at the Eagle's Nest because he enjoyed wearing a tux, dressing up, being in charge. Fortunately, Sam Farrell had seen that in him, recognized it immediately and let him run the restaurant his way, which was why they got along so well. Henry Lowell also had let him do whatever he wanted. And it was a good thing, or else he'd have left long ago. For, if he so chose, he'd never have to work another day in his life.

Leaving by the back door, Trevor smiled with a tinge of sadness. Mother had always said that women would underestimate men like him. And she'd been right.

Chapter 5

It had been raining all day Tuesday. Not storming, but a quiet, gentle rain. By late afternoon, it was still coming down. As he walked along the winding path, Giff noticed that Hayden Road Park was nearly deserted because of the weather. One lone fisherman sat on a concrete ledge, his line dangling in the water, probably in the belief that fish were more likely to bite on an overcast day.

Neil was already on the bench where they'd met last time, huddled into a leather jacket, sitting on a folded newspaper. Giff walked over to him. "Sorry to drag you out on such a lousy day."

"I've been out in worse." Neil's pipe was missing today and his gaze kept sweeping the area nervously.

"Anything wrong?" Giff asked, sitting down beside him.

He reached inside his jacket and pulled out something wrapped in a brown paper bag. "I got what you wanted."

Giff took it, noticing the weight and thinking the piece must be good-size, and stuffed it inside the nylon jogging jacket Tony had given him before he'd left Tucson. Fleetingly, Giff wondered if he'd ever be able to afford nice clothes after paying back Tony. And now he owed Neil, as well. "No numbers, no trace?"

Neil shot him a narrow look. "You think I'm stupid?"

"No, I don't, and I'm sorry." His friend seemed out of sorts. "Is something bothering you?"

"You could say that. I'm an officer of the law who just slipped a convicted felon an unmarked piece. A felon who's hell-bent on revenge and might get himself killed in the process."

Giff ran a hand through his hair, brushing off the rain. "Have you ever known me to do anything rash? To go off half-cocked? To move first and ask questions after?"

Neil huddled deeper into his unzipped jacket. "I guess not."

"If I get caught with this, there's no way someone could trace it back to you, right?"

"Right."

"Then relax. Besides, I'm not going to do anything dumb. I don't have a death wish. I just want to settle a score. Do you blame me for that?" Hell, he'd thought Neil was on his side, that he knew how much catching the men who'd wrongfully put him in prison meant to him. What had happened?

"All right. I just worry about you, that's all." He jammed both hands into his pockets. "How well do you know Trevor Ames?"

That was a question Giff hadn't been expecting. He watched the fisherman reel in a small one before answering. "Not very. He doesn't like me. I think he's a stuffed shirt who's overly impressed with his mickey mouse job." One late night, Giff had broken into Roxie's office and read the file on everyone working at the Eagle's Nest. "He's from England, has no family here and he's very protective of Roxie. Maybe even in love with her, in his own prissy way. Why? You have something?"

"He doesn't have a record, as I told you earlier. But I did a little checking, just to satisfy my curiosity. Did you know he lives in a very expensive house up a mountain? The property's worth about a million, and it's all paid for."

Giff let out a low whistle. He hadn't recognized the address in Trevor's file as being in a posh area. "He could have inherited money."

"Or he could be in on the whole operation with Sam."

Giff chewed on that a minute. "He's worked for the Lowells for something like seventeen years, since before Sam was dealing. Sam only came to the Eagle's Nest three months ago. Is this house a recent purchase?"

"No. He's had it for years." Neil watched a skinny dog amble past them, his nose sniffing the ground. "Maybe he's the kingpin. Maybe he's the one who got Sam up from Tucson in the first place."

Giff couldn't buy that. "Would a guy who has access to millions of dollars' worth of dirty money spend seventeen years managing a neighborhood restaurant? Come on, Neil."

"Hey, I'm just telling you the facts. Why would a guy worth so much be working at all?"

"I don't know. Some guys win the lottery and keep on working." Thoughtfully, he gazed up into the gray sky. "Look, I don't think much of Trevor, but I can't see him heading an international drug-smuggling operation. He doesn't strike me as the type who likes to get his hands dirty." Giff wanted to get on to other, more important things. "I don't suppose you heard any more about where Phil might be?" That was one man he badly wanted to talk with.

"I was down in Tucson yesterday. Ran into Mick Norris. You remember him?"

Mick had been the desk sergeant at the precinct that Giff and Phil had worked out of. "Sure."

"He's retired now. I asked him about Phil and he said that Phil had a lot of trouble after he got shot. Wound up with a limp, turned bitter. He moved down to Mexico for about a year. Mick heard he was back in Arizona, but he didn't know where. Not working in law enforcement that I know of."

"I'd sure as hell like to run into him."

"Forget him. Concentrate on things at this end."

"Yeah, right." The fisherman was calling it a day, packing his box and leaving. Giff couldn't blame him. It wasn't cold, but the rain wasn't letting up. "So, what did your snitches come up with?"

"Thursday's the night."

Giff turned to look at him, suddenly energized. "*This* Thursday, day after tomorrow?" No wonder Neil was nervous.

"That's what my most reliable informant tells me."

"I'm not surprised. Mondays and Thursdays are our slowest nights. How big?"

"He couldn't say, but said it was worth a bust."

"So what do we do?"

"You said there's a phone in the storeroom?" At Giff's nod, he went on. "Make sure you close up alone on Thursday night. When everyone's gone, get into the storeroom and call me, then stay in the shadows. Once I get that call, I'll be able to get some backup. We'll get there and be nearby. Then we wait."

He'd have to pretend to check out the storeroom with Roxie, maybe even see her home, then double back.

"Keep the girl out of it. And *don't* do anything until I show up. You got that?"

"Yeah." Giff's mind was racing. "Why is this one so big?"

"I understand their border location's in jeopardy. They're going to have to find another point where they can cross easily, so that'll mean cutting back for a while. They want the accumulated shipment over here before they have to regroup."

It made sense. "And this informant's on the level?"

"Hey, as good as any of them are. He's been right on in the past. This info cost me five big ones."

Out of his own pocket, since this was so far unofficial. "I'll pay you back."

Neil clapped him on the shoulder and stood. "I know you will. Just keep your nose clean and steer clear of Sam."

Giff didn't see any point in telling him about his arrangement with Roxie and their nightly checks in the storeroom. Neil was plenty nervous as it was. He got up and held out his hand. "Thanks, buddy. I owe you."

Neil shook his hand, turned and walked back to his car.

Giff stood watching him, then zipped up his jacket, the heft of the gun inside reassuring. Close. He was getting close. Two more days. He'd waited more than three years for this chance.

He sent a prayer up to a God he wasn't sure was listening to him any longer that nothing would go wrong this time.

The piece was as clean as could be, Giff thought as he sat examining the gun in the privacy of his locked apartment. The serial numbers had been neatly filed off, and it was oiled and ready to roll.

He'd had one of these before, a nine-millimeter Beretta. He preferred automatics. Slipping out the magazine, he checked it over. Fifteen rounds. Neil had given him extra ammo. He could take out a roomful of people with what he held in his hand.

Provided his aim was still good.

Giff got up and closed the blinds on the window overlooking the backyard. Without the clip in, he practiced drawing from his belt line. Not up to the speed he'd once had, but not too shabby, either. He wanted to wear it from now on, and the best place was in the small of the back, close to his body. Even someone patting you down rarely found a piece carried there. But bartenders didn't wear jackets, so that left that out.

At well over two pounds and about nine inches long, the Beretta was too big to strap to his ankle. He'd have to take it in inside his jacket, then find a hiding place for it behind the bar during work hours. It was risky, but the best he could do.

Rewrapping the gun in the cloth, Giff wished he could fire off a couple of rounds to familiarize himself with this particular piece. Every weapon was different, with varying characteristics. Some pulled a little to the left or right, some hesitated a fraction, a few jerked. There were shooting ranges in town, he knew, but going to one was too dangerous. He couldn't chance being caught out in the open with the piece on him. They'd put him away before he had his revenge. That he couldn't handle.

Checking his watch, he decided he had just enough time to locate Trevor's house and drive by. He still didn't believe the officious little man could head such a big operation, but stranger things had happened.

Roxie leaned back in her desk chair and smiled. "Nikki! It's so good to hear your voice. How is our little mother-to-be?"

In Sedona, Nikki Kendall rearranged her bulk on the sofa facing a roaring fire. "As big as a house, thank you very much."

Roxie still could hardly believe her best friend was married and about to have a baby. She and Nikki had grown up in the same neighborhood, attended college together and even shared Roxie's condo for a while after her divorce from Brad. "And loving every minute of it, I'm sure. Is Adam still spoiling you rotten?"

"I wouldn't say that. He's finally finished putting the addition onto the house after nearly a year at it. He's got four more horses, so now he's expanding the barn." Nikki pushed aside a lock of dark hair as she looked over at her husband reading on the other end of the couch and wrinkled her face at him as he glanced up. "Then there's his painting. He scarcely has time for little old us.'' She ducked as Adam tossed a pillow at her.

Roxie laughed out loud. ''That'll be the day. Seriously, are you doing all right? No problems with the pregnancy?'' She'd had so little time to talk with her friend since her father's death.

''I'm doing just fine. We're in countdown now, though. Only a couple of weeks to go, so I'm pretty clumsy. Why don't you drive up next weekend and veg out with me? We could sit around, eat everything in sight and stay up half the night talking, like we used to do. Remember?''

A wave of nostalgia washed over Roxie. All that seemed so long ago. ''I do remember. I keep meaning to make time for a visit, but I've been so busy at the restaurant.''

''You must be. Every time I call you at home, you're never there.'' Nikki paused a moment, thinking her friend sounded distracted. ''Is everything all right?''

Terrific. If you didn't take into consideration that her family's business had been taken over by drug runners and there was an ex-convict cop working her bar who was getting under her skin far more than she'd thought possible. ''Oh, you know me, I roll with the punches. How's Lindsay?'' Adam's daughter from his first marriage was a cute redhead who would soon turn ten.

Nikki glanced over at the bedroom door of the daughter she'd grown to love as her own. ''She's great. I've taught her how to knit and we're busily making little sweaters and caps and booties.''

''You always were the domestic type. What have you decided about your law practice? Giving it up?''

''Heavens, no. I've taken on a partner, though, and she's handling things for a few months, until after I stop nursing the baby.''

Roxie felt a pang of envy. Would she ever have a family like Nikki did? For years, she hadn't wanted to settle down. Then, when she'd finally decided to, it had been with a man who hadn't wanted the same things she did. "You sound happy, Nikki. I'm glad."

"I am." A low moan came from the rust-colored beagle that lay on the rug near her feet. "You won't believe this, but Maudie's going to have puppies again. I think she was jealous of all the attention I've been getting."

"Must be something in the drinking water up there."

"Since we're on that subject, how's your love life, old friend?"

"What love life?" Roxie asked with a chuckle.

"No Mr. Tall, Dark and Handsome hanging around?"

She hesitated as Giff's image popped into her mind. No, she thought, dismissing the picture, he was definitely not family material. And the next time she got involved, she'd make sure they both had the same goals. Besides, Giff's single-minded focus on clearing his name and getting the bad guys rounded up left little time for thoughts of romance. "No, afraid not."

She'd hesitated a tad too long, Nikki decided. "Are you sure? Or are you holding out on me?"

"Would I do that? Honestly, there's no one I'm seriously interested in at the moment. You'll be the first to know when there is."

"All right, if you say so." Nikki still didn't believe her, but decided to let it go. "When *can* you come up? Are you going to wait until our child's in college to come see us?"

"Nikki, the baby's not even born yet." Glancing at her calendar lying open on her desk, she speculated for a moment about paying her friend a visit then decided she simply couldn't go away and relax with all that was happening right now. "Just as soon as I can see my way clear, I'll give you a call."

"Promise?"

"Absolutely. Give Adam and Lindsay a hug for me. And that promiscuous dog of yours, too. And tell that husband of yours to call me the moment the baby's here."

"I will. Love you, Roxie."

"I love you, too, Nikki. Bye." Hanging up, Roxie blinked rapidly at the unexpected tears that blurred her vision. She'd never been overly sentimental. Why now?

It was all this business with Sam and Giff, with her caught somewhere in the middle. It was making her crazy and she wished it would end soon. Her emotions were so close to the surface that if someone looked at her sideways, she was sure she'd burst into tears.

Enough! She had too much work to do to sit around feeling sorry for herself. She'd been coming in later these days, around four most afternoons, since she always stayed through closing for her inspection of the storeroom with Giff.

It was only ten p.m. and she still had to work on two weekend catering orders. They'd had a full house tonight in the restaurant, including a rowdy party of twenty attending a wedding rehearsal dinner. After eating, quite a few of the guests had gone into the bar. Through her open door, she heard the sound of a woman's high-pitched laugh and the drone of other voices.

Roxie decided that after she finished, she'd wander out and see how things were going. She was getting mighty tired of her own company.

The tall brunette on the bar stool was beautiful, Roxie had to admit. She had long black hair and eyes as green as her friend Nikki's were. If one were to judge by the woman's expensive black dress and heavy gold jewelry, she wasn't short on cash. And judging by the way she was smiling at Giff, she wasn't a shy little thing, either.

Roxie walked over to the corner table and stopped to chat with the Greens, a couple in their sixties who were old friends of her parents'. As she brought them up-to-date on how her mother was faring in Florida, she kept the bartender and his customer in her peripheral view. Not that she cared that the silly woman was all but spilling her cleavage onto the top of the bar. Obviously, just because a person had money didn't mean they had good sense, she thought huffily.

"Mother and Aunt Marian have a lot in common," she told Hannah Green. "They spend time walking on the beach and playing bingo at a local church." She watched Giff serve the brunette a martini straight up with two olives. Like something out of a bad movie, the woman grabbed his hand and pretended to read his palm. Lord, how obvious!

"Has she joined some kind of a support group for widows?" Hannah wanted to know.

Roxie pulled her attention back to the table. "It seems I remember her mentioning that the two of them go to some sort of a friendship group every week, where people talk freely about their loss." How could Giff just stand there and let that woman stroke his palm like that? Wasn't he embarrassed?

"That's good," Fred Green commented. "When my first wife died, I joined a group like that. That's where I met Hannah." He took his wife's hand in his own. "Perhaps your mother will meet someone, too."

Shocked and annoyed, Roxie looked at him. "I seriously doubt it. My father's been dead only six months." Wasn't it just like a man to think that a new widow was already out looking for a replacement? She glared in Giff's direction and caught his eye. He had the good grace to pull back his hand and look chagrined.

"It's hard to live alone, Roxie," Hannah told her. "Especially when you get old."

"My mother's only fifty-four. That's not old. And she's not alone. She's with Aunt Marian."

"I didn't mean to upset you," Fred said apologetically.

Perhaps she was overreacting. Roxie found a small smile. "I know, and I'm not upset. It's just that I can't imagine Mother with... with anyone but Dad."

Fred nodded knowingly. "Life goes on, Roxie."

"I suppose." She glanced up at the clock and saw it was ten minutes to closing. Only the Greens, the brunette and three members of the bridal party at a round table remained. She wished they'd all leave so she could.

Fred drained his beer glass and reached for his wallet. "Well, Mama, do you think you're ready to head for home?" He turned to Roxie. "It's our tenth wedding anniversary. Between us now, we have ten grandchildren."

"That's great. Congratulations." She rose. "Put your money away, Mr. Green. Allow me to buy your drinks as thanks for celebrating with us."

The Greens thanked her and left. Roxie stifled a yawn as she walked to the back. She watched a man from the bridal party stroll over to the brunette, slip his arm around her and say something. Apparently, the woman didn't like his suggestion for she shook her head, then smiled at Giff who'd walked over to the other end of the bar to wash glasses.

"Run along, Rick. He'll take me home," the brunette purred. "Won't you, honey?"

His hands in soapy water, Giff frowned. "Afraid not. You'd better go with your friend."

Her red lips moved into a pout. "I don't want to go with him. I want to go with you."

"Not this time." Giff glanced over to where Roxie was watching the exchange with cool eyes. Now, what was eating her? Didn't she know that every bartender got propositioned almost nightly by some bored woman who'd had one too many? And why should Roxie care, anyhow?

"Come on, Paula," Rick said, taking her arm and helping her off the stool.

Paula shook Rick's arm off and made her unsteady way over to where Giff was now drying glasses. "If not tonight, then when, honey? I'm footloose and fancy-free, and I like your type."

A good bartender also never riled a customer. Bad for business. He gave her a smile. "You come back some evening, and we'll talk about it."

To Giff's relief, that seemed to satisfy Paula. She drained her martini, pursed her lips and blew him a kiss. Finally, she turned and let Rick lead her to the door where their friends were waiting.

Ginny cleared the table and walked to the bar, slipping off her shoes and stretching her aching feet. "She's sure hot to trot, Giff." She grinned at him as she pulled her vouchers from her pocket. "You sure you want to pass on taking her home?"

"Yeah, I'm sure." Hanging up the towel, he glanced at Roxie. Unsmiling, she gazed at him a long moment, then turned and walked toward her office. He almost swore aloud.

Impatiently, Giff waited for Ginny to tally up and leave. He checked the lighting, then looked into Roxie's open office. She was standing, staring out the window at the dark night. "You ready?" he asked.

She whirled and picked up her keys. "Yes." Hurriedly, she breezed past him and headed for the storeroom.

At the door, he watched her make two stabs at getting the key in. "Is something the matter?"

"Not a thing." She swung open the door, flipped on the light and stood there while he moved inside and checked each row of cartons. She hoped he wouldn't find anything tonight. She wasn't up to more cops-and-robbers stuff right now.

Finished, he came out, told her he hadn't found anything out of the ordinary and waited for her to lock up. When she walked to the back door without another word, he followed and grabbed her arm, pulling her around to face him. "What's eating you?"

"Nothing. I'm tired."

Somehow, he didn't believe that was all. "How about a cup of coffee and a little conversation?" What was wrong with him? Giff asked himself. Neil had warned him to keep her out of it. With this sudden show of temper, she'd probably stay away from him for days, which was just what he wanted. Why, then, was he asking her to stay?

"Not tonight." She turned and unlatched the back door.

"Come on. Just one."

"Why don't you go find your brunette barfly and have coffee with her?" The moment the words were out of her mouth, she wanted desperately to call them back. Instead, she pulled open the door.

He shoved it shut and glared at her. "What the hell's going on? You're really off base if you think I'm interested in that tipsy dame. And even if I were, what's it to you?"

The unreasonable anger she'd been struggling with for the past hour drained out of Roxie, leaving her feeling embarrassed and awkward. He was absolutely right. What he did away from here was none of her business. She couldn't ever remember acting quite this stupid before. "You're right. It's your business." She just wanted to get away, to go home. Her fingers closed on the doorknob.

Giff swore under his breath, took her other hand and tugged until her body came up tight against his. In the harsh overhead light, he searched her eyes and didn't like what he found. "Didn't you tell me a few nights ago that you weren't going to get involved with a guy like me again?"

She could feel his heart beating next to hers, could smell his hot male scent. Roxie swallowed hard. "Yes. And I'm *not* involved. So you can let me go."

"Uh-huh." His arms around her tightened.

Two could play this game. "Didn't you tell me the day we met that you weren't interested in women?" she said pointedly.

"Right. I'm not. Not at this time in my life, that is."

"Terrific. Then let me go."

Why did she have to feel so damn good in his arms? Why had he ever touched her in the first place? "I don't need this right now. And neither do you."

"Exactly." She wished he'd let her go. She wished he'd *never* let her go. The way her insides were churning was making her light-headed.

Giff felt as if he were losing himself in those soft brown eyes. He shifted his gaze to her trembling lips and knew instantly that that was a mistake. "Ah, hell," he said, and took her mouth.

It wasn't like before, Roxie thought. It was better. When he'd kissed her in the parking lot, he'd crushed and plundered and ravaged. Now, his arms held her loosely and his mouth on hers was soft, gentle, persuasive.

Which made the kiss so much more deadly.

She could have moved her head aside or pushed him away, she knew. Instead, she opened to him, her lips loving the feel of his, her tongue welcoming his. With a sigh, she let him take her up the roller coaster to the summit.

His first thought was that she fit so well with him. All her sweet curves seemed to melt into the hard planes of his body as if made for him alone. He couldn't alibi away this kiss, say that it was for Sam who might be watching. No one was around. No one to take the blame. Except himself.

And he wanted her. God, how he wanted her. Her scent that drove him crazy each time he passed her wrapped around him up close and had his blood singing. The special taste of her that already was familiar exploded on his tongue. And Giff knew he was lost.

He needed to explore farther and sent his mouth on a journey of her face. He felt her shiver, her hands at his back gripping him, and returned to her mouth to feast again. His head was swimming and he felt as if he were drowning. Drowning in her and his suddenly huge need.

Pulling back at last, Roxie eased down from her tiptoes and looked at him, then felt her breath back up in her lungs. His eyes were hot, hungry and locked on hers. He was everything she'd ever longed for and everything she shouldn't want. She took a step backward, then another.

She needed air, she needed time and space. God help her, she needed him.

Without bothering to adjust her clothing, she opened the door. "I've got to go. You lock up." And she hurried out.

"Roxie, wait, please." He felt as if he should do something, say something, explain. Only he had no answers.

"No," she said. "I can't talk about this now." Almost at a run, she rushed to her car through a lightly falling rain.

Giff watched her go, his fists balled at his sides.

It was an unseasonably cold night for October, Roxie thought, probably because it had rained all day. She wrapped herself in her long white terry-cloth robe and belted it, shook out her damp hair and walked barefoot to the kitchen to put the kettle on for tea. She felt better after a long, hot shower. Maybe the tea would relax her enough to allow her to sleep.

She'd no sooner poured boiling water over the tea bag in her mug when she heard her front doorbell. It was nearly three in the morning. Her heart was pounding as she padded through the living room, turned on the porch light and peered out her peephole.

Giff was standing on her front stoop, brushing rain out of his hair, his shoulders hunched against the chill. Roxie took in a deep, calming breath. What on earth did he want at this hour? Perhaps she could plead fatigue. She didn't feel up to round two.

She unlocked the door and opened it a crack, leaving the chain in place. She didn't speak, just looked at him.

He felt stupid, but he'd come this far. "I couldn't sleep so I thought I'd drive around. I saw your lights and thought you couldn't, either." She looked small and fragile in the deep folds of her thick robe, her hair damp and loose. Her face was clear of makeup, making her look younger, more vulnerable. "I don't suppose you'd have a cup of coffee?"

She could refuse and, considering that it was the middle of the night, she could hardly be thought rude. Yet, for the first time in the weeks she'd known him, she thought he looked like a young boy who'd lost his way. She eased the door closed, removed the chain and swung it open.

It felt good to get in out of the rain. Giff removed his jacket and rubbed his hands together. "It's cold out there. Good night for a fire."

She gestured toward the corner fireplace where the logs were stacked and waiting. "You can light it if you want while I make the coffee. I was just having a cup of tea."

"Tea would be fine." He wasn't much of a tea drinker, but then, he hadn't really come for the coffee, either. Why had he come? Giff asked himself as he picked up the box of fireplace matches on the hearth and removed one.

He'd come to set the record straight. He'd come to tell her why it could never be between them, at least not now. Maybe never. Maybe something would go wrong and he wouldn't get Sam and the others this time. Then he'd have to wait for them to surface somewhere else, go after them again. He couldn't, *wouldn't*, ask any woman to wait all that time. He didn't want to hurt her.

No matter that she had a stake in getting them to justice, too. No matter that it was her family's restaurant that scumbag had chosen to desecrate and that just maybe he'd even had something to do with her father's untimely death. Basically, it was *his* fight, *his* war.

Giff opened the flue, held the match to the papers and kindling bunched under the logs and watched them catch. When he was certain the fire was going, he straightened and closed the wire-mesh curtain. On the way over, he'd told himself that he needed to talk with her, to let her know he didn't want to take advantage of her. He didn't want her to care for him even a little.

Sex was one thing, caring another. What he'd seen in her eyes tonight had been more than desire. It had been deep-down need, the kind that went to the soul and reached out to another. Roxie wasn't a quick-roll-in-the-hay, see-you-around type of woman. And he couldn't afford any other kind.

It had been a long time since anyone had cared for him—really cared for him—aside from his brother. He'd thought Carla cared, but he'd been wrong. She'd taught him that he didn't *want* anyone to care for him ever again. Someone cared for you and before you knew it, you started to care back. And then you were vulnerable, fair game for anyone who wanted to hurt you. And there were plenty who wanted to hurt him.

Better an easy letdown now than a more painful withdrawal later.

Roxie brought in the two mugs of tea, placed them on the table in front of the fire and curled up in the far corner of the couch. She saw that he'd changed out of his work clothes into faded jeans that lovingly molded to his strong thighs and long legs and a white cotton sweater with the sleeves pushed up on his strong arms. Except for the day she'd met him, she hadn't seen him out of his white-shirt-and-black-pants bar outfit, and she had to admit the casual outfit suited him more.

Roxie watched him sit down next to her, not close enough to touch, yet not at the other end. As he angled his body toward her, she took in the black curly hair in the V-neck of his sweater, the faint dark stubble on his chin and the small scar there, the piercing blue of his eyes. Dropping her gaze, she reached for her cup and saw that her hand was less than steady.

Giff took a swallow of tea, wondering why he felt like a damn teenager facing his first real-live girl. Setting the mug down, he cleared his throat and stretched his arm along the couch back. "I want to tell you a story."

"All right."

He paused, wondering where to begin. "About a year before the drug bust that ended my police career, I met a woman. Her name is Carla Prinz. She was born in Nogales, Mexico, didn't know who her father was, was abandoned by her mother in her early teens and was left alone to grow up on the streets." Giff forced himself to take a breath, to talk dispassionately, almost as if he hadn't been involved. "But she rose above it.

"We had a lot in common. My mother left us when I was barely ten. My father's name was Tony and he was the original owner of Tony's Bar and Grille. He got killed during a robbery when I was fifteen. My brother took over the bar, working long hours, so I sort of raised myself from then on. And I did my share of running on the streets, too."

Now Roxie understood how he'd been able to relate so well to Ginny's troubled young son. She also saw how difficult it was for him to reveal this much about himself.

Giff looked over and saw she was watching him intently, her hands curled around her mug. He wondered what she was thinking, and pushed on before he could change his mind. "Anyhow, my partner, Phil Weston, introduced me to Carla, and I fell pretty hard. She's small, with all this black hair and beautiful brown eyes. Like yours."

Silently, she waited for him to go on.

"Carla tried to get me to quit the force, but I wouldn't do it. We fought about that a lot. Then, when I was arrested and went to trial, she didn't come around. Finally, I called her and that's when she told me. She was going back to Mexico. She couldn't handle waiting around for me to get out of prison." His mouth a hard line, Giff gazed out the window behind them into the darkness. "Another one I owe Sam and his friends."

Roxie didn't see it quite that way. "You blame Sam for Carla's not standing by you? Don't you think, if she'd have cared enough, she'd have waited, no matter what? Aren't you the one who told me that Brad couldn't have cared enough for me or he'd have never let me go?"

His blue eyes bore into hers. He knew she was right. It was just so damn hard to accept. "Yeah. So we both thought we had someone who cared, and they took the easy way out, right?"

"I guess so." She set down her empty mug. "Why did you come over tonight to tell me this?"

Giff moved closer to her on the couch, intent on making her see, unsure why it was so important to him that she did. "Because I wanted to let you know that letting yourself care for me would be a mistake. Correct me if I'm wrong, but I

thought that's what I saw in your eyes tonight. That's why
you ran from me, isn't it? Because you realized it, too.''

He saw the truth on her face, but she didn't answer. A log
in the grate shifted and she jumped, her nerves on edge.

"I don't want to hurt you, Roxie. And I'm not going to
lie to you. I want you badly. But I don't have anything to
offer you. Not love, not a future, not hope. My life's on
hold, in limbo. I can't concentrate on what I have to do to
clear my name if I get wrapped up in you. I can't afford a
diversion.''

Her eyes grew wide with hurt. "Is that what I would be,
a diversion?''

Frustrated, Giff ran a hand through his hair. "I'm saying this badly." He saw the moisture cloud her eyes and felt
like a heel. "Please don't cry." He watched her turn away
from him, from the truth she hadn't wanted to hear.

"Damn it, I can't seem to do anything right." Moving to
her, he pulled her into his arms, settling her head against his
chest. His hands smoothed her hair and he felt her heart
pick up its rhythm. As his had.

Shifting to look into her face, he knew he was about to
lose the battle and probably the war. Slowly, he lowered his
mouth and kissed her.

With a catch in her throat, Roxie reached for him, returning the kiss with all the emotion that had been churning inside her since she'd left him at the bar. He'd been right
to warn her, right to tell her just how it was. The problem
was that the warning had come too late.

She hadn't wanted to care for this hard, desperate, troubled man. She'd been cautious all her life and yet, here she
was, pressing herself shamelessly to him. She'd steered clear
of relationships since Brad, thinking it was better not to love
at all than to love and be hurt again. But from Giff's first
touch, she'd thrown out her own rule book.

Blood rushed through Giff's veins like a runaway train.
He was losing ground, losing control. He'd been kidding
himself that his desire was so strong because of his years of

celibacy. He no longer believed the lie. He'd been out two months and could have had any number of women if physical release alone was what he craved. But he hadn't had to struggle for control unless it was Roxie's arms around him, Roxie's mouth pressed to his, Roxie's soft sounds he heard.

Breathing hard, he eased back to trail kisses down her throat and into the opening of her robe. She smelled so good and her skin was softer than silk. She moaned as he continued, and he dared to raise his hands and part the folds of her robe above the knotted belt, discovering she had on nothing underneath.

Pale and beautiful in the firelight, her breasts shimmered, their peaks hardening under his heated gaze. He filled his hands with her swollen breasts and closed his eyes on a rush of pleasure. "You are so beautiful," he whispered, then lowered his mouth to one rigid peak.

Roxie's restless hands settled in his hair as she pressed his head closer to her yearning flesh. The ache of desire raced through her, seeking fulfillment, longing for more. The pleasure was so intense that another low sound escaped from her.

Giff returned to kiss her face, then to her waiting mouth as he crushed her breasts against his chest. He wanted to rip off his sweater, to feel her against his skin. He wanted to carry her upstairs to her bed, to bury himself inside her, to love her all night long while the rain beat on the roof above them. He wanted this feeling to never go away, this woman to never leave him.

Only she would.

Reality intruded, jerking him back. She would leave because he still had to walk through hell before he would be free, and he needed to walk alone. He couldn't risk having still another woman turn from him because she couldn't wait. It would be wrong of him to ask Roxie to go through that.

With shaky fingers, he drew the folds of her robe over the breasts he hated like hell to cover, then sucked in a deep breath before meeting her eyes. "I can't tell you how hard it is for me to walk away from you tonight."

She would not beg, would not even ask him to stay. And she could not trust herself to speak.

He knew he'd hurt her already, but this was nothing compared to what might come. Giff tipped up her chin with one hand. "Say something, anything."

Roxie closed her eyes and shook her head as her hands grasped her upper arms and she hugged herself, shrinking into the corner of the couch away from him.

He wanted to swear, to hit something hard. Instead, he got to his feet and picked up his jacket. He saw a lone tear trail down her soft cheek, and felt like a sonofabitch. Quickly, before he lost his courage, he left her house.

Leaning her head onto her bent knees, Roxie let the rest of the tears fall.

Chapter 6

The Wednesday-night drinking crowd was light, which gave Giff plenty of chances to walk out from behind the bar and wander into the restaurant with one excuse or another, unobtrusively checking on Sam. Wearing a powder-blue suit with navy shirt and white tie, Sam table-hopped, sitting down with this customer and that, his usual congenial self. Just once, Giff thought he'd seen those shrewd dark eyes studying him from behind his glasses. Then he was laughing with the table of out-of-towners and Giff wondered if he'd imagined the look.

Back at the bar, his eyes kept checking everyone out more than usual. For some reason, he felt jittery. Probably anticipating tomorrow night's stakeout, he told himself.

Roxie hadn't come in until after his shift had begun at six, wearing sunglasses even though it was cloudy out. She'd immediately holed up in her office and the few times he'd passed her open doorway, she'd been bent over paperwork. She hadn't spoken a word to him since he'd left her so abruptly last night.

Giff placed two tall vodka and tonics with wedges of lime on Ginny's tray and handed her the bill.

"You're a million miles away tonight, Giff," Ginny told him. "You feel okay?"

"Yeah, fine." He turned to hand a glass of beer to a brooding bald man seated on a bar stool.

Fine wasn't exactly how he felt, Giff acknowledged. Nervous was more like it. Edgy, irritable, tense. All of the above and more. Mad at himself for the way he'd botched things up last night. He'd gone over to her place with the best intentions, to set things straight between himself and Roxie, and then had nearly taken her right there on her living room couch.

It was a damn good thing she was avoiding him tonight. If he looked into those huge, hurt eyes, it would surely unravel his renewed promises to himself. He'd be more than distracted. He'd want to chuck the whole matter, say to hell with trying to break up the drug ring, take her hand and run away somewhere quiet where no one knew either one of them.

But he had debts, both of money and of honor, that he needed to repay. To Tony and to Neil. And most of all, to himself. A man had to examine himself in the mirror every day, and it was damn hard to shave when you couldn't look yourself in the eye without cringing.

He glanced at his watch and saw it was only eight. The Suns were beating Seattle on their home court on the television over the bar, but the sound wasn't loud. Giff found himself wishing it was tomorrow night.

In her office, Roxie reached for a pen and knocked over a half-filled cup of coffee. Swearing at her own clumsiness, she jumped up and reached for the tissue box she kept in her drawer. Mopping up, she swore again when she realized she'd ruined her only copy of next month's schedule that she'd just finished. Now she'd have to dry it off and redo it.

She dropped the soggy tissues into the basket and sat down. Nothing, but nothing, was going right today. She'd cut her finger opening the coffee can this morning. She'd ruined a brand-new pair of panty hose when she was putting them on. And she'd nearly run out of gas on the way here, chugging into the gas station on fumes.

Whatever had happened to her marvelous organizational skills?

They'd flown out the window when Giff had breezed in the door. Whoever said that having a man in your life muddles your mind knew what they were talking about.

She'd cried it all out last night and finally come to a couple of decisions. Giff had been absolutely right about at least one thing: their tenuous relationship had nowhere to go. Their attraction was too new, too nebulous to survive the current complications. The loneliness she sensed in him reached out to her, perhaps because occasionally she felt a similar bleakness. But that was hardly a basis for a serious relationship. He was hell-bent on getting Sam and the others; she was equally determined to discover if Sam was somehow responsible for her father's death.

That had to take priority over her other, more personal needs. They could never have anything worthwhile to build on until their past problems were cleared up. Her analysis seemed correct, seemed the right way to proceed.

Then why did she feel depressed?

Because she'd allowed herself to care too much too soon, a new failing of hers. The last time she'd thought she cared a great deal for a man, she'd had years to know and assess Brad. And the relationship hadn't fared any better. Was she just a lousy judge of men or did the men who came into her life just not care enough? Roxie wondered.

It was a moot point. Giff had told her yesterday that tomorrow was the night of the stakeout. He didn't want her around for it, but that decision wasn't up to him. Roxie would not only be around, but was determined to play an active part. Sam may have stolen three years of Giff's life down in Tucson, but he may have robbed her father of far more.

Roxie badly wanted to even the score.

So, for now, she'd put her feelings for Giff aside until they cleared up this mess. Then, they'd talk and decide if there was anything of lasting value in what they shared. Roxie had gone to bed and actually slept well after having reached that conclusion last night.

But she was still edgy, knowing tomorrow was the day. Giff may be used to all this tension in trying to trap criminals, but she was not. Aside from her own fears, she was afraid he'd get hurt again, which was why she intended to be nearby with her weapon at the ready. She knew he dismissed her as merely a woman toting around a silly little gun for show. Little did he know she went regularly to a shooting range and was an expert markswoman.

Still, she prayed she wouldn't have to use the gun. Hitting a target was one thing. Firing at another human being was quite another. The fact that she never had didn't stop her from forming her plan. Just as her confidence in her shooting ability didn't prevent her from being scared silly.

Rising, she decided to go into the kitchen to see if there was any coffee left and maybe a piece of fruit. She hadn't eaten since lunch. It was hours till closing and she could probably use something in her stomach.

As she passed through the swinging door, she almost turned around and walked back. Sam was adding whipped cream to two Irish coffee mugs. He looked startled to see her, Roxie thought as she walked past him to the coffeepot. "I thought they made those at the bar," she commented.

Sam recovered quickly. "Giff was busy so I thought I'd make them up myself. From the private stock I keep in my desk drawer," he added with a wink. "A friend is visiting from Tucson and we've just finished dinner. I took him into my office for a nightcap."

"I see." She walked to the refrigerator and gazed in.

Sam came alongside and replaced the whipped cream container. "Have you switched to working nights? You're not around much during the day anymore," he said.

Roxie sent him a cool look as she reached in for an apple. "I don't believe our arrangement specified that I be here certain hours. I get the work done."

"Hey, I wasn't complaining. Just commenting. Why are you so touchy?" He picked up the tray and sent her a questioning look.

She'd reacted and shouldn't have. The last thing she wanted was for Sam to get suspicious, especially now. "Sorry. Must be the full moon, or something." She held the door open for him. She gritted her teeth as he brushed against her unnecessarily as he passed. Roxie felt like letting the swinging door bang into him, but refrained from indulging herself.

In the hallway, she saw Trevor coming toward her and smiled a greeting. There was a time when she'd spent half an hour or so evenings just chatting with him, and she felt bad that she'd neglected her old friend. "How are things, Trevor?"

"Fine, just fine." He smoothed back his thin hair in a gesture of vanity that Roxie had noticed he often displayed in her presence. "You're looking so much better, more rested. And I love that suit."

It was dark green, a shade that went well with her coloring, Roxie knew. "Thanks. Are you leaving?"

"Unless you'd like me to stay and close up? I don't mind."

"No. Giff will do that. You have a good evening, what's left of it." She turned and was about to go into her office when a big man stepped out of Sam's doorway, his face stormy. Close on his heels was Sam. Curiosity had her rooted to the spot.

"Uh, Roxie," Sam said, noticing her, "this is—"

"Johnny," the big man said, extending a beefy hand. "And you must be Sam's pretty little manager." His eyes drifted down to her legs, then journeyed back up, and he lost his frown.

Swallowing the quick retort that sprang into her mind, Roxie managed a smile as she gave his hand the merest of shakes. He had a poor complexion and thick lips—a thoroughly repulsive man. "I understand you're from Tucson."

Johnny glanced at Sam, then to her. "Yeah, Tucson."

So much for small talk. She'd met a few other friends of Sam's and they all seemed about as interesting. "Well, enjoy your Irish coffee."

Sam locked his office door. "We don't have time for it, after all. A friend called and we're off to see him." He gave her a tight smile. "See you tomorrow."

Roxie stood watching them rush toward the restaurant and the front door, a puzzled frown on her face. What, she wondered, was Sam up to?

Giff was jumpy with nerves tonight, Roxie noticed as she relocked the storeroom door after their inspection. Worse than she herself was, which was unusual. "Is something wrong?"

"No. There are no new cartons in there." Slowly, Giff walked to the back door with her, surprised that she'd picked up on his tension. Nothing seemed amiss, yet he had this *feeling* that everything wasn't right. Call it a hunch or perhaps it was his naturally suspicious nature. The fact that Roxie could read him so well after knowing him less than a month bothered him almost as much as this persistent sense of foreboding.

"I don't mean in the storeroom. I mean otherwise. You seem . . . I don't know . . . jittery . . . tense."

He opened the back door, planning to walk her to her car, then double back. He just wanted to check things out one more time alone. "Probably because tomorrow's the night. I've been waiting for this chance a long time."

She believed that much, at least, and hoped there wasn't something else he wasn't telling her.

The Mustang was in the parking lot. Giff had advised her not to park on the side street anymore because Sam would become suspicious and ask why she wasn't using the lot even though she stayed late most nights. She opened the car door, then paused. "Sam had a friend in tonight."

Giff was immediately interested. "Did Sam introduce him?"

"He started to, but the man interrupted and said his name was Johnny. No last name."

"What did he look like?"

"Like something off the old "Munsters" TV show. Big, hulky. Thick brown hair, small eyes, bad skin."

"What time was this?"

"Shortly after ten."

"Did Sam make it a point to find you and introduce you?"

"No, I bumped into them leaving his office. They seemed in a big hurry and I got the feeling they'd been angry or quarreling. Do you know this Johnny?"

Giff shook his head. "Probably not his real name. There was one big man at the Tucson restaurant that night, and one much smaller. But all three of them wore ski masks. I'll run the description by Neil next time we talk."

She'd run out of things to say. Besides, he looked preoccupied. "Would you like a ride home?" she asked.

"Thanks, but I like to walk."

Still, she hesitated, studying his closed expression. She might as well have been waiting for a granite wall to give her a sign. She closed the door and started the engine. "See you tomorrow."

Giff watched her drive off, then started slowly walking toward his apartment in case she was watching or doubled back to check on him. Almost there, he realized there were no cars in sight. Quickly, he walked back to the Eagle's Nest and let himself in the back way, locking the door.

With just the usual night-lights on, he retrieved his gun from its hiding place behind the bar and stuck it into his belt at the small of his back, hiding it with his cotton jacket. Then he moved through every room, beginning with the restaurant itself. He couldn't have said what it was he was looking for. Some telltale evidence that would account for his feeling of unease, some small thing that wasn't where it should be. Silently, he surveyed the corners, the offices, the kitchen, the barroom.

Finally, he returned to the storeroom and was bending low to open the lock with his small tool when he heard a car drive into the parking lot and park close to the door. A vehicle with a large engine idling. Hurriedly, he entered, locked the door and hid behind two large cartons in the farthest corner. Had Sam gotten wind of the sting and decided to move a day early? Was the man named Johnny that Roxie had seen involved? Apparently, his gut instinct that had drawn him back tonight was still on target, Giff thought.

But if he was right, how the hell was he going to notify Neil?

Scarcely daring to breathe, Giff waited, listening to the back door open and muffled male voices.

When he heard the back door open and footsteps come toward the storeroom, he reached for his gun and removed the safety.

The light flashed on and Sam entered, followed closely by a large man with heavy footsteps. Giff was so familiar with the storeroom that he could track their movements without actually seeing them. Since they were a day early, they wouldn't be expecting any trouble. For a moment, he entertained the idea that they were unarmed, but then dismissed that thought. Could that hulky Johnny, or whatever his real name was, be the top man?

"Put them over there on that empty shelf," Giff heard Sam say.

The other man grunted over the sound of cardboard boxes clunking down on metal shelves. "Do we wait for the pickup?"

"We better. Remember last time when we left early?"

The big guy groaned. "I'd rather not."

"Maybe we better check these." Sam got out his knife and Giff heard the sound of the blade ripping through cardboard.

It took Giff only a few seconds to decide what to do. Apparently, they were waiting for a pickup truck tonight. He didn't know how many boxes they'd lugged in, but by the sound of it, there were several. There'd be no point in staying out of sight until still more men arrived and letting them cart off the goods. He had to act, act fast and act now.

Silently, he crept out and moved to the end of the aisle where he could see them. Gripping his Beretta in shooting stance, he braced his legs. "Stop right there!" he ordered.

The big man ducked into a crouch, but Sam's hand went for his belt line without turning around.

"I wouldn't," Giff said, his voice steely. "Get your hands up high, both of you." His back to the open doorway, he inched around so he had both of them in his full view.

Sam got the message, turned slowly and raised his hands. His face registered no surprise that the man behind the gun was Giff. "You're in over your head, cowboy," he warned.

"Just stand perfectly still, both of you." Never taking his eyes from them, Giff moved to the wall phone.

"Don't be stupid," Sam told him. "After Tucson, do you think the cops will believe you?"

So Sam knew who he was. Why hadn't the man acted sooner? Giff wondered. He grabbed the receiver, but before he could punch in a single number, a shot rang out from the hallway behind him. He felt the hot bullet rip through his back below his shoulder, the force knocking him to the floor. He angled around, aimed in the general direction of the hall and squeezed the trigger.

And nothing happened. Hell of a time for his gun to jam, Giff thought with a surge of frustration. The effort had cost him and he fell face forward, the pain taking over, the blackness of oblivion reaching for him.

Suddenly, in the distance, sirens could be heard, the shrill sound coming closer. From the hallway, someone shouted, "Hurry!" Through a red mist, Giff heard heavy, uneven footsteps retreating as if the gunman had moved out, then the back door slamming shut.

The big man walked to Giff and kicked him in the side. Giff didn't move. "Looks like he's gone."

On his stomach, Giff kept his eyes closed, hoping Sam would believe his friend. If they thought he was dead, he might yet have a chance.

The sirens screamed, nearing. "Damn, I thought we'd taken care of the cops," the big man mumbled, then moved to the other aisle and the boxes he'd placed on the shelves.

Torn between checking Giff's condition and gathering up the expensive white powder, Sam made a hasty decision and followed his friend.

Straining to listen, Giff heard them shuffling around one aisle over. Seizing the moment, he braced himself against the pain and, making as little sound as possible, got to his feet and left the storeroom. The bar seemed the best bet. He hurried there, crouching down out of sight. His shoulder hurt like hell, but he couldn't let the ache distract him. Anchoring his gun hand, he kept the doorway in sight and his weapon ready.

"They're coming closer," Sam said, cocking his ear. He dropped the box he'd been carrying and moved toward the doorway. "We don't have enough time."

"There's going to be hell to pay if we don't take the goods," the other man insisted.

Sam knew he was right. The boss didn't like screwups. But he'd discovered a bigger problem. "What the hell?" he asked, looking around. "Where's Garrison?"

Coming up behind him, the big man looked around. "I thought he was a goner. We gotta find him. You search the kitchen. I'll go up front." From the direction of the parking lot, they heard the *beep-beep* of a car horn honking.

"We'll never make it if we don't go *now*," Sam said urgently. Sure he wanted to get Giff. But he wanted to save his own skin more. Sam opened the back door and gazed out. Through the open window, the driver of the van motioned them to hurry.

"The boss ain't going to like this," Johnny said.

"Do you think it would be better if we wound up in a squad car? Come on." Sam rushed out, leaving the door ajar.

Muttering to himself, the big man hurried after him.

Behind the bar, Giff had listened to the exchange, but didn't dare move. He heard two car doors slam, then wheels squealing as the vehicle left the parking lot. Grabbing hold of the counter, he eased to a full standing position and drew in a ragged breath.

He could feel blood oozing onto his shirt in back. Already, his knees were weak and his hands not quite steady. His face was bathed in perspiration. He had to get help.

But from whom?

Walking with difficulty, he moved to the back door and carefully peered out. No car in sight. The sirens were still shrieking, but the sound seemed farther away. Or did it just seem that way because he was getting light-headed?

He staggered toward the storeroom, trying desperately to think. Should he call Neil? Why hadn't Neil known the delivery would be today? Had they gotten to his last friend? And there was the fact that the gun he'd been given had jammed.

Giff struggled with a wave of dizziness, bending low, trying to stay conscious. Roxie. She was his only hope. He didn't want to involve her, but he couldn't stay here like a sitting duck and wait for the police to find him with those boxes of cocaine. It would be like last time. And he couldn't let that happen, not again.

With his last ounce of strength, Giff dragged himself toward the phone, fighting the blackness that threatened to engulf him. He looked up through the sweat pouring into his eyes and saw the receiver dangling. At the wall, he stretched to reach it.

God, it was so far away.

By nature, she wasn't a worrier, Roxie reminded herself. Or hadn't been before her father's death and all this business with the restaurant takeover had begun. Nikki used to call herself the worrywart and had labeled Roxie the carefree one. Most all of their friends would agree.

Then why was she pacing her living room at three in the morning, wondering why Giff didn't answer his phone?

She'd called to . . . well, to talk. To hear more about what was to happen tomorrow night. After all, they could hardly discuss the whole operation at the Eagle's Nest where the walls had ears. But he wasn't answering his phone, the damn answering machine beeping on.

He could be out walking, or driving as he had the other evening when he'd told her he couldn't sleep. Or he could be with some woman who was less complicated than she, who would willingly jump into bed with him, then kiss him goodbye without a second thought. She had to give him credit. He'd quickly spotted that that wasn't her style.

She frowned, gazing out her window into the peaceful darkness, the moonlight filtering through the palm trees, their fronds shifting in a cool night breeze. He'd seemed so restless tonight, so distracted. Of course, the schedule of events for tomorrow night had to be worrying him, especially since the last time he'd been up against these men, everything that could go wrong had done exactly that. And this time, he had her to worry about, as well.

She paused, considering. If she knew his home address, she'd drive over. But he'd never given it to her. She hadn't left a message on his answering machine, uncertain exactly what to say. Maybe he just wasn't answering the phone.

Finally, she could stand it no longer. Shrugging into her light jacket, she went outside and climbed behind the wheel. She decided to drive by the Eagle's Nest to see if perhaps she could spot Giff walking in the neighborhood.

But the lot was deserted. She drove up close to the back door, nerves tingling along her spine. Grabbing her purse with the gun inside, she got out.

The first shock was that the door was unlocked. At that, she pulled out her gun and stepped into the back hallway. The storeroom was wide open with the light on. A man was sprawled on his back on the floor almost in the doorway. His face was turned away, but she could tell by his clothes that it was Giff. The fingers of his one hand were curled around a gun.

Her thoughts racing, Roxie ran to him and stooped down, feeling for a pulse. Her heart began again when she found that his was beating steadily. Had he just been knocked out? There were signs of a struggle and several boxes were lying on their sides nearby. And one of those plastic bags containing white powder was on the floor. Sam must have suspected they were on to him and moved the delivery date to tonight. Giff must have caught him at it and . . .

It was then that she saw the blood seeping onto the floor from beneath his right shoulder. "Oh, Lord, you've been hurt."

She heard Giff moan. Quickly, she went to the kitchen, soaked a towel with cold water and grabbed another dry one. Back beside him, she wet his face, trying to bring him around. "Giff, wake up. What happened? We need to get you to the hospital. What's your friend's name at the police station? Neil something. I'll call him and—"

His eyes opened, darkly commanding and filled with pain. "No, don't call anyone." He groaned, trying to sit up, but a wave of dizziness had him closing his eyes and grabbing her arm.

She tucked the dry towel onto his wound in an effort to stop the bleeding. "You need medical help." She knew it was difficult for him to talk, but she needed to know. "Was it Sam who did this?"

"There were three of them." His breath huffed out as he struggled to clear his head. "Sam and that big guy you mentioned. Another guy in the hall."

"I thought you trusted this Neil. Why shouldn't I call him?"

Holding on to her, Giff pushed himself to his feet. "Don't know who my friends are right now. I've got to get to a safe place where I can think."

"All right, first things first. Let me get you into my car and we'll plan what to do when we're away from here." When had she decided to help him? She wasn't sure. She only knew that she had to.

Giff looked down at the Beretta still in his right hand. "Damn weapon jammed, or I'd have winged one of them."

She put her arm around him and they made it to the back door. "Check around before we go out," he said, leaning against the wall.

Roxie did and found everything quiet. She helped him into the passenger side of her Mustang, tilting the seat back so he'd be comfortable. She still wanted to get him medical help.

Giff grabbed her sleeve. "Those boxes, plain, unmarked. Three of them in the aisle. Not too heavy if you carry one at a time. Put them in the trunk."

"Oh, Giff, what for? Let them have the damn stuff."

"It's our only bargaining chip." His voice was weak, but his eyes burned into hers.

She might have known something like a second bullet wound wouldn't stop his quest for revenge. She shut his car door, went back for the boxes and put them side by side into her trunk. She returned one last time for several more towels and a bag of ice, plus a couple of cold drinks. Just as she was getting behind the wheel, she heard a shrill sound coming closer.

"Sirens," Giff mumbled. "Heard 'em earlier. Don't know what happened." Talking was getting to cost too much. The other sirens must have gone elsewhere. Had Sam called the police anonymously as soon as he got clear of the Eagle's Nest and reported a robbery, hoping Giff would still be somewhere on the premises and he'd get caught with the coke?

"They sound like they're coming closer." Roxie put ice in a towel and placed it behind him on his wound, then popped a can of soda open for him. His mouth looked so dry.

Hurriedly, she drove out of the lot. They were perhaps three blocks away, turning onto a main thoroughfare when they saw the police cars heading in the opposite direction across the median strip.

"Keep going," Giff told her, "but don't speed. Don't call attention to us."

"I'll try not to. I'll take you to my place and fix that wound."

"No!" His voice had somehow regained its authority. "Can't involve you. Just drive. Up north. We'll find an out-of-the-way motel, or something."

As she headed west toward Interstate 17, an idea came to Roxie. "I have a better plan. I have these friends in Sedona. Nikki and I grew up together. Her husband used to drive an EMS wagon." Adam was the next best thing to a doctor.

Giff closed his eyes, feeling bone-weary. He was running out of viable choices. He hated like hell to drag Roxie into this, and now her friends. But those black-and-whites had been headed for the Eagle's Nest, sure as hell. "Can you trust them?"

"I would, with my life." As she said the words, she realized that was exactly what she was doing, only she was doing it with his life. "Can you hold on for a two-hour drive?"

He winced at the pain as he tried to find a comfortable position. "Yeah, I'll be fine."

There was so little traffic, she could easily maneuver the wheel with one hand. With the other, she searched in her large leather bag for a tin of pills. "Here, take one of these. Tylenol with codeine. I use them for bad cramps. They'll help with the pain."

Giff put one in his mouth and washed it down with a long swallow of soda. Carefully, he settled the towel beneath his shoulder. "I hope I'm not bleeding on your upholstery."

"That's the least of our worries."

He moved his left hand and touched her arm. "Roxie, maybe this isn't such a good idea. You can't just leave your work, everything, abandon your life like this. Why don't you drop me at the nearest motel and I'll find a way out when I feel better. This is my fight, not yours."

She gripped the wheel tighter. "No, it's my fight, too. You've been shot twice because of that man, and I just know that Sam had something to do with Dad dying so suddenly. I can't get on with my life until I know he's caught and punished."

His eyes were beginning to close, but he fought it. "Are you sure that's the real reason?"

She shot him a glance. "What other reason would I have?" She returned her attention to the driving. "Get some rest."

Chapter 7

The hazy sun was trying to break through some dark rain clouds hovering over the red rock hills in Sedona as Roxie turned onto the winding road leading to the Oak Creek Canyon area. She was too keyed up to be sleepy, though she knew fatigue would probably hit her later in the day. A glance at the clock on the dashboard told her it was just six a.m.

In the bucket seat next to her, Giff was in basically the same position as when they'd started out over two hours ago. She couldn't tell if he was asleep or if he'd passed out. However, from time to time, she'd reached over to check the pulse in his neck and found it strong.

The main street of the town was almost deserted on this gloomy morning with only a few cars parked in front of a western-style eatery that served early breakfast and one lone truck ambling along behind them. She'd finished her can of soda on the drive and was dying for a cup of coffee, hot, strong and black. Adam was an early riser and would probably be up. She wasn't sure about Nikki's hours since her friend was in the last month of her pregnancy. Then there'd be Lindsay who'd probably be getting ready to leave for school.

Lord, but she hated to burden her friends with this overwhelming problem. But she could think of no one else who'd help them with a minimum of fuss and few questions asked.

She crossed a small bridge, glanced again at Giff and placed her right hand on his cheek. His face was flushed, his skin warm. Of course, since the night had gotten colder as they'd driven north to the higher elevation, she'd had the heater on.

Sedona was beautiful in late October with the red, gold and rust-colored leaves on the trees just beginning to fall. Oak Creek swirled and gurgled along over assorted rocks alongside them as the road paralleled the stream. Roxie wished she were here to enjoy the autumn colors instead of on this dangerous mission.

If only she had some medical training, Roxie thought with a frown. Was Giff feverish because the bullet was still inside him? Was lead poisoning a possibility? Had the bullet hit a vital organ or severed an artery? The bleeding seemed to have abated, but he was slumped down and she couldn't see behind him. What about tetanus shots or antibiotics? Would he need a blood transfusion? She prayed that Adam would know.

At last, she found the dirt road that led to the Kendalls' cabin. A rush of memories hit her as she turned onto it, recalling the cottage some distance over from the Kendall place that used to belong to her family. She and her parents had spent many happy weekends and even whole weeks in the summer here, especially during her youth. But when times had gotten tough, her father had had to sell the cottage. She didn't even know who'd bought it, but she hated the thought of others living there. It rankled that life didn't always cooperate with our wishes.

The path led through evergreens and palo verde trees as well as the indigenous tall oaks from which the area got its name. The Mustang bounced fitfully over the ruts and Roxie was amazed that Giff didn't stir, though he groaned with the movement of the car. Finally, she came into a clearing and saw Adam's Bronco in the carport. The cabin was a wooden structure with a wide front porch where two rockers sat cozily facing a newly painted railing. The house was much larger than the last time she'd visited, and looking past the fenced corral, she could see that the barn was under renovation. A beautiful black stallion whinnied a welcome, his breath huffing out in the chill morning air. There was a light frost on the grass.

At least she knew Adam was up since he'd already tended to the horses, Roxie thought as she pulled into the carport and let out a sigh of relief. So far, so good. Now came the hard part.

She unfastened her seat belt and leaned over, touching Giff's face, his throat. He didn't move. She'd need help getting him inside, Roxie decided as she got out. She stretched, getting the kinks out, then shivered. She was wearing only jeans, a cotton shirt and a light jacket. It hadn't occurred to her to grab warmer clothes. But then, when she'd changed last evening, she hadn't known she'd be on the run.

Roxie was about to knock on the side door when it swung open and Adam Kendall stood behind the screen. When he recognized her, his handsome face broke into a wide, welcoming smile.

"Well, well. Look what the wind blew in." He pushed open the screen, inviting her inside as he called over his shoulder. "Honey, come see who I found on our doorstep." He pulled Roxie into a big hug. "If you were hoping to surprise us, you have."

She allowed herself to enjoy the momentary comfort of his strong, friendly arms, then turned to see her friend coming toward her in black sweatpants and a huge Mickey

Mouse sweatshirt that draped around her swollen stomach. Furry red slippers completed the dazzling outfit. Roxie felt tears sting her eyes as Nikki embraced her. Too much had happened in too short a time, she supposed as she clung to Nikki, causing her emotions to go into overload.

Stepping back, Nikki looked at her friend, concern apparent in her green eyes. "What's happened?"

She always could see through her, Roxie thought. "I need your help." Her eyes flew to Adam's worried frown. "Both of you. A friend of mine's in the car and . . . and he's been shot."

Nikki glanced over her shoulder out the screen door. "Shot? How bad is it?"

"I don't know." With a trembling hand, Roxie brushed back her hair from her face.

"Let me get my shoes on and we'll take a look," Adam told her as he reached behind into the hall closet.

In as few words as possible, she quickly told them about Sam Farrell taking over after her father's death, about Giff Jacobs coming to work at the Eagle's Nest a little over three weeks ago, and his problems in Tucson that had cost him his job and three years of his freedom. And then she explained what they'd been planning to do when everything had fallen apart last night.

"What a bizarre story," Nikki commented. "I had a feeling the last time we talked that there was something not quite right. Do you really think this Sam Farrell might be responsible for what happened to your father?"

"I wouldn't put it past him. We can only guess that he must have gotten wind that Giff was on to him and moved the delivery date up. Giff had already left the bar, but on a hunch went back to check things out. They must have happened on him in the storeroom."

"But you weren't there?" Adam asked.

"No, but I got worried when I phoned and couldn't reach him. So I went looking and found him passed out on the storeroom floor. He's been shot in the back." She looked

down at her hands and noticed spots of dried blood on them
from when she'd helped him to the car. "All we want to do
is get Sam Kendall and the men he's working with and see
that they're punished. I know it looks bad, but Giff didn't
do anything illegal. He's been a police detective for years
and he can't rest until he's cleared his name. He's been shot
twice now and...and he doesn't deserve this." She was
about at the end of her rope, nerves frayed, body exhausted. They simply had to believe her, had to help her.

Nikki got the picture first. Roxie was in love with the guy.
She slipped her arm around her friend's waist. "Don't
worry. We'll help." Her big green eyes sought her husband's gaze. "Won't we, Adam?"

His shoes finally on, Adam walked through the door and
around the Mustang with the two women close on his heels.
A light rain had begun falling. "Where did you say he was
hit?"

"In his back, just below his right shoulder. The bullet
might have passed through, but I'm not sure. There's no
blood in front." She watched Adam peer through the window. She was reluctant to presume upon their friendship,
despite her desperation. "If you feel you don't want to get
involved, I'll understand."

"Your word is good enough for us, Roxie," Adam said.
"Maybe you'd better open the door so the first thing he sees
is a familiar face. Then I'll help him inside."

But when she pulled back the door, Giff's eyes opened
and he grabbed her hand. "Where are we?" he asked, trying to focus, feeling disoriented.

"In Sedona, at my friends' home. They'll help us." She
turned to include the Kendalls. "This is Adam and his wife,
Nikki. I don't know if you can make it inside alone. Let
Adam help you."

The effort cost him, but Giff straightened and moved one
leg out. "I can make it."

Biting back a retort about stubborn macho men, Roxie
offered him her hand. He ignored it and braced his arm on

the car door, then pulled himself upright. He looked at Nikki, then Adam, his mouth a thin line as he struggled with the pain. "I hate like hell to bother you both."

"It's no bother." Adam knew the man wasn't about to let anyone help him. "This way," he said, walking to the door.

Roxie and Nikki shared a look that said exactly what they thought about men who refused assistance, then followed Giff into the house. Nikki pulled out a kitchen chair and watched Giff sit down heavily. His face was very white.

"Where's Lindsay?" Roxie asked. "Maybe she shouldn't—"

"Not to worry," Nikki assured her as Adam scrubbed his hands at the kitchen sink. "She spent the night at a girlfriend's house. They're working on a science project that they'll be taking to school this morning." She turned to the pot plugged in on the counter. "I'll bet you both could use a cup of coffee." Quickly, she filled two mugs as Adam helped Giff out of his jacket.

Giff winced as the torn and bloody garment was peeled from him. The shirt would be worse, he guessed, since some of it was probably stuck to his skin and would likely start the wound bleeding again. He watched Adam closely as he freed the buttons. "So you've had medical training?" With his left hand, he lifted the mug and took several long swallows. He welcomed the heat and the caffeine jolt.

"Yes," Adam answered. "I had two years of med school left when I quit. My father's a doctor and I thought I wanted to be one, too. Found I didn't have the dedication."

"He does have the dedication to be a very fine artist, though," Roxie interjected. "I'll show you some of his paintings later."

Adam worked at removing the shirt slowly, carefully. It didn't look good. He'd been shot in the back and there was no exit wound. That had to mean the bullet was still in there. "Honey, get me some clean cloths and the bottle of antiseptic. And put on some water to boil, would you, please?"

"I'll put on the kettle," Roxie offered.

Adam kept talking, low and unhurried, hoping to distract Giff from what he was doing, as he'd been taught years ago. He could see particles of material stuck to the wound, which was already opening again. That was good in a way, for it would flush out some debris. "I operated an EMS wagon for three years. Ran into just about every kind of thing you can imagine."

Nikki walked over with clean white strips of cloth, a big package of gauze and tape, and the antiseptic, placing them all on the table. Behind her waddled a sleepy-eyed, rust-colored beagle who looked ready to drop her puppies momentarily. She wagged her tail in what passed for a show of excitement these days, causing her entire back quarters to sway.

Roxie bent to pet her sleek head. "Maudie, I was wondering where you were."

"She sleeps almost as much as I do," Nikki said with an affectionate smile. "Adam's nervous that we'll both deliver on the same day."

"No, I'm not," Adam said, his mouth twitching as he poured antiseptic on a piece of cloth, "I'll have to choose Maudie. She was here before you."

Nikki punched his arm. "We delivered her last litter together." Meeting her husband's eyes for a brief moment, she saw that he remembered that night as well as she.

As Roxie bent to pet the animal's sleek head, a rumble of thunder in the distance had her glancing worriedly out the window. "Looks like we're in for a storm." And they had to leave, to find a safe place. They couldn't endanger the Kendalls. But where could they go?

Adam cleaned the wound, poured in a bit of antiseptic and probed the area delicately with a finger. He could tell that Giff Jacobs was used to pain for he'd been stoical, not making a sound. He'd just taken huge gulps of coffee now and then, and sucked in deep breaths.

Adam stepped back, surveying the situation. Roxie had been right. It could hardly be Giff's fault since he'd been ambushed. "Looks like you ran into somebody nasty, Giff. The bullet entered in the back, probably passed through deltoid muscles under the sternum." His hand moved around front as he pointed. "From what I can tell, the trajectory was upward, meaning the shooter was crouching or rather short. The bullet went in, either hit the scapula bone or perhaps a rib, was deflected somehow and got lodged somewhere in this front muscle band, the pectoralus major, just below your clavicle."

Giff clenched his jaw. "What does all that mean?"

"The bad news is that the bullet's still in there since there's no exit wound." He placed his fingers on Giff's chest below his collarbone. "The good news is, I can almost feel it right beneath here. It shouldn't be too big a problem to remove. I'll call my friend, Matt Towers. He's a general practitioner and—"

"No!" Giff's voice was suddenly strong and brooked no argument. "I've already risked too much coming here. No doctors. If you can't get the bullet out, it'll just have to stay in there."

Roxie moved to his side. "Giff, you're risking blood poisoning or infection if you don't get that bullet out."

Giff looked up at Adam, hating to be indebted to still another person. "Can you get it out?"

"Probably, but I'm not sure what we'll find in there. If it's deeply imbedded in a muscle, I might cut something and you'd be impaired as it healed or—"

"I'll take the risk. Let's just do it."

Adam looked at his wife, then met Roxie's eyes. He remembered being as stubborn as Giff at one time, and as certain that his way was the only way. Nikki had helped him get past all that. It seemed as if Roxie cared a lot about this guy, even though they hadn't known each other for very long. He had great respect and affection for Roxie. He couldn't turn from someone she cared about.

"Nikki, do you know where my medical bag is? I can't remember where I put it. We'll have to sterilize the probes and tweezers."

Giff swallowed hard as he looked up at Adam Kendall. "Thanks, I owe you."

"You owe me nothing." He turned to find Roxie beside him, her eyes suspiciously moist. She gripped his hand, squeezed it, then turned away. He looked at his new patient. "I think we'll need to do this on a bed."

"I'll help Nikki get things together," Roxie said, following her friend to the bedroom. She needed a moment to compose herself. Lack of sleep was making her weepy.

"I don't have any pain medication in injection form, just a few strong pills," Adam told Giff. "Or we could do it the old-fashioned way and fill you full of booze."

Giff braced the elbow of his good arm on the table. "Roxie gave me a codeine pill when we left Scottsdale, but it made me fuzzy. I don't think I'd better mix it with booze."

"You're right. In a hospital, they'd probably give you a pint of blood to replace what you lost, just to be on the safe side," Adam told him as he poured more coffee. "But since we're not in a hospital, we'll have to do without it. You'll be a little weaker, maybe take a day or two longer to get your strength back." He walked over and set the coffee mug in front of Giff, then refilled his own.

Giff took a long swallow of the hot liquid and grimaced as pain sliced through his shoulder. He looked over at his host, wondering how much they'd learned about him before he'd awakened. "Did Roxie tell you how all this came about?"

Adam nodded. "Some. Seems like you've had some rough years."

"You could say that."

"Anything I can do to help you get those guys, just ask." That surprised him. "Why? We just met."

"Because Roxie's good people. She was there for my wife when she needed someone. Me, too, for that matter. I don't forget."

He could buy that. "I don't forget, either." He took another swallow of strong black coffee and frowned. "It'd probably taste better with whiskey, though I don't care much for the stuff."

Adam sat back, propping his left ankle on his right knee. "I did, once. Liked the way it made me forget things I didn't want to remember. Drank myself stupid regularly and finally wrapped myself and my car around a tree real good one night. Took me six months to recover. The body's an amazing thing."

"I hope so. Right now, mine hurts like hell."

"It'll hurt even more before we're through." He stood and held out an arm to assist him. "They've probably got things ready by now. Let's get you into the bedroom."

Stripped to the waist and minus his shoes, Giff lay on his back on the guest room bed on a white sheet placed over a plastic one, his eyes watching everything. The coffee had him wide-awake and very aware. Despite her temporary bulk, Nikki moved with grace, placing the tools she'd sterilized in boiling water on a clean white towel. She was beautiful, with dark, curly hair and the greenest eyes he'd ever seen. He could see she was nuts about her husband.

Giff felt a pang of unexpected envy. Adam had it all—a lovely wife, baby on the way, ten-year-old daughter, nice house, good career. Even a family dog. Would he ever have that kind of serene life? Did he even want it? His eyes shifted to where Roxie sat, her brown eyes worried.

What had he ever done to deserve a woman like her worrying over him? Giff asked himself. Not much. Dragged her away from her home, her work. Involved her up to her gorgeous eyelashes in trouble. Seen to it that she, too, was on the run, from drug smugglers and from the police. Yeah, she'd sure latched on to a bargain in him.

She smiled at him then, and it felt incredible. She was so lovely, and she deserved more than the grief he'd given her. But, selfish man that he was, he didn't want her to leave. Not just yet. He tried to smile back, but didn't quite make it.

Roxie went to get a cold cloth and returned to place it on his forehead. As he'd lain down, she'd noticed a three-inch puckered scar on his lower back. Undoubtedly, the other wound he'd received from Sam Farrell and his friends. Anger rose in her, hot and heavy. If it was the last thing she did, she'd see to it that they were caught.

Sitting near Giff's head, Roxie reached to grip his hand. "When it gets bad, just squeeze."

Adam snapped on the rubber gloves he'd taken from his kit and picked up the probe. "Here goes, buddy. Hang on."

Nikki adjusted the lamp so it shone right where Adam wanted it, then stepped back. It wasn't that she was queasy, at least not yet. She wanted to keep it that way, so she sat down across the room.

It apparently didn't take Adam long to make a small incision and find the bullet, although, Nikki thought, it must have seemed like forever to Giff. She saw the perspiration on his face and watched Roxie patting his face gently with the cloth. The distress on her friend's face was worse than the pain on the patient's.

Adam held the probe in his left hand and reached for the long tweezers with his right. In moments, they heard the plink as he dropped the bullet into the basin. With a sterile pad, he absorbed the blood, then set down his instruments and reached for the antiseptic.

Nikki could see Roxie visibly relax now that the worst was over. She could also see something else—love on her friend's face, in her eyes, in her touch. Roxie had had such a bad time after her marriage to Brad, the self-doubt the divorce had left her with, the bruised ego and the painful rebuilding of her self-esteem. In their last conversation, Nikki had specifically asked, yet Roxie had denied that there was a new man in her life.

Apparently, her feelings had been too new to talk about. Nikki only hoped that this man—already troubled and in trouble—wouldn't hurt Roxie. Strong as she appeared, she wasn't sure her friend could survive another betrayal of her feelings.

Adam carefully stitched together the small wound, coated it with antibiotic ointment, placed a sterile Teflon gauze pad on it, then taped it in place.

"I can't believe you even sew people up, Adam," Roxie commented.

"You'd be surprised at the things EMS attendants learn to do over a period of time," he told her. Then, turning to Giff, he said, "These stitches can be removed in about a week. If you can manage to sit up, I think it best that I clean that point-of-entry wound, as well, to prevent break-through bleeding."

"Do you think he could have gotten blood poisoning?" Roxie wanted to know as Giff squirmed around and sat up.

"Doubtful. Bullet wasn't in him that long, and I've really doused the wound with antiseptic. Let me see if I have any antibiotics on hand. We usually do, for the animals." Adam finished bandaging, and cut tape to keep the ends in place.

"And I have pain pills in my purse," Roxie said.

"We'll need to check this twice a day to make sure there's no further infection and change the bandages. You've lost some blood so you should drink lots of fluids," he told Giff.

"I'll see that he does all that," Roxie said.

Adam pulled off his rubber gloves. "That should do it. I've got some clean clothes if you'd like to change. And I can help you into the bathroom if you'd like to clean up."

"I would, thanks," Giff said, "but I can manage."

"You are the stubbornest man," Roxie told him. "Why is it so hard for you to let us help you?"

"You already have, all three of you." He moved his feet off the bed and eased up, testing his strength.

Nikki rose, too. "I think we could all use a good breakfast. How do bacon and eggs sound?"

Giff looked at Roxie. "We've got to go. We can't stay here." He glanced at Adam and his wife. "I can't thank you enough, but I won't put you in further jeopardy. As you may have noticed, these men mean business."

Adam stepped back. "You can thank us by eating breakfast, taking the pills and getting some rest before you move on. Too much jostling right now, and you could open that wound again."

"I'll take my chances." Giff took an unsteady step, then had to grip the bedpost as a wave of dizziness washed over him.

Roxie moved to his side and helped him sit down again. "No, we're not doing this. Listen, I've gone along with all your plans, but now, you're going to listen to me. We're going to do exactly as Adam and Nikki suggested. Eat and then rest. After that, when it gets dark again, we'll move on." Exactly where, she wasn't sure.

Adam picked up his medical kit. "You could stay here. We're pretty remote. I doubt that anyone would think to look for you here."

Roxie wasn't convinced. "They might. Everyone at the restaurant knows that Nikki and I are close. This is one of the first places they'd look. Giff's right. We can't risk involving you further than we have."

"Do you have any ideas where you might go?" Adam asked.

Roxie brushed back her hair wearily. "Not really."

"I have a suggestion," Adam offered. "I'll tell you about it over breakfast."

Adam slipped half a slice of bacon under the table into Maudie's waiting mouth, then wiped his hands on his napkin. "Honey, stop boring these people," he admonished his wife good-naturedly. "They don't want to hear about my work."

"A one-man art show and I wouldn't want to hear about it?" Roxie asked. "I think that's wonderful, Adam. When is it going to be?"

"In three weeks," his proud wife answered. "You should see the painting he did of Lindsay on her horse. You expect her to open her mouth and speak, it's so real."

From the corner of her eye, Roxie watched Giff scoop up the last of his three eggs with a section of toast and pop it into his mouth. He'd said he wasn't hungry, but he'd almost eaten the design off the plate. She picked up her coffee mug and turned back to Adam. "No nudes of Nikki, *before* her altered state?"

Adam winked at his wife. "In my private collection."

Nikki shook her head at him. "In your dreams." She picked up the pot. "More coffee, Giff?"

Pushing his plate aside, he sat back. "No, thanks. That was terrific, Nikki." Surprisingly, he felt sated, drowsy and almost human, despite the dull throb in his back, which he knew would pick up steam as soon as the second pain pill Roxie had insisted he take wore off. He'd cleaned up and dressed in clothes he'd borrowed from Adam. Now, if he could sleep undisturbed for about a week, he'd be all right again.

And if he could just turn off his mind, he'd be even better. "What was your suggestion about a place to go?" he asked Adam, thinking he should find out before his eyes got much heavier.

Adam slipped his last bite of toast to Maudie before answering. "There's a woman who rents cabins up in Jerome, less than an hour's drive from here," Adam explained. "I've known her for years. She used to live in Phoenix and was a patient of my father's a long while ago."

"Of course," Nikki concurred. "Why didn't I think of Sunny's place? It's a perfect hideaway."

"Why is it so perfect?" Roxie wanted to know.

Adam fought a smile. "It's called Honeymoon Haven. She rents only to honeymooners—or those who might need to pretend they are." At the look on both their faces, he rushed on. "Sunny Thatcher is a widow, a wonderful lady, somewhere in her sixties. She's a little birdlike woman with huge blue eyes and she's always smiling. She raises desert flowers and fills each cottage with them daily. There are no phones, no outside interference, although she delivers a paper each morning."

Nikki had to add her two cents' worth. "She's got this kind of orange hair. Well, I've never seen all of it because she always wears a hat. Big, floppy straw ones in the summer with flowers pinned on, velvet cloche hats in the winter with narrow brims. And her cottages are out of this world, only twelve of them, each with a fireplace and a different decor. Early American, traditional French, southwestern. She stocks the place with romantic records, homemade jam, quaint little pillows with folksy sayings embroidered on them."

Despite the dangerous nature of their trip, Roxie had to smile at the description of this fanciful retreat. "It does sound as if no one would think to look for us there." She turned to Giff who was leaning quite heavily on the armrest on his good side. "What do you think?"

"Can she be trusted?" he asked Adam.

"To keep people from disturbing you? Absolutely. However, I would tell her you're on your honeymoon and want to be left alone pretty much. She needn't know anything more about your circumstances." He looked from one to the other. "I'll call her if you like, see if she's got a vacancy."

A honeymoon cottage hadn't been on his agenda, Giff thought. But then, neither had a wild run from the police and Sam's men. He'd run out of options. "I think it sounds fine."

Adam pushed back his chair and went to the kitchen phone.

"Do you like cats?" Nikki asked Giff. "Roxie's allergic to cats, but Sunny's pet won't bother you if you don't want him around. He's a bit old and kind of grumpy, like his namesake, Sunny's second husband, Clancy. She'd buried three others, that I know of."

Roxie's eyebrows raised. "Three? Maybe we shouldn't eat her jam."

Nikki laughed. "You'll love Sunny."

Giff was studying Roxie. While he'd been cleaning up down the hall, she'd showered in the bath off the master bedroom and changed into cocoa brown slacks and a turtleneck in the same color, apparently borrowed from Nikki. Her hair was down and fell past her shoulders, framing her oval face. She was so lovely she took his breath away.

But she had faint dark smudges beneath her eyes from lack of sleep. He felt a pang of guilt for having helped put them there. If not for him, she'd have spent the night in her own home, curled up in her soft bed, not roaring along a highway on the run. He would make it up to her. One day.

His hand over the mouthpiece, Adam came back to Giff. "How long would you want to stay? Keep in mind that you won't be in good shape for another week at the least, and your right arm will be stiff for four or five days."

His shooting arm. Damn, he wanted this over with. Still, it might be best to lie low a bit, get hold of Neil, set up some kind of showdown with Sam. "How about four or five days?" he asked, looking at Roxie for confirmation. "You can leave me there if you need to get back."

"I don't need to get back any sooner," she said softly. Get back to what? Coping with Sam alone? Talking with the police about a robbery? "I'll call Trevor and make up something."

Adam walked back to the kitchen as Giff returned his attention to Roxie. "What else are you allergic to besides cats?"

"Only stubborn men who refuse help," she answered with a straight face.

He almost smiled.

Adam returned. "You're all set. I registered you as the Joneses. Thought that would be safer. I told Sunny you'd be checking in around nine this evening, if that's all right. You can leave after dinner, after dark."

Roxie took over. "That's great, thanks." She stood and moved to Giff's side. "Let me help you get settled in the guest room. You really need to sleep."

Surprisingly, he didn't fight her, but went quietly after thanking both Nikki and Adam again. Despite his wearing Adam's corduroy pants and flannel shirt, he felt chilled and didn't object when Roxie pulled the heavy plaid blanket up over him. On his back, he looked up at her. "This isn't how I pictured it, you know. The first time we're alone in a bedroom, and I'm ready to pass out."

Roxie wished she felt more like smiling at his weak joke. She sat down on the edge of the bed and tucked the covers around him. She noticed the hint of pain at the corners of his mouth and could see how he struggled against letting her see. "Go ahead and pass out. I'll be in the next room if you need anything."

With his good hand, he reached up to run his fingers through her hair. "It doesn't seem enough to say thanks."

"Then don't say anything. Not now." She leaned down and brushed her lips across his.

When she would have withdrawn, his hand settled in her hair and he brought her back. This kiss was deeper, more intimate, his tongue twining with hers briefly but thoroughly.

Through misty eyes, she looked at him. "I thought you were ready to pass out."

"I'm tired, not dead." He gave her one of his quick smiles.

"Get some rest." She rose and walked out, leaving the door ajar.

Giff closed his eyes and was asleep in seconds.

* * *

The rain hadn't let up. It wasn't storming, just a steady, quiet rain that farmers always seemed pleased to see. They were probably the only ones, Roxie thought as she stood looking out the window at the gloomy late afternoon.

"Come sit by the fire," Nikki invited from the couch. "I've made some tea." She poured them each a cup, dropped a lemon slice in hers and rearranged her cumbersome self. "Are you worried about the drive to Jerome?" The road to the small hillside town was good, but it wound and twisted up the mountainside, which, slick with rain and after dark, could be dangerous. "Adam could drive you both."

Roxie shook her head as she sat down and picked up her tea. "I'll be fine. I've been through Jerome before, so I'm familiar with it." Truth be known, she was more than a little worried about spending four or five days closeted in a small cabin with the man still sleeping in the guest room. She'd napped, though fitfully, but her nerves wouldn't calm.

Watching her over the rim of her cup, Nikki decided to plunge in while Adam was out back seeing to the horses. "Roxie, am I your best friend?"

Surprised, Roxie looked up. "Yes, you know you are."

"And best friends tell each other everything, right?"

Roxie saw where this was headed. "Do they?"

"They should. How else can your best friend poke her nose into your life? In the nicest way, of course." They shared a smile. "Are you in love with him?"

Roxie set down her cup, leaned back and closed her eyes. "The sixty-four-thousand-dollar question. I've been so afraid, since Brad, to let myself care for any man. And, when I thought of a man in my future, he wasn't anything like Giff. But..."

"But. Ah, yes. That old familiar *but*. But you can't stop thinking of him, wanting him, needing him. And so on." She cocked her head. "Am I close?"

Roxie curled into the corner, propping an elbow on the couch back. "Right on, dear friend. Any words of wisdom you'd like to share?"

"Just two. Be careful. I don't want to see you hurt again." At the suddenly moist, vulnerable look in Roxie's eyes, Nikki was afraid her warning had come too late.

"I'm trying to be careful. I believe in him. I know he's telling me the truth. After...after this mess is over and once he's cleared his name, I guess we'll see." She picked at the fringe on a nearby toss pillow. "Then again, maybe he'll just say so long and leave. He's already warned me not to expect anything from him, that he needs to focus everything he's got on catching these men."

"I see." Nikki set aside her cup, wishing there was something she could say to ease her friend's pain. "I remember being in your shoes once and telling you about Adam. Do you recall what you told me? You said, if he's wrong for you, dump him. If he's right, if your gut feeling says he's the one, then go for it and the rest of the world be damned. Even if he leaves, he'll come back, you said. Because what's more powerful than love?" She smiled at Roxie. "Remember?"

Roxie's eyes were damp, but she smiled back. "Yes, I remember." She reached out and hugged her friend. "I love you, Nikki. Thanks."

Pulling back after a moment, Nikki reached for a little levity. "I remember something else you asked me when I was struggling my way through my feelings. Is he good in bed? you asked. Well, is he?"

Uncharacteristically, Roxie felt the color rise in her face. "I don't know."

Nikki sent her a shocked look. "Roxie, you're slipping." This time, they both laughed.

Chapter 8

"Do you think you can handle my Bronco?" Adam asked Roxie as they stood in the newly completed garage alongside the barn still under renovation.

"Actually, I think it'll be easier than my Mustang on these mountain roads." Roxie tugged up the collar of the fleece-lined denim jacket she'd borrowed from Nikki against the chill night air. She glanced out the double doors. "I wish it would stop raining."

"Probably won't for a couple of days. We get a lot of rain up here this time of year. And by next month, it'll turn to snow." Adam pushed back a lock of blond hair from his forehead. "If you won't let me drive you, then I'd really feel better if you took the Bronco. I'll put your Mustang in here and keep the garage doors locked so if anyone comes snooping around, they won't spot it."

Roxie looked over at Nikki's green Fiat convertible. "Can you manage with just one car for a few days?"

"Sure. Nikki isn't driving anywhere alone these last few

weeks." He smiled as he took Roxie's arm and led her out of the garage. "She can barely get behind the wheel."

But, as she dashed toward the back door through the rain, Roxie was thinking of the three boxes in her trunk, cartons containing illegal drugs. Should she tell Adam about them or would it be better if the Kendalls knew nothing so they could reveal nothing, should it come to that? Entering the warm kitchen, she decided she'd talk with Giff about it after dinner.

She was sitting cross-legged on the thick rug in front of the blazing fireplace petting Maudie's head as it lay on her knee when Giff came out of the guest room. He could hear Nikki moving about the kitchen and didn't know where Adam was. Bracing his left arm against the doorjamb, Giff stopped to listen to Roxie's soft voice as the dog's trusting brown eyes gazed at her adoringly.

"I shouldn't be doing this, you know," she told Maudie. "I'll be sneezing all night because of you." She touched the long, velvety ears. "Ah, but you know just how to get to me, don't you?" Reaching, she stroked the dog's distended belly. "Feels like you've got quite a family in there, girl. I hope you get to keep some of them. I'd take one of your babies if I could, you know that, don't you?"

Giff watched Maudie snuffle as if in answer and shift closer. Despite her allergies, Roxie couldn't keep away from the pregnant pooch. *I like living things,* she'd told him the day they'd met. She'd been talking about her plants, but he could tell that her home would probably be filled with pets if her health permitted. She didn't hear him, so absorbed was she in her conversation with Maudie.

"You're lucky, you know. Having your little ones here, in this safe place. I know you used to roam the streets, and that must have been terrible. But you've found a home and people who love you." Maudie stretched so she was half in Roxie's lap, her big tongue licking her chin in a wet kiss.

"And I know you love them, too." Bending, she lay her cheek against the dog's sleek head. "So lucky, all of you."

He didn't want to be moved, Giff told himself. But Roxie Lowell was an odd mix of cool, efficient businesswoman by day and warm, sentimental mush when it came to friends, family and stray animals. He didn't want to admit what a touching picture the two of them made huddled together by the fire. He didn't like the way the cozy cabin and thoughts of Roxie made him feel.

As if he'd been deprived of something warm and wonderful all his life. As if keeping himself from caring had kept him from really living. As if the world had thrown a party and he hadn't been invited. As if he were still the kid on the outside looking in, the one pressing his face to the candy-store window.

A piece of log in the grate hissed and fell sideways, sparks flying. The sound startled Roxie and she looked up, then over to the doorway. Before Giff could change it, she caught a glimpse of pure longing on his face. Had he heard all she'd said to the dog, heard her speak of her own need to belong? Probably, and her words had moved him, but he didn't want her to know he'd been affected. She watched as he quickly closed himself off behind that cool facade he preferred to present to the world. Rising, she walked over to him. "How do you feel?"

Giff shook off his introspective mood, embarrassed at being observed, and pushed away from the jamb. "Like I've been run over by a truck." The shadows were still under her eyes, increasing his guilt. "Did you get any rest?"

"Some." She slipped her arms around his waist, then reached up to touch his face with the back of one hand. He hadn't shaved and the dark stubble was bristly. "You're quite warm. Time for more medicine."

Damn stuff made him so weak and tired that he allowed her to assist him into the kitchen just as Adam came in the back door. "We should get going," Giff said, noticing how dark it was outside.

"Right after dinner," Nikki said, putting a large bowl of mashed potatoes on the table.

"You haven't lived until you've tasted Nikki's pot roast," Adam said as he hung his jacket on a hook beside the back door.

Roxie noticed the worried frown on Giff's face and squeezed his hand. "As soon as we eat, I promise."

Later, as Roxie folded the last of the clothes Adam and Nikki were lending them into a small suitcase, she saw that Giff's color wasn't very good despite his hours of sleep and the meal he'd scarcely touched. Adam had told them at dinner that Giff would be weak, feverish and possibly nauseated for several days and would need to rest almost continually. She didn't mind caring for him, but wished he'd cooperate and let her.

She told him about her conversation with Adam in the garage.

"It's probably a good idea to switch vehicles," Giff said, mopping his damp forehead with a handkerchief. "But we need to transfer the boxes. On the off chance they'd think to look here, I don't want to endanger the Kendalls. At this point, I know those men would kill to get the stuff back. It's a big haul."

"Yes, I suppose you're right." She snapped the suitcase closed and turned to where he was sitting on the edge of the bed. "Are you sure you're up to this drive? The Bronco's not a very smooth ride and the road twists and turns."

Giff reached for the heavy jacket Adam had insisted he take. He felt cold even though he was sweating. "I'll be fine." He shoved his left arm into a sleeve. "I hate it that I don't have the strength to drive."

She helped him into the jacket, reaching for a little humor to help his pride. "Why, Mr. Jones, are you afraid to ride with a woman driver?"

He wasn't in the mood for jokes. "You did a hell of a job on the way here."

"How would you know? You slept the whole way."

His hands settled on her arms. "That's probably all I'll be doing for the next few days. Are you sure you don't want to just drop me off in Jerome? I'm not much good for anything right now."

She knew he was feeling useless and dependent, and hating the feeling. "Giff, we all have moments in our lives when we need to lean on someone. It's not a crime or a sin."

"Not you. I've never known a stronger woman. You're not afraid of guns, or blood or an ex-con who's hauling around a great deal of baggage. And I don't mean the cartons in the car. You'll tackle anything."

"Well, I am afraid of creepy, crawly things, especially spiders."

He wasn't about to be diverted. His hand trailed down the silk of her cheek. "You're amazing."

Is that how he honestly saw her? "There are a lot of ways to need, not all of them physical."

He was unsteady on his feet, undoubtedly feverish, uncommonly vulnerable. And he wanted her. He was unquestionably out of his mind—from the pain, the medicine, the rise in his temperature. He would blame his need for her on that, knowing his weakness would be temporary. "I owe you a great deal, and it isn't over yet." The list of people he owed was growing, and he hated it.

"Do you hear me complaining?"

"You should be. You should send me packing, drop me off, out of your life and—"

"You talk too much. Save your strength for more important things." On tiptoe, she pressed her mouth to his.

This kiss was different. She tasted his frustration, a need he struggled against, a yearning that had his arms wrapping around her, drawing her against his trembling body. She'd meant to kiss him lightly, to end the words she didn't want to hear. But his tongue entered her mouth and plundered, as if he needed to be in charge in this one thing when he couldn't be in so many other ways right now.

She let him dominate, let him seduce her, returning the fierce pleasure of his mouth on hers with demands of her own. She felt him gentle, and the kiss became soothing, a balm for their separate pain.

When he released her, she saw the desire in his eyes, and something more. Confusion. Reluctance. He didn't want this, didn't want to want her, yet couldn't stop himself from reaching for her. Roxie didn't know whether to laugh or cry.

She stepped back. "I need to call Trevor. Why don't you go with Adam and have him load the boxes into the Bronco?"

Giff brushed a shaky hand over his stubble, wondering why she had this stunning effect on him, sick or well. "Yeah," he muttered, and left the bedroom before she could offer assistance.

"Roxie, I've been calling all over looking for you." Trevor's clipped British voice was ripe with concern and a hint of censure. "Where are you?"

Roxie stood by the wall phone in the kitchen, searching for the right thing to say. She'd formulated a rather vague story to tell her manager, and hoped he wouldn't ask too many questions. "You've been telling me for days how tired I look, so I decided to go away for a few days and rest up."

"But without letting me know, without leaving a note?" Now he sounded hurt.

Roxie closed her eyes, reaching for patience. "I am sorry about that, but it was a spur-of-the-moment decision. Haven't you ever had an impulse to just get away?" She was certain the regimented, superorganized man never had.

"I suppose. But where did you go?"

"Up into the mountains. A friend has a cabin I'm borrowing for a while. It's remote, peaceful and quiet, just what I need."

"You're alone then?"

"Now, who would I have taken with me?" Evasion. She hated it. She rushed on before he could ask more. "How are things?'' She waited, hearing the familiar noises of the restaurant in the background. She'd deliberately called in the evening when she knew Trevor would be distracted and unable to spare much time.

"I'm afraid I've got some bad news. We had an attempted robbery last night."

"Oh, no. What happened?" In all the years that her family had run the Eagle's Nest, they'd never once been robbed. She guessed that Trevor was shocked. Curling the cord around her fingers, she moved to sit down at the table. She could see Nikki stretched out on the sofa in front of the fire, Maudie on the floor alongside.

"Nothing, it appears. Apparently, they were attempting to take things from the storeroom when something frightened them off. By the time the police arrived, no one was around. We've taken inventory and they didn't take a thing."

Roxie tried to come up with the right questions so he wouldn't suspect she knew anything. "When, exactly, did this occur?"

"Sometime during the night, three or four, I'd guess. But there's something puzzling the police."

"What's that?"

"They found quite a lot of blood on the storeroom floor."

She'd been waiting for that. "Oh, Lord. Who was hurt?"

"Must have been one of the intruders. Perhaps they quarreled among themselves and one had a knife. The police couldn't find evidence of a bullet hitting anywhere. It's a puzzle."

"Maybe this will prove to Sam that we ought to have a burglar alarm system installed." She didn't want to talk with Sam, but she knew it would look odd if she didn't. "Is Sam there?"

"No, he hasn't come in yet. When the police couldn't locate you, they called him and he hurried over. He stayed until about noon, then called me in and left, saying he'd be back sometime tonight. Why don't you give me your number and I'll have him call when he gets in?"

She felt relieved and had her answer ready. "There's no phone in the cabin. I'm calling from a pay phone at a gas station."

"Well." Trevor hesitated, finding the whole business distasteful. "The police want to talk with you."

Roxie had been afraid of that. "Listen, Trevor, tell them I'll be back in a couple of days. I left home right after closing yesterday and obviously didn't know a thing about this until now." The lies were becoming entirely too easy to come up with. She had to keep in mind that she couldn't afford to trust anyone until they had Sam and the others in custody. For Giff's safety, and perhaps her own. Not that she suspected Trevor, but he might inadvertently let something slip. "I'll call again soon."

"Something else, Roxie. Giff didn't show up for his shift tonight." He cleared his throat, clearly uncomfortable. "Do you suppose he had something to do with this?"

"Now, why would you think that?"

"I don't know. I've never trusted that man. We don't have his address or phone number, oddly enough. You closed up with him. Did he perhaps quit, or mention leaving?"

"No, he didn't. I don't believe Giff would rob us." At least she could be truthful about that. "Look, Trevor, please just handle things until I get back. I . . . I really need to rest and regroup." And that wasn't an untruth, either. She wished they were already up in Jerome and she could sleep around the clock.

Trevor's concern for her kicked in. "Of course I'll take care of everything. You take your time. I'll tell Sam you'll be calling and I'll phone the officer who left his card and update him."

That rang a bell. "What is his name, Trevor?"

"Just a moment." He took the card from his vest pocket. "A Lieutenant Tom Burke. Might you know him?"

She was surprised it wasn't Giff's friend Neil. "No, I don't. Thank you, Trevor. I appreciate all you're doing."

"It's no trouble, really. Take care of yourself, Roxie."

She hung up the phone and let out a long breath, wondering how many more lies she'd have to tell before all this ended.

"You could leave them, you know," Adam told Giff in the garage. "I have half a dozen places around here I could hide those boxes where no one would find them."

Giff shook his head. "I won't put you at any more risk than I already have. I'm not letting these out of my possession until I can turn them over to the police." He didn't think even a man who'd been around as much as Adam would guess that the street value of the contents was well over a million dollars. Men had been killed for far less.

They'd backed up the Mustang so that the rear faced the open garage door. He unlocked the trunk and reached for the first box.

"Here, I'll move them. You shouldn't be lifting." Adam unlocked the hatch of the Bronco and lifted the shield over the storage compartment. "Sunny's cabins have carports attached to each one, but I think these'll be safe in here." He hoisted the cartons one by one and placed them in the Bronco, then snapped the security cover back in place. "If you're worried about a break-in, you could always put them inside the cabin."

"I'll decide when we get there." Giff closed the trunk of Roxie's car and handed Adam the Mustang keys. "It seems I have a lot to thank you for."

"There is a way you can thank me."

Giff kept his expression even. "And what would that be?"

Adam wasn't especially comfortable bringing up the subject, but knew he had to let his feelings be known. "You can be good to Roxie, take care of her. She means a great deal to Nikki and me."

Despite his wound, which was throbbing like hell, Giff's eyes were clear. "I know that. She means quite a lot to me, too." He turned aside, looking out into the rainy night. "More than I'd planned."

So that's how it was. Adam relaxed a bit. "I know exactly how that feels. And it happens to the best of us. I didn't mean to speak out of turn, but I don't know you very well and I'd hate to see Roxie get hurt. She likes people to think she's a rock, but underneath, she's a softie."

Giff swung his gaze back. "I'm beginning to find that out. I promise I'll take care of her."

Adam clapped him on his good shoulder. "Good enough. I'll move the Bronco over by the side door and garage the Mustang. Go inside before you get a cold."

Shivering, Giff did just that, praying he could live up to his promise.

Fatigue was beginning to catch up with her, Roxie decided as she spotted the first sign directing them to Honeymoon Haven. She'd been to Jerome before and had loved the quaint little town with many of its houses perched perilously close to the edges of cliffs that overlooked the valley far below. But at night, with the roads not terribly well lighted, the drive offered perils of another sort.

Surprisingly, Giff had remained awake for the entire drive and had assumed the job of navigator after they passed the city limits, directing her from the hand-drawn map Adam had given them. She turned onto the two-lane road indicated by the sign. "Shouldn't be too much farther now."

"About two miles, according to the map." He'd refused a pain pill when they'd left, preferring to have his mind alert. But he was paying for it, with the entire right side of his upper back on fire. They'd changed the bandage before leaving and there appeared to be no infection setting in. Why, then, was he drifting from shivers to hot flashes?

Hilly open fields were on both sides of the road, soggy with the rain still falling steadily and pooling in low spots everywhere. This was an old part of the country with thick-trunked trees, some with roots so gnarled that the road had been built around the lumpy exposed sections. The Bronco almost left the ground as they bounced over a huge rut. Roxie glanced at Giff and saw he was biting back his discomfort. "Sorry."

He didn't answer. He just wanted to get there.

At last, Giff saw the sign at the road's edge, the arrow below the nameplate pointing to a narrow path off to the left. "There it is."

Roxie turned, following the trail until she came to a wide stucco house, its glassed-in porch sporting a sign that told visitors that this was the office of Honeymoon Haven. As she pulled the Bronco to a halt in front, she could see several cabins behind, both right and left of the building. Wearily, she shifted into park. "I'll be right back," she told him, stepping out.

"I've been waiting for you, dear," Sunny Thatcher said as she rose from a bentwood rocker in the corner, gently removing an old gray cat from her lap and placing him on the rug. He didn't look any too happy at the disruption, meowing grumpily. "There now, Clancy. We'll go in and watch our movie shortly." She looked up at Roxie. "We've got *Casablanca* in the VCR for tonight. Clancy and I just love old movies."

Despite her fatigue, Roxie had to smile. There was a trace of the South in the woman's soft voice.

"Let's see now, Roxanne and Gifford Jones, right?" Curious blue eyes looked her over as Sunny tucked tufts of reddish orange hair into a frilly affair on her head that could only be called a nightcap.

"Yes," Roxie answered. "I'm sorry if we kept you waiting."

"It's no problem." Sunny bustled behind a free-standing corner counter and removed two keys from a small cubicle. "I've put you in number six." She smiled softly. "It's our Native American cabin. I hope that's all right."

As worn-out as they both were, Roxie thought, it could have been decorated in early depression era and neither would have minded. "That'll be lovely, I'm sure. Adam and Nikki asked me to give you their best."

Again the sweet, almost childlike smile. "Such dear people. They spent their honeymoon here, you know. I insisted. Adam's father saved my first husband's life years ago. A wonderful man."

Roxie wasn't sure which man had been wonderful and was too tired to ask. "If you'll point me in the right direction . . ."

"Certainly." Sunny opened the porch door and stepped onto the stoop beneath the overhang. "This rain is so good for my roses." Gathering her long sweater together across her chest, she pointed to the left. "Number six is down there. I've left the porch light on so you could spot it." She turned back to Roxie. "I've put in supplies and the refrigerator's stocked. I'll be by in the morning to see if you need anything else. I go to town every day."

"That'll be fine." She'd have to go in herself and find a bank to cash a check. She couldn't very well use a credit card since Sunny knew her as Mrs. Jones. "I don't know what Adam arranged about the fee, but—"

"He told me he was taking care of it and would collect from you later."

"Oh. Well, all right then." Adam had thought of everything.

Sunny peered into the Bronco, though she couldn't see much since the windows were somewhat fogged up. "Your husband is with you, isn't he?"

Roxie smiled nervously. "Of course. I drove the last hour. We're both pretty exhausted. The wedding and all, you know." More lies.

"I understand perfectly." She patted Roxie's arm. "I do hope you both enjoy your stay with us. Just come knock on my door if you need anything."

"Thank you." Roxie opened the Bronco and got behind the wheel. She could see Sunny peeking in and waving her fingers at Giff. Turning her head, she saw him wave back. Swallowing a smile, she shifted into gear and bounced along to cabin six.

It was on the edge of the cliff and Roxie guessed that the view in the daytime must be spectacular. She gave Giff the door key, waited until he maneuvered himself out of the car, looking pained, then backed the Bronco into the carport and gathered up her purse along with the small suitcase. After making sure the doors were locked, she went inside the cabin and locked that door.

Finally, she breathed a sigh of relief, feeling fairly safe for the first time in nearly twenty-four hours. She set down her things and removed her jacket, then looked around.

In the soft glow of a table lamp, she saw that there were several chunky candles placed around the room. The floor of the main room was terrazzo covered by a large Navajo rug in shades of turquoise, tan and yellow. The walls were richly paneled in oak and there was a lovely adobe corner fireplace with a leather couch the color of butter facing it. A variety of Indian artifacts were hung over the fairly cavernous opening and an assortment of bows and arrows decorated the area around a large picture window. There was a Pullman kitchen, a drop-leaf table for two by a smaller window and a door that probably led to the bathroom, plus an open closet area.

Over to the right, dominating the room was a king-size, four-poster bed carved from bleached pine, its sides fashioned like an outrigger canoe. And sprawled out on his stomach on the bed, lying crossways, was Giff, still fully clothed. He hadn't even removed his jacket or shoes.

Stifling a yawn, Roxie smiled, then checked out the couch. Yes, it would do nicely. She was bushed enough to sleep standing upright in a corner.

* * *

Nikki had wanted to lend her a long satin robe, but Roxie had opted for a warmer terry-cloth one in pale blue. Snuggled into it and furry slippers after her morning shower, she sipped her first cup of coffee and stared out at the fantastic view.

It was still drizzling and a gray haze hung over the valley, but the sight was still stunning. Tall dark evergreens jutted from adjacent hillsides reaching toward heavy clouds, and red rock mesas sat in the distance as they had for centuries. She felt as if she could see for miles, all the way to a thin ribbon of road winding around a faraway mountain.

Turning, she saw that Giff was still asleep, though he'd tossed off the feather comforter she'd placed over him when she'd removed his shoes and jacket. Walking over, she leaned down and touched his head. He was quite warm and damp. If he didn't waken soon, she'd have to get him up and get more antibiotics in him somehow. If he developed an infection, it would present more problems.

Earlier, she'd heard a noise on the front porch, like a rolled-up newspaper landing there. She opened the door and found she'd been right. Just as she removed the rubber band, she heard Giff moan as he turned restlessly. She placed the paper on the table and went to him. "Giff, you need to take more pills."

His eyes opened slowly and he brushed a hand over his face before attempting to sit up. Finally, he swung his legs over the side of the bed. Slices of pain shot along the muscles of his back. Even the small cut in his chest where Adam had removed the bullet ached like the devil. He steadied himself by gripping the edge of the mattress and sitting there a minute.

"How do you—"

"Don't ask. Like hell, that's how I feel." She had no right to look so damn terrific when he must look like something the cat dragged in. And felt worse. Angry with himself for his foul mood, mad at the world for his present predica-

ment, Giff eased off the bed and staggered into the bathroom.

Perhaps he wasn't a morning person, even under the best
of circumstances, Roxie mused. Certainly he had every right
to feel rotten after what he'd gone through. The so-called
surgery hadn't been done under ideal conditions, no numb-
ing anesthetic, no pain-killing injections. She wondered how
he was even able to get up and move around. The man must
have an iron constitution and a high pain threshold.

In the kitchen, she poured him a glass of fresh orange
juice and laid out his pills, then refilled her coffee cup.
Rummaging about this morning in search of something to
fix the two of them for breakfast, she'd found enough food
for twice as many people. A couple could literally hole up
here a week and never leave the cabin. Which, she supposed as she curled up on the couch and reached for the
newspaper, was exactly what honeymoon couples liked to
do.

Most of them, anyhow. She and Brad had gone to Ha-
waii. He'd gone deep-sea fishing the first day and gotten so
sunburned he'd spent almost the entire week in their room,
salved up from head to toe, moaning and groaning. It had
been less than ideal.

The bathroom door opened and Giff stepped out. He'd
rinsed his face, brushed his teeth, combed his hair and had
a talk with himself in the mirror. He'd decided that none of
this was Roxie's fault, that he had no right to take any of it
out on her and that if he didn't stop acting like a horse's ass,
she'd leave him.

The thought of not having her around had sobered him
quickly.

Still wearing his wrinkled shirt and pants, he walked over
to where she sat watching his approach with wide, wary
eyes. Trying not to flinch, he sat down next to her and
cocked up his chin, pointing at it. "Here. Hit me right
here."

The smile she gave him warmed her eyes, changed her face. "I don't want to hit you."

He reached for her hand, rubbed his thumb over her soft skin. "I can't imagine why not. I'm sorry I growled at you. I hereby give you permission to pop me a good one the next time I do. And there probably will be a next time."

With her other hand, she touched his forehead, then his cheek. "You're fever's back up. I'll get your pills." Walking was obviously painful for him. She got up, brought back juice and pills.

"I don't want any pain pills. They make me sleep."

"Maybe that's what you need, more rest."

He tossed down the antibiotic, then drank the juice thirstily. "I slept most of yesterday and all night. Great company, right?"

"Stop that. You're not here to entertain me. You're here to get well. Would you like some coffee?"

The aroma from her cup had his mouth watering. "Please." He picked up the paper as she rose, and spread it out on his lap. After he had some coffee, he'd take a make-shift shower and maybe even shave. Perhaps then he'd feel human again.

"In a little while, I'll make some breakfast," Roxie said from the kitchen. "Sunny's supplied us with sausage, bacon, eggs, pancake mix, milk, ham slices, homemade bread—you name it. What do you feel like having?"

"I'll be damned," Giff said, frowning at the newspaper.

Placing his cup on the table, she sat back down. "What is it?"

He held it out so she could read over his good shoulder. In the lower corner of the front page was a small black-and-white picture of a bearded man and a story describing how his body had been found in an alley in Phoenix late yesterday. It wasn't until she came to the name that she gasped. "Oh, my God. It's your ex-partner."

"Yeah, Phil Weston." The article was short, one paragraph on his career as an undercover policeman in Tucson a while back, detailing that he'd quit the force three years ago and had no known address currently. The rest of the piece had told how his hands and feet had been bound and he'd been strangled with a telephone cord.

Tossing aside the paper, Giff leaned back, then quickly sat forward as a shaft of pain tore through him. Bracing his elbows on his knees, he shook his head. "Damn, I wish I'd have been able to locate him after I got out. His murder *has* to be somehow connected to this thing with Sam."

Roxie felt a shiver race up her spine. "You think Sam killed Phil Weston?"

"Maybe he didn't do it, but someone connected with him probably did. After all, Phil was at that first sting in Tucson. Maybe he'd been nosing around and the man in charge ordered him out of the way. Whoever the hell *he* is." His hands clenched into fists. "How I'd like to know who he is."

"It does seem an odd coincidence that, after being gone for three years, Phil would surface on the day after your encounter with Sam at the Eagle's Nest. Do you think Sam knows your true identity?"

Giff took a swallow of coffee and gave a bitter laugh. "Oh, yeah, he knows. I'm sure he called the police after he left that night, tipping them off that he'd seen something suspicious at the back of the Eagle's Nest. He thought I'd still be there and get caught, like last time, with the coke on the premises."

The thought had Roxie wincing. "Could Phil have been the man in the hallway, the one who shot you?"

He narrowed his eyes thoughtfully, forcing himself to remember. "I have a vague impression of an awkward walk as the man in the hallway ran out."

"You said that Phil had been shot in the leg three years ago, which could have left him with a limp. Did it sound like he was walking with a limp?"

"Somewhat, yeah." Giff stood. All this time, had Phil been working with Sam? Was that why he'd testified against Giff? "I've got to talk with Neil. Where's the phone?"

Regretfully, she shook her head. "Only in the office." She rose, taking his arm. "First, let's get some breakfast in you, then a pain pill." When he started to protest, she cut him off. "The pill won't put you out if your stomach isn't empty. Then, you can get cleaned up and I'll drive you to the office phone."

He opened his mouth again, then closed it. He supposed waiting another hour wouldn't hurt, and he did feel hungry and grungy. "Did I ever tell you that I've never gotten along well with bossy women?"

"Tough," she answered, then whirled past him to the stove.

"On special assignment?" Standing in the front office, Giff gripped the phone, his back to the doorway leading into Sunny's living quarters, where Roxie was telling their hostess how wonderful her place was. "What do you mean, Neil's on special assignment?"

Lieutenant Tom Burke repeated himself. "Just like I said, he's somewhere near the border, but I can't tell you exactly where. A case he's been working on blew wide open and he left yesterday morning. Who is this?"

"A friend of his." Giff was well aware that a lot of people called undercover cops and never left a name—contacts, snitches, other cops working undercover. "When will he be back?"

"Couple of days, I guess."

Giff stared out at the wet limbs of a nearby tree, his lips a thin line. How could Neil have left yesterday when the sting they'd set up had been scheduled for that night, if nothing had gone wrong the day before? And Neil hadn't known of the fiasco, had he? What the hell was going on? "Is there any way I can reach him? It's important."

"Not really. Listen, if you've got information Neil's been waiting for on a case, I can take it down for him. He'll take care of you later."

So the lieutenant thought he was an informant selling information. Good. He'd let him. "No, I only talk to Neil. I'll call back in a couple of days." He hung up and turned to look for Roxie. He wanted to go back to their room and think this through.

Sunny poked her head through the archway. She was wearing a truly silly straw hat with a bright pink scarf threaded through the sides of the broad brim and tied under her chin. "I hear you love my raspberry jam. I make it myself."

Giff removed his frown and smiled at the woman who couldn't have been an inch over five feet. "It's wonderful." He waved his hand, indicating the area. "This is a great place you've got here."

Sunny beamed. "I'm so glad you think so. Your missus tells me you've been a bit under the weather, working too hard before the wedding. I'll make some chicken soup this afternoon and bring some over for your supper. Nothing like soup on a chilly evening."

The wedding? His eyes met Roxie's over the woman's head and he caught her lips twitching. "That would be awfully nice of you. Ready to leave, *honey?*"

Playing the game, Roxie moved to his side. "Absolutely, darling." She smiled at Sunny. "We'll see you later."

Slipping behind the wheel of the Bronco, she saw from his expression that the news wasn't good. "Neil wasn't there?"

"He's away on special assignment and they say he can't be reached till he comes back in a couple of days." He ran a hand over his hair and let out a frustrated whoosh of air. "One curve after another. I don't know what to make of it. I'll bet you're sorry as hell you ever came back to the Eagle's Nest that night and got involved in this mess."

She started the Bronco toward number six. "I'm not in the least sorry."

He looked at her, honestly puzzled. "Why? Why aren't you?"

She waited until she'd parked alongside their cabin before answering. "Don't you know?"

Chapter 9

Giff awoke to the muted sounds of Elvis Presley asking listeners if they were lonesome tonight. He rolled over slowly, feeling the ache in his back spread through his limbs as his body stretched out. He'd cleaned up before lying down, but he hadn't shaved and his mouth had a lingering medicinal taste. The song ended as he eased his legs over the edge of the bed and stifled a groan, just barely.

"I'm sorry if I woke you," Roxie said from the corner of the couch where she was sorting through a stack of albums. "Sunny's got quite a collection of golden oldies here."

"It's all right. I need to get up. All I do is sleep." He shuffled into the bathroom.

He returned to the strains of Patti Paige asking how much was that doggie in the window. He poured himself a large glass of lemonade from the pitcher in the fridge and drank it before walking over to the picture window. "It's stopped raining finally." Afternoon clouds still hung over the valley and a weak sun was trying to break through. The view made him feel as if he were standing on the edge of the earth.

"Need some more pills?" Roxie asked, coming to stand next to him. He'd spent the whole afternoon in bed, which had been just fine with her, especially after that bombshell she'd laid on him in the Bronco. *Don't you know?* she'd asked, coy and cutesy. Can't you guess why I dropped my life to go with you? Good Lord, whatever had made her say something so blatantly stupid?

And, in typical Giff fashion, he'd ignored the question, the inference and her, walking inside and climbing under the feather comforter. She prayed that his mind was too pre-occupied with thoughts of Sam and too befuddled with medicine to remember her momentary loss of good sense.

She hadn't meant to challenge him, especially since she wasn't certain exactly how she felt. She only knew she was inexplicably drawn to this man, to help him right his wrongs, fight his battles, mend his wounds. More explanation than that, she didn't want to explore just now.

"What I need is some fresh air." Giff turned from the window and found her soft brown eyes watching him. He looked away, but he still saw them, just as he'd seen them in his restless dreams. Waiting, watching, worrying. "Want to go for a walk?"

"Sure, if you feel up to it."

"I've felt worse." He remembered his first few months in prison, a big ox named Willie who kept at him with not-so-subtle comments about dirty cops. They'd finally been paired on the road gang and Willie had seen his chance. Giff had had no choice but to take him on. The fight had been vicious and blessedly brief before the guards had separated them. He'd felt far more battered from Willie's powerful fists than he did now with a bullet wound in him, yet he'd had to go right back out and work the next day. Yeah, he'd felt plenty worse before.

There was a red-rock wooded area not far from the cabins, and a winding path that led alongside a stream. Roxie hadn't been able to get pills into Giff before they'd set out, but she did take his hand as they climbed the incline. Holding on to him, perhaps she could sense his fatigue if he overdid things, she thought.

They wound in and out of tall pines still dripping rain onto the path from a murky sky. But Giff gazed up with a kind of wonder, anyway. "You have no idea how badly a person can miss looking up at the sky when your freedom has been snatched away from you and you no longer can."

He was right; she could only imagine that kind of frustration. "But you're here now, at least."

He was, yet he worried he might lose that freedom again. As they moved into a small clearing, a shaft of sunlight turned the slug piles along the streambed into a dusty turquoise.

Scampering onto a large stone, Roxie bent to pick up a piece. "Kind of pretty, isn't it?"

Standing beside her, Giff reached to examine the piece she handed him. "Left over from the copper mines around here, right?"

"Yes." Roxie straightened, dusting off her hands as she squinted along the streambed. "There's a place in town that has a relief map of the whole town of Jerome. It shows all the tunnels beneath many of the streets and even under the houses and business district. I've often wondered how it is that some of these homes haven't caved in, since the foundations are so shaky. The place is a big sinkhole just waiting to happen."

Giff tossed aside the slug and shoved his hands into his pockets. "Sort of like relationships that seem to be strong to the casual observer, but underneath, the foundation's shaky. Bound to collapse sooner or later."

She should have guessed his cynicism would surface. "Then again, this is a very old town and not a single tunnel has caused a building to collapse yet."

"It will, one day. Wait and see."

Roxie pulled up the collar of her coat against a sudden chill wind. Or was it the turn their conversation had taken that had her feeling the need for additional warmth? "You think it's inevitable, then. Don't you know of *any* relationships that stand on a solid foundation?"

"No," he replied immediately. "Do you?"

"Many. My parents had a very strong marriage...and you saw Nikki and Adam, to name a couple of relationships that weren't doomed."

Giff raised his eyes to watch a cloud drift by. "The Kendalls have only been married a little over a year. Time will tell. They're well-off now, in love, a baby on the way, not hurting for money. But what would happen if something devastating happened, something that would jar that foundation, make one of them lose faith in the other?"

"They'd weather it and *not* lose faith in each other." She shook her head at him. "Why is it that you always expect the worst?" She knew why, or thought she did. The woman he'd loved who hadn't stood by him when he'd needed her to believe in him. "Not all women are like Carla, Giff."

He gave a bitter laugh. "Yeah, well, you couldn't prove it by me." He started walking on a bit farther, his conscience nagging him. Roxie *was* different. She'd left everything to come with him. She hadn't turned tail and run. But he couldn't think like that. Wouldn't. Life had taught him that most people had ulterior motives. Everyone looked out for number one.

Could she be the one exception?

Roxie followed, wishing they'd never started this depressing conversation, wishing she knew a way to convince him that he was dead wrong.

A few minutes later, Giff stopped and peered across the stream at an underground opening. "Is that one of the mining tunnels, you think?"

Roxie followed his gaze. "I don't know. Possibly."

The opening was barely large enough for a man to crawl through, and there were wooden supports on each side and overhead. Giff could see only darkness inside. It looked deserted yet oddly inviting, or perhaps it was just his mood dictating that impression. "A good place to get away from it all. Peaceful and quiet, where no one could bother you."

She'd about had it with his pessimism and his negative remarks. "So's a coffin, but that still doesn't make it very appealing." Positioning herself in front of him, she scowled up into his face, noticing that with several days' growth of beard, he looked even more dangerous than when she'd first met him. "What is it with you? You've had a few rough breaks, I'll grant you that. And some bad years, through no fault of your own. Well, mister, no one promised you—or me or anyone else—a rose garden. Life, at times, is unfair and rotten. That's just the way it is."

His frown was menacing. "Rough breaks? Bad years? Lady, you don't know the half of it."

"Perhaps not, but I do know that when lousy things happen to us, we have two choices—cave in or get over it. Which one do you pick?" Turning on her heel, Roxie started back for their cabin.

They ate Sunny's chicken soup in virtual silence, then cleared the table and loaded the dishwasher, being very careful not to brush against each other. Giff read the paper from front to back while Roxie curled up with an old copy of *Wuthering Heights* that she'd found in Sunny's bookcase.

Giff fell asleep in the chair. Roxie went on reading. Giff woke up to the sound of the shower running in the bathroom. Yawning, he tossed down his pills with more fruit juice, peeled down to his briefs and got under the feather comforter. Why fight it? he asked himself as he closed his eyes. He wasn't fit company for man nor beast. And certainly not for the woman in the next room.

A woman he had no right to be wanting.

Roxie came out brushing her hair. She saw that he was already asleep. Good. At least she wouldn't have to sit there with the air around them thick as the fog that was swirling through the valley outside the window. She prepared her bed on the couch, tossed her robe onto a nearby chair and got under the blankets.

With a sigh, she picked up the book and opened it to where she'd left off. Fool, she reproached herself. Just what else had you expected?

The sound woke her quickly, unexpectedly. Roxie sat up, listening hard. There it was again, an angry retort followed by a moan, coming from the direction of the bed. She snapped on the table lamp and rose.

Giff was thrashing around in the covers, his head jerking back onto the pillow, his fists balled at his sides. The bandage was stark white against his tan skin and the black curly hair as his chest heaved with his labored breathing. Fierce, guttural sounds came from deep in his throat as his hands grasped handfuls of sheet. "No," he growled. "Don't come any closer."

"Giff, you're dreaming," Roxie said, daring to lean over him. She touched his arm and squeezed a little to get his attention. "Wake up."

His eyes flew open, and there was such rage in their blue depths that she took an involuntary step backward. "No, you don't. Get out of my face!" he raged. Again, his head snapped sideways as if he'd received a sharp blow to the chin. He sat up, staring ahead at a vision she couldn't see. "Touch me again and I'll finish you. I swear I will." He took in quick, shallow breaths, his fingers bunching and unclenching.

Roxie moved closer and sat down near the foot of the bed facing him. "It's all right, Giff. It's me, Roxie. You're having a bad dream."

He didn't seem to hear the words, just the sound as he swiveled toward her, grabbing her upper arms in his powerful hands. "Why can't you leave me alone? Why won't you go away?" He shook her, hard, then again.

Taken off guard, Roxie was shaken, but she wasn't about to give up. Her hands moved to his chest, soothing, caressing as she raised her head to look at him. "It's all right. It's over. You're safe now."

His eyes, those hard, cold eyes stared into hers for a very long moment. Then she saw awareness return as he blinked and loosened his hold on her. "Roxie?" he asked, then looked down at his hands gripping her. "Oh, God, Roxie." And he pulled her to him, gently now, easing her closer. His fingers smoothed her hair while his other hand stroked along her back. "I'm sorry. I'm so sorry."

Her head tucked under his chin, she closed her eyes. His skin felt chilled, clammy. Her arms slid around him, trying to share her body warmth. "Don't be. It was a nightmare."

He pulled back, checking her arms, her face. "Did I...did I hurt you?"

She shook her head. "Do you have these dreams often?"

He didn't answer, just continued to stare at her hair, golden in the dim light of the lamp. Helpless to resist, he threaded his fingers through the silken strands. Her skin up close was as delicate and fine as a thin china cup that had been in their cabinet, the one thing left over from his mother's short stay in his life. He trailed his fingers along her cheek and found her flesh sleepy warm and lightly flushed.

Giff frowned, still unconvinced. "I'd never hurt you, not knowingly."

She believed him. "You didn't." Remnants of the effect of the hellish dream were lingering in his eyes, she noticed. She could see he was forcing it back, determined to conquer the demons that plagued him. She reached to take his hand, to lace his fingers with hers. "You couldn't."

He felt the anxiety drift from him and in its place came an unexpected and unwelcome rush of tenderness for the woman who'd cared enough to comfort him, who'd set aside her fear to come to him. Only a misguided woman or a desperate one would want him. Roxie was neither.

Yet in her dark eyes, he saw a simmering desire barely awakening. He'd been lonely so damn long. Maybe even before prison and that hated night. Perhaps even when he'd been lying to himself that Carla had cared for him. Lonely and needy. Dare he reach out and take what this fragile woman was offering? he asked himself.

"You're the most perfect thing that's ever happened to me," he said, his voice no longer gruff but low, husky.

"I'm not perfect. I'm only a woman. A woman who cares about you." Roxie knew she was stepping into a mine field, but it was too late to be careful. She let her heart speak for her. "A woman who wants you."

His hands framed her lovely face, his thumbs caressing the satin of her skin. "Make me clean, Roxie. Make me whole again. Make me forget."

It was what she'd been waiting for, what she realized she so desperately wanted. She closed the gap between them, her lips opening to his, her arms circling his waist. She needed him more than she'd ever needed anything before. And she needed to give to him. She tumbled into the kiss, going deeper, falling all the way.

Her mouth was like honey, sweet and warm, drugging his senses. Giff drank from her, knowing even as he supped that he could never get his fill. She was nourishing his soul and cleansing his mind, absolving him of guilt, real or imagined. In one hot, hungry kiss, she was erasing his past and offering him hope, making him feel like a man again.

He was a volcano, ready to overflow, churning too long, denied too frequently. Roxie felt the trembling inside him as he fought for control, a battle made all the more difficult as she thrust her hands into his hair and drew his head down to her breasts, already throbbing and heavy with arousal.

His blood racing, Giff ripped the thin gown that she wore, exposing her breasts to his greedy mouth. Her low, throaty moan drove him on as he feasted, devoured, ravaged. Like a man consumed, he eased her onto her back and felt her arch upward as with teeth and tongue he teased each quivering peak.

The heady feminine flavor of her skin had him breathing in deeply, had his head swimming. But he needed to see more. Shifting, he tore the rest of the gown from her and tossed it aside. The lamplight shimmered across her flat stomach and her incredibly long legs as his eyes reveled in her perfection. The years of celibacy had been worth the wait for this wondrous view. His briefs strained to contain a need almost too huge to control. He wanted desperately for this to be good for her.

When her arms reached to bring him up to her, he ignored her and skimmed his lips along her thigh. Guessing his intention, she reached to stop him. "No, not like that. Together."

Giff raised his head. "Not this first time. I...it's been so long that I have a feeling we might not finish together. Trust me."

She understood and let herself trust, turning herself over to his care. In moments he had her climbing, an aching sob caught in her throat. Unable to clutch him, her hands fisted in the sheet as the awesome sensations buffeted her.

He heard her cry of stunned release and felt a masculine satisfaction that was like no other. He watched the sensual flush darken her cheeks and saw her struggle to catch her breath. He knew he couldn't wait another second. Shoving free of his briefs, he rose above her, his arms trembling with tension.

"Open your eyes," he whispered and when she did, he filled her in one powerful stroke. He tried to keep his gaze locked on hers, but his body too long deprived had a mind of its own. He felt his vision blur in moments as he hurled out of control, gasping for air. Boneless, he collapsed onto her, praying it had been long enough for her to share the ride.

When he thought he could move again without quivering, he lifted his head and saw brown eyes still adrift in passion. He couldn't prevent a smile as he rose on one elbow and brushed back a strand of hair from her damp face. "Are you all right?"

"What do you think?" she managed on a huffy breath.

His smile broadened as his arms gathered her to him, sharing the afterglow. He was warm and a little sweaty, but not from fever or pain. A rich contentment he hadn't felt in far too long enveloped him as he rolled to his back and took her with him. Letting out a deep sigh of fulfillment, Giff closed his eyes.

He didn't sleep, couldn't sleep. He didn't want to miss a moment of the pleasure of just holding her. Had it been so much better because it had been so long, or because it had been with this woman? This very special woman.

He could tell by her breathing that Roxie wasn't asleep, either. He felt stunned by the thought that she wanted to be here, too. Had it been a fluke, or would it be just as good the second time they made love?

Giff shifted his head on the pillow, tilting her face up so he could look into her eyes. "Are you sorry?" he asked, still unable to believe she'd wanted him as badly as he'd wanted her.

"No. Are you?"

He tightened his hold on her. "What a silly question."

"My thought, exactly." He was relaxed now, feeling better, she knew. Perhaps he would talk with her finally. "Tell me about the dream, Giff."

He shifted his gaze toward the window where tree branches were swaying in a wind that was picking up. Thunder rumbled in the distance and the rain had returned. He shrugged with his good shoulder. "Nothing much to tell. I guess we all have nightmares occasionally."

One-handed, she drew the sheet up over them. "This was more than a mild nightmare. You were furious and frightening."

He swallowed. "What did I say?"

"You were warning someone to stay away or you'd do something drastic to them. Were you back in prison?"

"Yeah." He withdrew from her, running a hand through his hair.

Wrapping the sheet around her, Roxie sat up facing him. "Who was tormenting you?"

Giff moved one arm above his head. "Lots of guys. Cops who go to prison aren't anyone's best buddy. The inmates hate you and the guards look for opportunities to make your life miserable."

"But you hadn't done anything wrong. Doesn't that count for anything?"

He smiled at her naiveté. "There are no guilty men in prison. Everyone claims they're innocent. It doesn't mean a thing."

"Yet everyone assumes the other guy's guilty?"

"Right."

She wanted to keep him talking. "Did you have a cell mate?"

"Cops who've been sent to prison have their own cells or they probably wouldn't make it through the first night. But there's mealtime, the exercise yard and whatever work you're assigned to do."

"What did they do, start fights with you?"

He shook his head. "Too smart for that. They kept at me, quiet jabs that the guards never heard, calling me a dirty cop and much worse. That sort of thing wears on you, day after day. The man in the cell next to mine was an okay guy. Luther heard a lot of it and kept telling me to keep my cool."

"What was he in for?"

He didn't know how to pretty it up so he told her. "Murder one. Killed the man who lured his son into heavy use of drugs. Luther's wife walked away from him during the trial..."

Like Carla had, she finished for him silently. Roxie imagined that there weren't all that many women who stood by men who were convicted. But there had to be some. "Did you listen to Luther and keep your cool?"

"Most of the time. There was this big dude named Willie on the road gang. Wouldn't let me be. Outweighed me by fifty pounds at least." He smiled at the ceiling. "But I got in a few good punches before the guards took him off me."

She tried to control an involuntary shudder. "You worked on a road gang?"

His eyes flew to her face, wondering if he'd see revulsion. He saw instead a heartbreaking sympathy. "It wasn't so bad most of the time. Got a nice tan."

He didn't fool her with his breezy explanation. Roxie took his hand in hers and examined it slowly. "I knew that first day that you hadn't gotten these cuts and calluses from bartending." She lowered her head and gently kissed his palm.

Giff felt his emotions shift as he watched her hair fall like a golden curtain surrounding his hand.

Roxie touched the scar on his chin. "Did you get this in prison?"

His face hardened, remembering. "Souvenir from a guard everyone called Blackjack. He used to patrol at night with a long, pipelike stick. My bunk was along the side wall, but his stick could reach through the bars quite a ways. If you were unlucky enough to fall asleep with any part of you within reach, you could wake up real quick with a sharp jab of that pipe, and by the time you knew what hit you, Blackjack was three cells away. Sadistic sonofabitch."

"What recourse did you have against men like Willie and Blackjack?"

"None. Who'd believe a prisoner over a guard? And in Willie's case, he said he slipped on the wet grass and I jumped him." He saw the anger and disbelief on her face and went on to explain. "You see, it's real hot working on the road chopping down weeds, the temperature over a hundred sometimes. At night, the men are penned up together, and by day marched outside and linked together by leg chains to work along a highway where people who are free are whizzing by in their cars without a care. Frustrations, anger, emotions run high. Fights are common and the guards really don't care who's at fault. Their answer is to whack you each a good one, then separate you. Until the next time."

Propped up on one elbow, she toyed with his chest hair with her other hand. "Was the dream specifically about someone? Whoever it was, you seemed so angry with him."

The dream had been about Eddie, a middle-aged drug pusher Giff had put away a year or so before he'd joined him in prison. Somehow, Eddie had managed to steal a table knife and grind it down to razor sharpness. He'd cornered Giff one late afternoon in the exercise yard, even though Giff always stayed to himself and usually within clear range of a guard. Eddie had jerked him to the ground and taunted him while his buddies created a diversion across the field. Giff had been a second away from being stabbed when he'd managed to free a leg and ram his knee into Eddie's groin.

This was the first time he'd dreamed of that particular day, though other incidents drifted in and out of his consciousness, both awake and sleeping. He saw no reason to share more with Roxie. "Nah. Just flashes." He swiveled to encircle her. "Can't we think of a more pleasant subject?"

He wasn't telling her all of it, she was certain. Perhaps that was for the best. What he had shared with her had quietly horrified her. She wondered how he'd survived prison and emerged such a gentle lover. "Where did you learn to make love so beautifully?" she asked, knowing the question would certainly distract his thoughts.

He smiled. "Now, that's a leading question if ever I heard one. I take the Fifth."

She ran a lazy hand along his back and encountered the bandage. Suddenly concerned, she realized she'd forgotten to be careful of his wound. "Are you hurting? Is there anything you need?"

His smile was blatantly sexual. "What I need is you." Grasping her hand, he moved it down between their bodies, directing her fingers to curl around him. "Since you asked, this is where it's hurting, but I think you can make the pain go away."

Color stained her cheeks, but she smiled back. She raised her face for his kiss while her hands worked magic on his burning flesh. She felt him flinch on his right side as if he were hurting. "We shouldn't be doing this," she said, easing back. "We're going to open that wound and have it bleeding."

"Some things are worth a little discomfort." He stretched to resume the kiss.

"Wait." She maneuvered around him. "Are you all right lying on your back?"

"I'm fine. Will you forget my injury and—"

"No." Gently, she poked at his chest until he lay back. "Just let me do the work this time."

He grinned. "Gladly. Don't hurt me, will you?"

Her lips twitched. "I promise to be gentle." And she bent to her task.

Earlier, his mouth had skimmed along every inch of her skin, lighting fires, stoking needs. She could do no less. Her lips explored his face, all of it. A kiss on each of those startling blue eyes hidden by heavy lids, along cheeks bristly with a growth rapidly forming into a beard that she found enormously appealing. She found it wildly sexy to brush her mouth through the short patch and kiss the small scar not yet completely buried.

But when he raised his face to capture her lips, she evaded him and shifted her attention to his throat before investigating the hard ridges of muscles in his chest, then trailing downward.

Giff felt the breath whoosh out of his lungs as she busied herself learning him with her soft hands, her incredible mouth, her small, white teeth that nibbled and left a trail of love bites. Fascinated with her, he watched her touch and taste and kiss her way back up to his waiting lips.

She swept her mouth along his from corner to corner, then deepened the kiss, her tongue easing inside and gently dueling with his. There was no hurry, she seemed to say. Let's not rush this. Let us savor and enjoy.

The kiss was slow, luxurious, so tender that he felt his strength ebb away, along with his tension. The blood no longer pounded through his veins, but rather flowed warm and easy and sure. The sweet scent of her wrapped around him, replacing life's harsher smells that he'd inhaled for too long. The wondrous sight of her delighted him, removing old, bitter mental pictures that tended to swamp him. More thoroughly than he would have dreamed possible, he drifted under her spell.

The kiss turned dreamy, offering possibilities he'd forgotten how to pray for. The touch of her hands on his flesh seduced him long after there was no need. He felt himself surrendering happily, completely.

She lifted then, watching him watching her. She guided him inside her while his hot eyes devoured her. He arched, joining them more deeply, and she felt her vision cloud. Tossing her hair back, Roxie began to move. Gently at first, then picking up the rhythm. The raw hunger on his face aroused her almost as thoroughly as the hands that closed around her breasts.

He wanted to rush to completion, but she would have none of it, controlling the pace. Her eyes challenged him as she deliberately slowed, prolonging the pleasure, drawing out each separate ounce of passion. She held nothing back from him and, because that was so, neither did he. Trusting her, he let her lead the way.

She knew the moment he surrendered. Not a subservient surrender, for his hands on her sent pleasure waves throughout her system, and his body arching into hers had her biting back a moan, and his mouth when finally he drew her down to him all but sucked the breath from her body. It was more an acceptance of her power over him. The same power she knew he had over her.

How easy it was now to see everything clearly, Roxie thought with the small portion of her mind still able to reason. She saw her marriage for what it had been, a need for a home, a family, such as the one she'd been raised in. She'd been motivated not so much by love as by a nesting desire, a reaching out for the familiar. It hadn't come close to the potency, the power of her feelings for Giff.

He moved within her, patiently, steadily, lovingly. Staring into his eyes, she couldn't stop the smile as the world began to slip away. Roxie closed her eyes, knowing that all she'd ever wanted lay within the circle of her arms.

Giff watched her splinter and let himself join her, the soft sound he made an echo of hers. The explosion rocked him to his core. As he drifted back to reality, he felt a frown forming.

He'd had sex before, many times. But always, he'd kept a small part of himself from becoming completely involved, unable to relinquish everything. Tonight, with Roxie, he'd given her his all.

And it worried the hell out of him.

It didn't matter that he'd done it willingly, although not without trepidation. He knew now that what he'd had with Carla had been a rush of hormones, not a burst of devotion. He'd fallen in lust with her, not love. Bought into a nightmare, not a dream. But he'd protected himself with Carla.

Somehow, Roxie had gotten under his skin, past his defenses, and into his heart.

But he couldn't let her know. He had too much to do yet. He had to heal, to get the people who'd so callously stolen precious years from him, to obtain justice and clear his name. Feeling about her as he did, he couldn't risk hurting her. Later—if there would be a later—he would think about what to do about Roxie.

Maybe nothing. Maybe when all this was over, he still wouldn't be able to adjust to someone in his life. He'd gone it alone so long, trusting few, suspecting everyone. Maybe he'd only be able to share himself physically.

And Roxie deserved more.

Gently, he eased her over, but kept her curled up against his heart, his arms holding her close. She made as if to rise, but he pressed her head down. "Stay with me, Roxie. Don't leave."

He felt her draw in a deep breath, then settle down. "I'm not going anywhere."

Giff kissed the top of her head, then shifted his gaze out the window where the rain was streaming down in restless rivulets.

Why was it that whenever he got a glimpse of heaven, he knew that it would never last?

Chapter 10

It was a lovely morning. Roxie walked along the path leading from Sunny's small office to the cabin under an incredibly blue sky. A hummingbird, its tiny wings a blur of motion, moved among the wildflowers as it scavenged for breakfast. Just ahead of her, a pinecone dropped from an evergreen and lodged in a tuft of grass. She inhaled deeply, the clean woodsy scent most welcome after yesterday's heavy, humid air. One of the amazing things about Arizona was that rain could fall all night long, but after a couple of hours of sunshine, it looked as if there'd been no storm at all.

She carried a covered dish of warm cranberry muffins carefully. After breakfast, she'd gone to use the phone and found Sunny removing the fragrant tray from her oven. The little woman had insisted Roxie take some back to her "husband." Feeling a little giddy after the night she'd spent in Giff's arms, Roxie had smilingly agreed.

Was the sunshine brighter because she felt so thoroughly, so beautifully loved? Of course, despite the fact that

they'd made love several times throughout the long night.
Roxie wasn't fool enough to believe that Giff loved her. She
was painfully aware that very little had changed.

Except in her own heart. She loved him. She acknowledged that truth finally. The problems they faced were many
and vast, and not apt to be cleared up easily. She wasn't a
naive woman who felt that making love was the same as being loved. However, last night, logic and reason had fled
when instinct and desire had taken over. For Giff as well as
for her.

Roxie knew that the most he wanted from her was a
physical relationship, and even to that he'd succumbed
grudgingly, when his body's needs had taken over his mind's
iron resolve. He wanted her, of that she was certain. But he
didn't *want* to want her.

As for her, she'd shared a night of love with him such as
she'd never known. She'd never given herself to men easily
or often, although she sometimes gave the impression that
she knew a lot of men. Which she did, but not in an intimate way. Because she'd left home at an early age and had
traveled extensively, her friends assumed she was worldly. It
was a facade she'd fostered. In fact, she'd been extremely
cautious, trying to protect her heart from further injury,
especially after Brad.

Giff had slipped past her defenses without even trying,
where others, who'd tried valiantly, had failed to get to first
base. There was no explaining these things, Roxie thought
as she stepped around a fallen branch. Chemistry, karma,
fate—who knew? She only knew that though she had denied her feelings from the start, she'd been attracted to Giff
from day one.

He'd seen too much of the sordid side of life, been hurt
by too many people he'd trusted—his mother walking away
when he'd been so young, his partner turning against him,
Carla's disloyalty. Small wonder he trusted no one, not even
Roxie most of the time.

Roxie longed to soothe him, to erase the pain of his lonely past, to prove to him that life needn't be harsh and unforgiving. She wanted to make up for his disappointments, to offer him hope. She couldn't help but worry that he'd built such a high wall around his feelings that he might never be able to tear it down completely.

Still, she would have to try to penetrate each and every barricade he threw up.

Stepping onto the small stoop, she reached for the knob and pushed open the door. And almost dropped the plate of muffins as she stared into the barrel of Giff's Beretta aimed directly at her. "Oh!" she cried out.

Giff straightened from his shooting stance and lowered his gun. "Sorry. I didn't mean to scare you. I was practicing my draw."

Roxie let out a whoosh of air. "A highly unusual welcome, if you don't mind my saying so."

Giff rolled his sore shoulder, trying to loosen it. There was still pain, but he chose to ignore it. He couldn't afford to baby himself. "I'm going to walk into those woods up the road and try the gun out with live ammo. I think there's something wrong with it. The trigger keeps jamming."

Setting down the dish of muffins on the kitchen counter, she turned to him. "Surely your detective friend wouldn't have given you a gun he hadn't tested."

"Probably not, but maybe it's been a while since it's been used. I might have to take it apart and oil everything before it works smoothly." He stuck the Beretta into his waistband, distracted by a pleasant aroma. "What've you got there?" He lifted the cloth from the plate. "Mmm, smells good."

She'd fixed him a big breakfast a little over an hour ago and watched him eat like a starving man. He'd confessed that since his stint in prison, he couldn't seem to get enough of really good food. She handed him a muffin. "Sunny sent you these, hot out of the oven." She watched him take a bite and chew appreciatively, and she smiled. "You're like a little boy who's just been given a treat."

He felt a little like that, especially this morning. His blood was still humming from the wondrous hours he'd held her in his arms. She'd satisfied his appetite for food, and so much more. He'd learned every inch of her body. He'd like nothing better than to lead her right back to bed and spend the day relearning her. But already the soft look in her eyes was beginning to worry him.

He couldn't afford to let her care even more.

Finishing the muffin, he turned to look for the jacket he'd borrowed from Adam. "Did you get through to Nikki?"

"Yes. I told her we were fine and not to worry." She hadn't been able to say much more since the door from Sunny's office into her living quarters had been open, the small woman hovering nearby.

"Did you call Trevor again?"

"No. Should I have?"

He struggled into the jacket, mindful of his stiff shoulder. He had a few questions about the Lowells' old family friend and had been wondering just how attached Roxie was to Trevor. "I'm not so sure about him. Did you know he owns this big house up on Camelback Mountain worth about a million?"

"I didn't know how much it was worth, but I've been to his home and it is lovely." She frowned at Giff, not sure where he was going with this. Did he suspect everyone? "Surely you're not suggesting that Trevor had anything to do with the smuggling operation?"

"Maybe not, but how does a man own a home like that, free and clear, on a restaurant manager's salary? I checked out his file. He doesn't make that much."

That caught her attention. "You went through the files?"

Restlessly, Giff paced the length of the small kitchen. "Roxie, I *had* to. I'm working this case as if I were still a cop. I have to know all I can about everyone involved. And by the way, why is there no file on Sam? I couldn't find even an address for him, nor a slip of paper with his phone number on it.''

"I have his address and phone number in my Rolodex. Trevor has that information, too. We only keep files on the employees, not the owners." She was sounding defensive and hated it. But he had to have gone through the files in her office, and that didn't sit well with her, even though she knew that Sam was the criminal here and not Giff. "If you'd have asked me, I'd have told you.''

He couldn't have asked her when he'd first started on the job without arousing her suspicions. He could see she wasn't happy with the way he got things done, but that couldn't be helped right now. He had more important concerns. "Getting back to Trevor, do you know how he managed to pay for that big house?''

Roxie toyed with her bangs, hating to reveal personal things about an old friend, but needing to remove Trevor from Giff's suspect list. "He gambles.''

Giff's eyebrows shot up. "He gambles? Are you telling me Trevor paid off a million-dollar property by gambling?''

She nodded. "He goes to Las Vegas three or four times a year and he wins big. His home is filled with valuable paintings, a rare-book collection, expensive furnishings. Once, he let it slip that he'd worked out a system that paid off.''

"I don't believe this.''

Roxie shrugged. "It's true. He plays blackjack, and he rarely walks away with a loss. I'm the only one who knows, and I don't believe Trevor is aware that I've discovered his little secret vice.''

"How did you find out?''

"I have a friend who works at Caesar's Palace. Trevor always stays there, and his line of credit would amaze you. He's a high roller, believe it or not.''

"Is he doing it under the table?''

Roxie sighed. "Look, I don't want this to go any further, because I don't have proof. But yes, I believe he is. I don't think he declares all his winnings, which is why he doesn't want anyone to know. He keeps a low profile, otherwise. And I think that's why he maintains his job at the Eagle's Nest."

Giff resumed his pacing. "I don't buy this. The IRS isn't easily fooled. It wouldn't take a Harvard professor to figure out that he could never afford to *rent* that house on his income as manager of a restaurant, much less own it outright."

"He tells the world he inherited money from relatives in England." The idea of Trevor as a criminal was so preposterous that she had to dismiss Giff's suspicions. "Trevor doesn't have the stomach for smuggling or guns or violence. He's…well, he's a refined man with intellectual tastes and artistic interests. I can no more picture him as kingpin of a drug-smuggling operation than I can imagine that Sunny Thatcher is involved."

Halting in front of her, Giff's expression wasn't amused. "Not every crook is an uneducated, muscle-bound gorilla. Some of the worst are the white-collar guys who give in to greed. I once pursued a guy who drove a Jag, graduated from Princeton, wore eight-hundred-dollar suits and had season tickets to the symphony. He was a slime ball who ran a prostitution ring involving over fifty call girls, all teenagers. Guys like him have others do the dirty work while they collect, big time. Now, do you still have a hard time picturing good old Trevor getting his manicured hands dirty?"

"Yes. I'd bet my last dollar that Trevor's clean."

His eyes narrowed. "And you're such a great judge of character? How come you couldn't read your ex-husband better? You'd grown up knowing him, after all."

It was all she could do not to visibly flinch. Was he just being the tough cop, or was he already trying to distance himself from her because of last night? "I loved Brad. People in love are prone to poor judgment. I admit to that very human weakness."

He just stared at her, knowing he'd delivered one below the belt, wishing he hadn't felt it necessary. He hated the hurt in her eyes, yet she didn't retaliate by reminding him about his own poor assessment of Carla when she easily could have. He felt rotten, as if he'd won the round, but lost the fight.

Turning, he zipped up his jacket and headed for the door. "I'll be back in a little while."

Roxie had been planning to offer to go with him, but their encounter had made her change her mind. Perhaps he needed to be alone for a while as much as she did.

Shrugging out of her jacket, she tossed it aside and curled up on the couch. She knew what he was doing. He was angry with himself for letting down his guard last night, for reaching for her, for admitting his need. He turned gruff and almost cruel to hide his softer feelings.

Perhaps prison had done that to him, taught him to hide behind his temper, his indifference. He didn't like her witnessing any signs of human weakness in him, such as his kindness to Ginny over her difficult son. He would deny all shows of tenderness, of a loving nature.

And she'd seen that side of him last night in spades.

In loving her, he'd been gentle, compassionate, sensitive, more interested in her pleasure than his own. Every woman recognized a selfish lover. Traits like that were hard to hide in bed. By the same token, a tender lover revealed an unerring kindness and consideration, a generosity of spirit that the rest of the world might not readily see.

Leaning her head back, Roxie sighed. She'd been wanting this nightmare to end. Yet she couldn't help wondering if when it did, the love she'd just discovered would end also.

Giff stood on Sunny's enclosed porch, frowning as he listened to Lieutenant Tom Burke at Scottsdale police headquarters on the other end of the line tell him that they still hadn't heard from Neil. "Isn't this highly unusual, an officer's being gone this long without contacting his commanding officer?" He'd been an undercover cop a long time and knew that no matter the assignment, each man found time to check in every day or so.

Burke took his time responding. "Apparently, you're not one of his paid snitches. Exactly who are you?"

No dummy this guy, Giff thought. He'd suspected that he might give away too much by his question. However, his concern ran deep enough to risk it. He'd spent half an hour firing the Beretta in the woods only to have the gun jam two out of three times. It could be, as he'd told Roxie, that the gun had been confiscated some time ago and not been used in a while. But his gut instinct had begun to smell a rat.

"I'm a friend of Neil's. I really need to get a hold of him."

"Is that a fact?" Burke's tone indicated he wasn't convinced. "Well, you're out of luck then. He can't be reached right now."

Something else had been bothering Giff. "I called his home and there's no answer. Do you know when would be a good time to contact Lisa?"

Burke paused before answering. "You can't be a good friend of Neil's or you'd know that he lives alone."

Giff felt a cold chill race up his spine. "Alone?"

"Yeah."

Hope I didn't wake Lisa or the boys by calling so late, he'd said to Neil the night he'd called from Roxie's condo. *No problem,* Neil had told him. Had his good friend, the man who'd sworn he believed in Giff, lied to him about his family, given him a defective gun and then disappeared just when Giff needed him the most? Or were there logical explanations to all of this—a malfunctioning gun, perhaps a trial separation from his wife that Neil wasn't obligated to discuss with him, an assignment that kept him too busy to phone?

"You still there?" Burke asked.

"Yeah, I'm here." Giff ran a hand over his unshaven face, wondering how to word his next question. "Lieutenant, did Neil ever mention working on something in Scottsdale with a cop he used to know in Tucson?"

"Not to me. What's the cop's name?"

"I'd rather not say right now." He needed help from the police and yet, the one cop he'd trusted had suddenly become suspect. How could he know who he could talk to without risk?

Burke had run out of patience. "If you won't trust me, I guess we're finished talking."

Maybe not. Giff turned his back toward the archway leading to Sunny's living quarters and lowered his voice. "Lieutenant, if I were to put you onto a large drug operation right in your own backyard, would you be interested?"

Burke's voice hinted at a cautious interest. "Maybe. Tell me more."

"I can't right now. But just as soon as I know what and when it's going down, I'll contact you. I know that isn't much to go on, and I wish I could be more specific, but..."

"Who was your captain in Tucson?"

Annoyed, Giff swore under his breath, realizing Burke had guessed he was the cop that had worked with Neil on the case in Scottsdale. There was no way he was going to get something without giving something. "Williams. A big man, six-four. Used to box in college and smokes these terrible cigars."

Burke turned that over in his mind. He knew Williams and the description was right on. The guy on the phone sounded undercover. He'd do some quiet checking. "All right. Are we talking a couple of weeks or a couple of days here?"

"Days. Two or three at the most." He'd have to push Sam, make him rise to the bait. But he had to get this over with.

Burke decided to gamble. "Let me give you my beeper number."

Giff wrote it down. He didn't think Burke believed him a hundred percent. Just enough to be interested, to be suspicious. That's the most he could hope for under the circumstances. "I'll be in touch."

He hung up, then walked to Sunny's doorway. She was sitting in her rocker, Clancy on her lap, watching television. "I've got to make another call, Sunny. But I'll get the charges and leave you enough money for all of them."

She adjusted her heavy hair net. "Help yourself, Mr. Jones. You young people today can't seem to relax, even when you're on your honeymoon. I didn't have phones installed in the cabins because I thought newlyweds would want to get away from everyone and everything." She sighed sadly, stroking the cat's fur. "But more often than not, one or both of you have to make call after call. In my day, we left the outside world behind for this short time and got to know each other." She snuggled her cat closer and sighed again. "Everything changes."

He didn't have an answer to that, at least not one Sunny would believe.

Giff checked his watch and saw that it was two in the afternoon. The lunch crowd at the Eagle's Nest would be thinning. Trevor probably wouldn't be in yet, but Sam would be. He dialed the restaurant. Ronnie answered from the bar and went to get Sam. He came on the line, his voice low and angry.

"Where the hell are you?"

"What's the matter, Sam, do you miss me?"

"I think you have something that belongs to me."

Giff's voice turned cold and hard. "Are you ready to deal?"

"If you're smart, you'll get those boxes back here. It's just a matter of time till I find you."

That was an obvious bluff that Giff decided to ignore. If Sam had had the slightest idea where they were, he wouldn't be hanging around the restaurant. "You're in no position to demand anything."

"I wouldn't be too sure."

"I want you to set up a meet with the man in charge. An even exchange. I bring the goods, and he reveals his face."

Sam laughed. "What makes you think we'd be stupid enough to play along with you?"

"Because I have the goods. With me. All three of them. You and I both know what they're worth. I'll hand them over after I chat with the big guy."

"You can hand them to me, and I'll see to it that they get to him."

He could almost feel Sam fuming impotently. "No deal. The top man or I turn these over to the cops and share with them all I know about you, Sammy boy. I'm sure their investigation will turn up the others."

The pause was longer this time. "What makes you think we'd show up like sitting ducks so you could haul in the cops?"

"No cops. I come alone with the merchandise."

"Right, and I'm the Easter Bunny."

"Listen, Sam, I don't have any police contacts I can trust anymore. I see somebody offed my old pal Phil." He waited but Sam didn't respond. "I couldn't talk a cop into showing up with the skimpy story I have. Not unless I turn over the stuff. Then, they'll listen, all right. But I'll give it to you, instead, as I've said, if you bring the head man in to meet with me."

"Why is it so important that you meet with him?"

"Let's just say that I like to know who's holding the gun that shoots me. Two days from now, in the bar at the Eagle's Nest, two a.m. Call your boss and set it up."

"I don't know if he'll go for this."

"If your head man wants his million bucks, he'll go for it. I'll check back with you at noon tomorrow. Be at this number." Giff realized that his hands were clammy as he hung up the phone. A quick glance told him Sunny was still absorbed in her television program. Taking a deep breath, he left the porch and started toward the cabin.

He was taking a hell of a chance, but he had to flush out the man in charge. Tomorrow, after he got the okay from Sam, he'd call Lieutenant Burke and bring him in on things. Even so, it was dangerous. Sam and his merry men could set up a watch and ambush him before he ever got inside the Eagle's Nest. Or shoot him down when he went in. Maybe Burke wouldn't play along. Giff's credibility was at an all-time low. The whole thing was damn risky.

But not if he planned it well. Not if he relocated the boxes to a place no one would think to look. It would be important to Sam's boss to keep Giff alive till he led them to the stuff. If luck was with him, that would give Burke enough time to move in.

Provided Burke was on the up-and-up.

Huddling into his jacket, Giff marched along the path. Then there was the problem of Roxie. He'd have to stash her somewhere safe until it was all over. He couldn't reveal his plans to her or she'd insist on taking part. That he couldn't allow. She'd be in the way, she could mess things up. But more important, she'd be in danger. These guys wouldn't hesitate to grab her, use her as a hostage or kill her.

That was a risk Giff was unwilling to take.

He stepped inside the cabin, his hand on the unpredictable gun, moving quietly, habit making him cautious. And found her asleep on the wide butter yellow couch.

He locked the door, shrugged out of his jacket, set the gun on the kitchen counter and walked to her. She was beautiful enough to take his breath away, to make his yearning heart swell. She was someone he might have had as his own once upon a time, if fate had been kinder. Even though they came from separate worlds, he knew she cared for him.

As he did for her. Finally, he could admit it, to himself only. He was in love with Roxie Lowell. What he felt was far more than affection, deeper than friendship, as it had been from the beginning. But he'd resolved not to let himself think it, much less say it aloud. Nor would he now.

He sat down alongside her and though she stirred, she didn't wake. She deserved a better man than he, a man who could give her the life-style she'd lived until her father's untimely death and Sam's unexpected entrance into her life...and his own appearance in her life. He'd dragged her into the world of drug smuggling, skipping out on a police investigation, running from the law, hiding out from family and friends.

Giff leaned closer and brushed back a strand of silken blond hair from her cheek. Her thick lashes contrasted against the pale ivory of her skin, where faint traces of fatigue still lingered. In sleep, she looked even more vulnerable than when she was awake.

He picked up one of her small hands, his thumb caressing gently. She brought out his protective instincts as no one else had managed to do in a long while. Since he'd known her, she'd acted unselfishly, with little regard to her own safety. And she'd believed him, believed *in* him. Because so few had, he found her hard to accept.

The best thing he could do would be to walk away from her right now. She'd hurt for a little while, but she'd get over him. If he stayed, if she got more attached to him, the parting would be all the more difficult for her. And for him.

He couldn't do it. He couldn't release the best thing that had ever happened to him. Not just yet. Not until he'd spent another night with those extraordinary long legs wrapped around him as he buried himself deep within the moist folds of her welcoming body. He was selfish enough to hold on to her just a little longer, to build a few more memories that would be all he would have to keep him warm through all the long, lonely nights after he finally walked away from her.

For walk he must. He would ruin her life, otherwise. If he made it through this next encounter with Sam and the men waiting to kill him, he still faced a long, weary road. He owed money to Tony, so much it would take years on a cop's salary to repay. And he had no job, no guarantee that he could convince the police that he'd been innocent all along and therefore deserved his criminal record expunged, reinstatement with back pay and full benefits.

What would he do? Tend bar the rest of his life? Go somewhere else, where no one knew him, and start over? Even if the law exonerated him, there'd always be those who would believe he'd been guilty. How could he ask Roxie to share that kind of existence? She deserved a man like Adam who could support her well, who could give her babies without the worry of passing along a tainted name. She deserved peace and a loving relationship, the kind Giff wasn't even sure he even believed in.

Roxie had pointed out some examples of couples who were committed to one another—her mother and father, Adam and Nikki—who lived together happily ever after. He'd stopped believing in that fairy tale the summer his mother had abandoned her husband and two sons, never again contacting any of them. In his work, in his life, the relationships that he'd seen, married or otherwise, had fared no better. Dare he believe it could be different this time, with this woman?

Roxie sighed softly and he leaned down to curl his hand along her cheek. She nuzzled into his touch, her warm breath heating his skin and his cold heart. She was the one person who'd made him wonder if it really could happen, if he could really have caught the brass ring this time around. She hinted of possibilities, of hope, of a future. With her, he could climb that mountain, leap buildings with a single bound, be a hero.

But he'd be dragging her down instead of pulling her up. The feelings she had for him would die as she watched him struggle to repay people, to earn back the respect he'd lost. He couldn't stand to watch the love in her eyes turn to pity.

But he could have this one more day and night. To grab a taste of what might have been, to love her, to give to her. Lowering his head, he touched his mouth to hers.

Roxie was involved in a dream, one so real that her blood was heating and her body shifting in restless need. Giff was there, with her, his lips tenderly on hers, his arms moving her closer to his hard, muscled chest. She reached out with both hands to capture the moment, to draw him nearer, to never let him go. It was so real . . .

Slowly, her eyes opened and she went from relaxed to responsive in seconds as she realized he was kissing her. A soft sound escaped from her as she deepened the kiss, participating wholeheartedly now that she'd awakened. His hands skimmed along her back, inching under her sweatshirt, trailing along her warm skin. The fire in the grate crackled and hissed but the fire Giff was lighting inside her was far hotter.

Breathless, she broke the kiss and stared into eyes deep blue and intense. The man was a paradox, stalking off angrily and returning lovingly. She didn't care. She'd take what she could, for she saw something else in his eyes. A determination to be free of her. He would find she was equally as determined to indelibly imprint herself in his mind and heart, so that leaving her would be the hardest thing he would ever do.

"Mmm," she whispered, "what a way to wake up. You could make alarm clocks obsolete."

But he wasn't in the mood to smile. His hands fisted in her hair as he brought her back to his waiting mouth. Driven by his own demons, he plundered, hoping that in doing so he would purge this insatiable need for her, knowing even as he did that he never could.

She tasted like a rich wine, her fragrance sweeter than the wildflowers outside their door. He scooped her into his arms, ignoring the stab of pain that skittered up his back, and carried her to the bed. Without breaking the kiss, he lowered her onto the feather bed and followed her down.

He knew it was impossible to devour her, yet he tried with teeth and tongue and lips that slid along the smooth column of her throat. Impatient with her clothes, he eased back, gripped the hem of her sweatshirt and yanked it off over her head. She wore nothing underneath and he stopped to feast on breasts that seemed to invite him to explore further.

Roxie floated in sensation, happy to relinquish control of her body to this man who could make her feel so much. The scrape of his light beard grazing her sensitive skin had her arching her body to his. When he reached to pull her jeans from her, she angled up off the mattress to help him. Then she felt his large hand move to the silken swatch which was all she wore, and reveled in the sexy feel of the sweet friction.

Driven by an overpowering need to be skin to skin with him, her clumsy fingers pulled at the buttons of his shirt until finally he raised his hands to assist her. This time when her hands settled at his waist, he stilled, waiting to see what she'd do. With agonizing slowness, she lowered his zipper over the bulge that pulsed beneath her feathery touch. Her eyes locked on his, she slipped her hand inside his briefs and closed around him, the involuntary sound that came from low in his throat egging her on.

Giff shifted to recapture her mouth while her clever fingers worked their magic. His tongue simulated a mating dance that had his blood churning with the need to unite with her in every way. He heard her gasp as his hand slipped the triangle of silk from her, his desire to return the favor overwhelming him. She jolted when his fingers found her damp and yearning, then settled as he paused, lifting his head to watch her face.

She squirmed, shifting, trying to move closer to the touch that promised a golden release, but he wouldn't allow it, teasing, then retreating, moving her to the edge, then withdrawing until she was wild and straining. Desperate, she dug her nails into the flesh of his upper arms as a whimper caught in her throat.

He was about at the end of his rope. With one swift motion, he rid himself of the corduroy pants and his briefs, then rose above her, the muscles of his arms quivering as his eyes sought hers. "I need you," he said in a ragged whisper, the confession seemingly wrenched from him.

Her hands caressed his shoulders. "I'm here. I'm right here. Come to me."

He filled her slowly, drawing out the pleasure, watching her eyes darken as she took him deep inside her. Her arms reached up to enfold him as he lowered to bury his face in her hair, his movement increasing. She adjusted to the rhythm as if they'd been lovers for years instead of days. He felt his vision dim and closed his eyes as he drove her as furiously as he drove himself.

When at last he shattered within her, he knew she'd joined him mere seconds later. His face contorted as he absorbed the shimmering waves of pleasure. It went on and on, yet was over too soon.

And Giff was left to wonder at the sudden rush of tears that had gathered behind his closed eyelids.

Chapter 11

"It's a very old ring," Roxie explained, holding her hand up to the late-morning sunshine coming in through the window. "It belonged to my father and his father before him. Dad had it cut down to fit my finger."

"What language are the engravings in?" Giff asked.

"Gaelic. It's a Claddaugh, a circle-of-love ring, or so my father called it. The words inscribed on it are friendship, loyalty, love. My grandmother was Irish and gave it to my grandfather who wore it until he died, passing it on to his only son."

Giff snuggled her closer to his chest as they lay in the big four-poster bed. It was moving on toward noon and they'd been in bed since late yesterday afternoon, rising only to eat and to share a shower. He knew they'd have to get going soon, yet he wanted to put it off to the last possible moment. "My dad used to say he wished he'd had a daughter who could have helped out with me after my mother left us. Not the most selfless reason to want another child. Do you think your father wished he'd had a son?"

"If he did, he never said so. My father was wonderful. He used to hold me on his lap when I was little and read to me by the hour. He'd make up nonsensical songs and sing me to sleep. I used to feel so safe in his arms." Tossing her hair back, she raised her head to look at him. "As safe as I've felt here with you these past few hours."

He didn't meet her eyes but reached instead for her hand and placed a gentle kiss in her palm. The unspoken words between them were that this idyllic time was about to come to an end. They hadn't talked about it, nor had Giff told her much about his conversation with Burke or Sam. But he could tell she knew in that instinctive way she had. "I'm going to hate leaving here," he said in all honesty.

"Yes, so will I." She scooted up him, crossing her arms over his chest, until she met his gaze. "You got through to Neil, right? And you've made some arrangements?"

"Not exactly. I have to make a call at noon. I'll know more then." Effortlessly, he rolled her onto her back and followed her over. "Until then, I don't want to talk about it." And he took her mouth in a stunning kiss that left them both breathless.

Roxie raised her arms and framed his face within her two hands, halting him. "Giff, you're the first man—the only man—who's ever tapped into all of me. I look in your eyes and I see all this passion. And I want it. I want you. But I know you've got scores to settle, so I'm not asking anything of you. I just want you to know that...that I make no demands on you. I want you to be free to do what you must without worrying about me."

She humbled him. "I can't be the kind of man you need, Roxie. I wish I could."

"How would you know what kind of man I need?"

He gave a mirthless chuckle. "Oh, I know, all right. A man free to make you promises, and one who can deliver on those promises. A good, solid man like Adam, with a stable income, a promising future, a respectable citizen with an unblemished reputation. One who can provide you with a home, children, the family dog."

"I'm allergic to dogs."

"I'm serious."

"So am I and you're wrong. Dead wrong. I require only one thing from the man I need."

He had a feeling this was leading into murky waters, but he played along. "And that is?"

"That he love me, only me, until the end of time."

Giff smoothed back her hair, his blue eyes dark with bitter disappointment. "I wish I could offer you that."

"I wish you could, too, particularly since I love you in just that way." Her fingers trailed along his short beard, as if committing the contours of his face to memory, as if touching him for the last time. "You're out of prison, Giff, but not really. There are walls all around your feelings that only you can tear down."

She was right. He knew it. But it wasn't something he could change, not now. "Maybe, when this is all over—"

She pressed two fingers to his lips. "Don't. Don't make promises. Let's just wait and see." She shifted her hips so they aligned more perfectly with his, then wiggled as she felt him come alive. "For now, make love to me. Let me feel how much you want me. Leave me something to remember after you're gone."

Feeling infinitely sad, Giff lowered his head to kiss her.

"Take it or leave it," Sam snarled into the phone. "Tonight at two a.m. or forget it."

A muscle twitched in Giff's jaw as he bit back a reply that would have ended the conversation. "I thought I told you to make it tomorrow night?"

"Yeah, but the boss says tonight or nothing. You don't want to play, fine."

It was hard for Giff to believe they'd walk away from a cool million or more, street value. Then again, though the money would be nice to have before they relocated and established another point of entry for the illegal substances they were selling, their sources to the stuff from South America were probably unlimited. He was in no position to challenge them further. "All right. Two. I'll be there."

"With the stuff. And no cops. Don't pull anything funny."

Giff hung up Sunny's phone and gazed out through the glass of the porch, seeing in his mind's eye the night he'd been shot in the storeroom of the Eagle's Nest. He'd had a fleeting glimpse—more like an impression than an actual sighting—of a large man with that peculiar walk that hinted of a limp, the man he'd aimed his malfunctioning gun toward. Had that man been Phil, his mysterious ex-partner who'd wound up bound and strangled? Soon, he'd know who they all were. Over three years of dreaming and scheming about to come to an end.

God, he could hardly wait.

Quickly, he picked up the phone and dialed Lieutenant Burke.

Roxie bounced on the seat of the Bronco as Giff drove over a bump in the road. "What do you mean, Neil can't be reached?"

He'd told her that much but hadn't yet revealed the rest of his plan. "Just what I said. I don't know if he's legit, if they got to him or even if he's lying in some alley somewhere as dead as Phil."

Roxie shivered involuntarily. Up until recently, the only violence she'd known had been on television, the occasional movie and some gory newspaper accounts. Certainly she'd never witnessed a shooting firsthand. Suddenly, she'd been thrust into the eye of the storm, and it was unnerving, to say the least.

"What's your best guess?" she asked, frowning.

Giff's lips were a thin line. "That Neil's crossed over to the other side."

She could only imagine how still another betrayal would affect him. "If he has, then he'll be there at the showdown, right?"

He shot her a quick glance. "What showdown?"

"Come on, Giff. I know the reason we suddenly packed up to rush back to Nikki's and pick up my car is that you've arranged a showdown. I don't know where or when, but I know that's what you've done."

He should have known better than to underestimate her. "And you're not going to know where or when. I want you out of this. Are we clear on that?"

"You don't have to tell me twice."

This time he turned to look at her hard. "Am I hearing right?"

"Yes. I find I have very little stomach for rough games. I'll just go home to my safe little condo, take a nice long shower and wait for you to return." And pray. Lord, how she'd pray.

"No, I don't want you at the condo. Sam knows where you live."

Annoyed, she frowned at him. "Then where?"

"I don't know yet. Let me think on it."

She settled back on the seat and closed her eyes. However, her restless thoughts wouldn't let her be. "If Neil's not around, then are you going to meet Sam and whoever without *any* police protection?"

"I told most of the story to Lieutenant Burke, the cop that was on the scene the night of the so-called attempted robbery at the restaurant. I also let him know there'd be a big drug bust going down, if we played our cards right. He agreed to back me up." That wasn't exactly true. Burke hadn't actually promised him anything. The lieutenant had said he'd see when the time came. Under the circumstances, Giff couldn't blame him. He only hoped when push came to shove, that the veteran cop would come through.

"This sort of thing takes split-second timing, I imagine. Right?"

Giff reached over and took hold of her hand. "Why don't you try not imagining? If it's me you're worried about, don't. I'm a cop. A cop without a badge and official gun right now, but still a cop. I know my job, and I'll do it."

"But you've been shot twice and—"

"And might well be shot again. But I can't dwell on that or I'd never leave home. Cops face danger every day. You learn to live with it." But you never quite get used to it, he mused. "This is one reason I didn't want you involved. You promised no pressure, remember?"

"Yes, I remember." Roxie sighed and closed her eyes again. It had been a stupid promise, one she'd known all along she couldn't keep.

"Oak Creek Canyon is up ahead. Tell me when we get close to the turnoff road to the Kendalls' cabin, will you?"

She sat up straighter. He'd insisted on driving from Jerome to Sedona. More damn macho stuff. Then another two hours to Scottsdale from Sedona. By the time they'd arrive, he'd be exhausted. She could tell by the occasional grimace on his face that he was still hurting. "How's the shoulder? Are you in pain?"

"No, I'm fine."

He was lying, and she knew it. What's more, he knew she knew it. But he'd slipped into his detective-in-charge mode, the lover he'd been for two days and nights seemingly forgotten. Small wonder women found it difficult to understand men. "On the left there, past that curve," she said. "Turn easy. The path is probably soggy from all the rain we've had." The thick growth of trees would keep the sun from getting through.

Roxie swayed toward the window as the Bronco bounced along the narrow path. She wished she could take time to have a good cry on Nikki's shoulder, to pour out her heart to her best friend. But she knew Giff wanted to get going.

Gripping the door handle, she prayed she'd find the strength to make it through this endless day and night.

* * *

"Giff's right, you know," Nikki said as they cleared the table. "You really should stay with us."

"But I'm not going to." They'd argued all through lunch over this, three of them against Roxie. But she wasn't budging. "Look, I know you're concerned, and I appreciate that concern. However, I need to be there, to know what's going on."

Nikki slipped a plate into the dishwasher, then straightened, rubbing her lower back. The baby was definitely making itself known today. "Things have changed between you two," she said, searching her friend's face. "Is it because you've realized you love him?"

"That's part of it."

"All the more reason you should stay here where it's safe and—"

"There's more to this, Nikki. I have every reason to believe that Sam may have been responsible for Dad's heart attack." She saw the shock register on her friend's face. "So I have a score to settle with Sam Farrell, myself."

Nikki knew her friend had a gun and the thought deepened her frown. "Surely you're not going to face these dangerous criminals alongside Giff. I know you're good with your little Smith & Wesson, but this isn't like practice on the shooting range."

Roxie sighed, wishing for a confrontation, but knowing she didn't have the intestinal fortitude for a showdown. "No, but I need to be nearby, so I can help Giff by making calls or whatever he needs."

Nikki's face, rounder in her pregnancy, softened. "So it's finally happened. Our wandering playgirl's fallen hard." Then her features settled into another reluctant frown. "But I'm wondering if this particular man might not be hazardous to your health."

Emotionally keyed-up, Roxie moved to awkwardly embrace her friend. "Don't worry about me, please. Giff and I are going to get through this, the bad guys are going to get what's coming to them, and..." She'd been about to say that they'd all live happily ever after, but that was too much of a stretch. "And things will work out somehow. I have to believe that."

Nikki gave her a squeeze, then pulled back as she heard the men approaching the back door. "I'll be thinking of you every minute. You'll call as soon as you can?"

Blinking, Roxie nodded. "You know I will." She smiled and patted Nikki's distended belly. "Take good care of your precious little package."

Adam came in, slipping an arm around both of them. "I'll see to it that she does." He kissed Roxie's forehead. "You take care, too, you hear?"

Vision blurring rapidly, Roxie hugged them both.

Over the heads of the women, Adam sent a warning look to Giff as he waited by the back door. Giff understood that look. They'd already talked outside. There was little more to say.

Giff had done everything he knew to try to persuade Roxie to remain with her friends, but she'd adamantly refused. He didn't know whether to be pleased or annoyed. But he did know that there were few ways around a woman as stubborn as Roxie.

She moved to him, reaching for the jacket she'd left on the chair back. "Ready?"

His mouth a grim line, Giff nodded. He led the way out to Roxie's Mustang with the cartons now locked in the trunk. Their goodbyes were swift and tinged with fear. He drove down the path away from the Kendall place, very aware of Roxie huddled in the seat beside him, looking fragile and frightened, wrapped in her own disturbing thoughts.

He would make all this up to her, he vowed silently.

The note was stuck to Giff's apartment door with a blue thumbtack. He removed it and read Clarence's shaky handwriting carefully. It seemed that his landlord had left two days ago and would be gone for a week visiting his brother in Yuma, taking his chatty bird with him. Giff was relieved.

It was four in the afternoon by the time they'd arrived at his apartment, the one he hoped no one had knowledge of. He'd parked Roxie's Mustang by the trees on the driveway apron with the engine running, wanting to check things out before taking her inside. On the long drive back, he'd decided that this was probably the safest place to have her wait things out.

Pocketing the note, Giff unlocked the door, then the dead bolt he'd installed shortly after moving in. Cautiously, he examined each room, having left things in a certain way that would have told him instantly if someone had been inside disturbing things. He found nothing amiss.

Just to be on the safe side, he went down and told Roxie to sit tight, then he jimmied the lock on Clarence's back door and let himself inside the old man's house. The blinds were drawn throughout, giving the interior a hazy look with the sun shining on the windows.

Giff inspected every room, every closet, moving slowly. The furniture was old and faded, and the house smelled faintly of dust and age. The whole place could have used a good airing. But the kitchen was neat and clean. And most important, it appeared as if no one except Clarence had stepped foot inside in some time. He left everything exactly as he'd found it.

Walking outside, Giff next went to check out the small, one-car garage. The heavy wooden door rolled up easily enough, after he picked the lock. At the back was a make-shift workbench with gardening tools hanging neatly on nails along both sides. Looking up, he saw a heavy cord hanging down near the rear and went over to pull at it. With a protesting squeak, a folding stairway creaked downward. It just might do for his purposes.

Testing the strength of the steps, he climbed up. The storage area was perhaps two feet high and smelled heavily of old dust. Two large cartons marked Christmas Ornaments were off to one side. It appeared that Clarence hadn't had much holiday spirit since his wife's death.

Moving back down the ladder, Giff left the garage and took Roxie up the stairs to his apartment. He didn't want her to know what he was about to do, feeling that what she didn't know, she couldn't reveal. Quickly, he turned the Mustang around and backed it into the garage. With no small effort, his wound throbbing with the exertion, he lugged each box from the trunk up the ladder and into the storage area. Ever-cautious, he arranged them so that the Christmas cartons faced the opening, hiding the other boxes from view should anyone just happen to snoop around.

Climbing down, he released the ladder and made sure it was snugly in place. He looked around the garage, which had been neatly swept out recently, and saw there was no sign that he'd been rearranging things. Outside, he lowered the door, locked it and went up to his quarters.

Giff found Roxie standing at the window looking out onto Clarence's small vegetable garden, dormant now, and a white wrought-iron bench set among the shrubbery and flowers. She dropped the rust-colored slat back into place and turned to face him as he locked the door. "It's so peaceful here," she said softly. "I wonder why I don't feel at peace."

He knew why and he was the cause. "Come here," he said, his throat thick, and took her into his arms. She felt small as she burrowed into him. He inhaled the sweet scent of her hair. "I wanted to spare you this," he reminded her. "I wish you'd listened to me."

Putting on a smile, Roxie looked up at him. "It's my fight, too. Besides, I'm not real good at following orders."

"That's an understatement." Despite the danger, the additional worry, it felt so good to hold her. "Are you hungry?" She shook her head and he wished he could remove the anxiety in her eyes. "Tired?"

"No. Why don't you tell me what you plan to do? I promise I'll stay put, but I need to know."

Taking a deep breath, he led her to the old corduroy couch, buying a little time as he wondered how much he dare tell her. "I'm going to make a couple of calls, verify the arrangements, then wait until dark."

"And then?"

"Then I'm meeting with Sam and whoever's in charge of the operation. With Lieutenant Burke backing me up."

Apparently, no matter how many times she asked him, he was sticking with that story. And perhaps some of it was true, Roxie thought. But there were big chunks he was leaving out. However, she'd promised him no pressure. If she could let him go do what he had to do without adding to his worries, he'd have a better chance of returning unharmed. If only she could . . .

She tightened her arms around him and closed her eyes. "By tomorrow this time, it'll all be over. Everything will be all right." She knew that thought was more hopeful prayer than anything resembling a real possibility, but she had to hope.

"That's right," he answered, reassuring her because he knew how much she needed to hear it. He could feel her trembling beneath his hands as he stroked her back. "Did I ever tell you about the time I single-handedly overcame an entire spaceship of invaders? Caught them all red-handed. Actually, their hands were more blue. Their feet were red and they had these cute pointed heads. I rounded them all up and put them behind bars. So how could a little caper like tonight's harm me?"

Roxie eased her head back on his shoulder so she could see his expression. His eyes were actually amused, something she hadn't seen before. She hadn't thought he had much of a sense of humor. And she warmed at the thought that he was dredging it up to take her mind off tonight. If only she felt like laughing, or even smiling. She couldn't quite manage it around the huge lump of fear in her throat.

"I love you, Giff," she whispered, her voice a mere breath.

The incredible blue of his eyes darkened. "Just for the record, lady, no matter how this comes out, I love you, too."

And he took her there on the lumpy old couch, frantically, feverishly, as if he might never have her again.

It was only seven in the evening, but already dark as pitch outside. Mid-November, Giff thought as he zipped up his jacket, and quite nippy out by evening. It was hard to believe he'd been out of prison well over a month.

He walked along Roosevelt in south Phoenix, his stride purposeful, his hands in his pants pockets, his head hunkered down into his collar, his eyes ever-watchful. This section of town was not for the fainthearted after the sun went down. Or maybe not even in broad daylight. Cheap bars with gaudy signs flashing and even cheaper motels with rooms for rent by the hour dotted this strip. A couple of all-night movie houses played porno films continually and an adult bookstore was doing a thriving business, he noted as he hurried past.

It wasn't an area one strolled along or lingered in, either. A dark-skinned woman wearing a blond wig, a tight short-sleeved sweater and an imitation-leather skirt with neon-blue spike heels stood in a doorway smoking, but she scarcely gave him a glance. The pros got so they knew who to approach and who to avoid. Giff walked on.

He wasn't here by choice. He'd tried tracking Neil again, using office, home and beeper numbers. Nothing. He'd talked with Burke who'd been somewhat vague, which worried Giff. However, the lieutenant had promised he'd be at a certain number waiting for Giff's call that night. Giff wished he unequivocably believed the man.

So he'd had to resort to other methods, getting what he wanted by going in the back door, calling in a few favors accrued years ago. He'd had to be very cautious, but he'd finally gotten the name of someone who just might be able to help him. The man, when they'd spoken on the phone, had been less than eager, but had at last agreed to ask around, then meet him.

As Giff neared the corner where the biggest topless joint of all had its doors spread wide open and music pouring out onto the street, he saw his man. Giff had purposely chosen this location having learned that Pepe, the owner of the bar, cooperated with the police for the most part. Giff was also aware that undercover vice officers were usually close by. He studied the man, who was standing half in shadow, as he slowed his approach.

Alexandro was many things, known by nearly every police station and cop in southern Arizona. He'd at various times been a numbers runner, a pimp, a dope smuggler and a well-paid snitch. He was short and skinny with a dark, pockmarked face and a shifty eye. Over the unseeing one, he wore a red patch like a proud banner, bragging that though he'd lost an eye in a fight years ago, the other *hombre* had fared much worse.

Giff wasn't crazy about snitches, but he knew they were a necessary part of his job. He also knew that a smart cop only believed about half of what one of them said. However, despite his less than impeccable rap sheet, Alexandro had a reputation for delivering the goods and only lying to save his own skin, a fact that most cops could overlook. The call he'd made to Alexandro earlier today had been a last-ditch effort to get at some ugly truths, though Giff hated it that his hopes hung on the pitiful excuse for a man now standing before him.

"Got a cigarette, man?" Alexandro asked, leaning casually against the stucco wall badly in need of paint.

"I don't smoke," Giff answered. "It's bad for your health."

Alexandro looked around nervously, his one eye scanning every car that drove by. "A lot of things bad for your health, Mr. Policeman. You got my dough?"

"Depends. You got my information?"

The little man sighed tiredly as if he'd known he'd have to deliver before being paid. "You want me to tell you about a cop. Hey, man, that cost you, big time. It ain't easy, poking around into a cop's life, you know."

Giff let his irritation show. "You got the goods or not? I'm not wasting time here if you can't deliver."

Alexandro grinned, showing teeth badly in need of work. "Hey, man, no use getting hot. When Alexandro says he'll deliver, you can believe it." He looked around again furtively, checking all sides, then moved closer to Giff. "Your pal, Detective Neil Kingston, he's not a straight shooter, you know. Not with the cops, not with you, not with the other side."

Giff felt like stepping back to avoid the man's foul breath, but he stayed put. "What do you mean, the other side?"

Alexandro stuck a toothpick between his uneven teeth. "You know what I mean, man. The boys who import the white powder."

Giff felt a chill race down his spine. "He's in with them?"

The swarthy man shrugged. "So they say on the street."

Music thrummed from the front of the building and a woman's shrill laughter could be heard as Giff digested Alexandro's news. "What about his family, a wife and two boys?"

Alexandro shook his head. "Gone, man. Divorced three years ago, maybe four. Word is Neil baby gets turned on by inflicting pain, you know. She went home to mama. He's got a new chickie, a real tough broad."

Betrayal was like a bad taste in his mouth. "You know her name?"

"Nah. Some Mexican sweetie, I hear. Works with her brother. They're all over Arizona, a little of this, a little of that. Word on the street is that they've made a few mistakes and their source is drying up. They may be in trouble."

"Do you know where Neil is now?"

"Nobody's saying. Could be they offed him. These are mean dudes, man." Alexandro sent the toothpick flying. "That's all I got. Gimme my dough. I got places to go."

Giff doubted the smarmy little man knew much more, or he'd have tried to hold him up for more money. He removed the folded bill from his pocket and handed it to Alexandro, watching while he examined it closely.

"Thanks, man. You need me again, you know my number." In moments, he'd disappeared in the shadows surrounding the garish building.

Giff waited while two inebriated customers staggered out of the bar, loudly quarreling about something. They made their unsteady way down the block. Leaving the questionable safety of the building, he retraced his steps, hurrying back to where he'd parked the Mustang.

He'd have time to go back to Roxie, have something to eat and maybe catch a nap, Giff thought as he climbed behind the wheel. But first there was one other stop he had to make, one other person he had to see. Shifting into gear, Giff prayed he wasn't trusting the wrong person again.

Chapter 12

"An hour's too long. Anything can happen in an hour." Roxie hated the pleading sound in her voice but felt helpless to lighten it.

Giff thought she was probably right. However, he hadn't intended to go even this far with her. "I'm giving you Lieutenant Burke's beeper number only if you promise not to call him before three a.m. I don't want this bungled. What if they're late, or someone lingered over closing? I need that hour, Rox."

If she didn't agree, he wouldn't give her the number, period. Feeling caught between a rock and a hard place, Roxie nodded. "All right." He was wearing black jeans and a black turtleneck sweater. His dark beard shadowed the lower half of his face and a generous lock of his black hair fell onto his forehead. She knew that her Smith & Wesson was tucked into his waistband at the small of his back. His blue eyes had darkened and were filled with impatience.

He looked more dangerous than she'd ever seen him. And more appealing.

He'd returned from meeting with his informant and given her a sketchy version of what had been said. At any rate, she gathered that his detective friend, Neil, had indeed jumped the fence to the other side. She'd seen the disillusionment Giff tried to hide, and her heart went out to him.

She'd opened a can of soup then, and they'd both attempted to eat, though neither had had much of an appetite. Then they'd lain down to nap, only resting side by side on his bed had turned to recreation, playfulness to passion. He'd made love to her slowly, beautifully, with such sensitivity but with an unmistakable hint of finality that it had brought tears to her eyes. Tears she hadn't dared let him see.

Afterward, they'd lain wrapped in each other's arms, neither able to sleep, until finally Giff had risen to shower and change.

Now, she reached up and touched the face that had come to mean the world to her. "I suppose it's foolish of me to ask you to be careful."

"No, it's not. I plan to be. Did you think I've come this far, spent three years waiting for this, only to blow it all in a careless move? I don't want to get killed, Roxie, or even shot again. I'll do everything possible to avoid both."

But so much could go wrong, she thought, as it had twice in the past. She didn't like the odds—Sam and that apelike Johnny and now maybe this Neil and whoever else was involved pitted against Giff and the nebulous Burke, who might or might not arrive in time. She didn't like the hour, either. Meeting at two in the morning seemed wildly dangerous to Roxie, but when she'd suggested a change, Giff had cut her off, saying it had all been arranged. Most of all, she didn't like waiting here in this sterile apartment—for the phone to ring, for news of what happened, for the nightmare to end. Even though she knew that though this would end, their life together might not begin, despite his whispered words of love.

Giff checked his watch and saw it was a little after one. The bar by prior arrangement had closed at ten. Curbing his need to be on his way, he bent his head and kissed her fingers one by one, then framed her face and kissed her waiting mouth. He tasted fear and frustration and the sweetness that was hers alone. She trembled in his arms like a captive bird, and he cursed himself anew for putting her through this.

Her eyes shimmering, she looked up at him, and it was almost his undoing. "I'll be back," he said. "Lock this door, both locks, and don't open for anyone but me. Promise me?"

She nodded.

He slipped out into the waiting night and stood listening. Finally, he heard both locks slam home. He pictured her leaning against the door, her eyes closed, her pale hair curtaining her troubled features. Turning, he scanned the area for several long seconds, then silently descended the stairs. In moments, the night shadows swallowed him.

Someone had turned off the two spotlights positioned on either side of the back entrance of the Eagle's Nest that usually lit up the parking lot. Or perhaps someone had unscrewed them, Giff thought, as he stuck to the shadows and walked the grounds. The air was cool with a wintry bite to the light wind. Half a block down, a dog barked, probably wanting inside. Turning up the collar of his jacket, Giff couldn't blame the mutt.

He could see no one around nor hear anything out of the ordinary. He checked the luminous dial of his watch and saw it was just past one-thirty. He peered at the high back kitchen window, the only one that faced the parking lot. Nothing stirred, nothing moved.

Were they already inside, waiting for him? Would he be the sitting duck, rather than they? Would they rush out of their hidey-holes the moment he stepped into view, their guns blazing? Would the big man really show himself tonight or had Sam lured Giff here on a fool's errand? Would Burke show or was he, too, on Sam's payroll?

Giff ran a hand over his beard. So damn many questions and too damn few answers.

He waited, watching and listening, another ten full minutes. Finally, moving with infinite care, he went to the back door, used his key and let himself inside. Gun in hand, breathing hard, he stood in the dark, orienting himself.

Again, someone had left off the back hallway light. Probably Sam, setting the scene. When his heart rate had normalized, Giff locked the door and began walking through the restaurant, his back to the wall as he went, his ears straining to hear the slightest sound.

It took another ten minutes to check every room, every nook and cranny, cupboard, closet and storeroom. Satisfied at last that everything was in order, Giff let out a relieved breath.

He'd thought a lot about what he'd do once inside and had decided on a plan of action that, while not perfect, seemed to give him the most advantage. He'd stay down low in back of the bar. There were two ways out from behind the large, curving structure, one at either end. There was a phone under the counter and several sharp knives, as well. There were ice cubes and crushed ice that could be thrown, should that become necessary, to disarm or surprise someone. Not ideal, but it offered possibilities.

Moving behind the bar, Giff checked the area to see if everything was in order for what he had planned. He dialed Burke's number on the phone, but hung up after the first ring. Now, all he'd have to do was punch redial and he'd get connected. Deciding that things were about as organized as he could make them, he located the short stool he'd kept behind the bar for slow times when the place was near-empty and he'd needed a break. Placing it just so, he tucked his gun into his belt, covered it over with his jacket and sat down.

It was then that he heard a loud rattling sound from the area of the kitchen.

* * *

At last, Roxie understood the saying that time stood still. She'd been pacing and checking the clock periodically, only to see the hands creep along with a maddening slowness. It was nearly two and her imagination, now more a hindrance than an asset, tried to picture the scene inside the Eagle's Nest.

Only the night-lights they always left burning would be on, if even those. It would be quiet except for the hum of the large refrigerators in the kitchen and the smaller one behind the bar. There would be the lingering smell of smoke and liquor, mingled with the soapy scent of the cleaning man's attention to the floors since this was his day to scrub.

Again Roxie glanced at the clock, noting that only a minute had passed. Giff would be inside by now, most likely. Where would he choose to hide, to wait for Sam and his cohorts? Not the storeroom since there was only one exit. Perhaps the far corner of the restaurant where there was an alcove with an abundance of plants for cover. Or maybe in the bar area. With only one lamp spotlighting the eagle above the bar and moonlight filtering through the skylight crisscrossing through the draped fishnet, the room always looked eerie after closing. Especially so tonight, she imagined.

With trembling fingers, she combed through her hair. Would Sam come swaggering in with that cocky gait he often affected, backed up by his pals carrying big guns? Giff had only her small Smith & Wesson. Dear God, they could blow him away before he could get off one shot. Why had he insisted on this madness?

Turning, she marched into his bedroom. It was as barren as the rest of the place, she couldn't help noticing. Not a picture or a plant to give a face to the person who lived here, not a book or magazine to personalize the apartment. It could have been a large motel room for all the character it displayed.

Then again, it was probably far homier than the cell Giff had occupied for three long years. She turned her mind away from that chilling thought, grateful he'd survived that chapter of his life, yet unwilling to allow herself to picture what he'd gone through. At least these living quarters were clean and smelled fresh.

She walked to the window and stared out at the fronds of a palm tree shifting in a light breeze. A partial moon shone down from an inky black sky, but she could see no stars. It looked cold and forbidding out there, yet she wasn't much warmer inside. Her frightened thoughts kept chilling her. If only she could relax.

Maybe if she took a hot shower, she'd feel better. And it would help pass the time. This waiting and pacing was about to drive her out of her mind. Quickly, she found the bag Giff had brought in from the Mustang and rummaged inside for clean clothes. There was a small radio on the dresser and she'd have appreciated the company of an impersonal night disc jockey's voice chatting between records. But she was afraid she'd miss Giff's call, should he need her.

Dragging the phone as close to the bathroom door as the cord would reach, she left it on the floor and went in to shower.

Lieutenant Tom Burke shoved back his desk chair at Scottsdale police headquarters and crossed one long leg over the other. He was a tall man, six-five in stocking feet, and he had trouble sitting for long at these regulation-size desks. Leaning back, he rubbed his right knee, the one with arthritis that bothered him from time to time.

Tonight was one of those nights. But it wasn't just his knee bothering Burke. He was wondering if he'd been scammed.

From his first conversation with the fellow who claimed to be a friend of Neil's, he'd had his doubts. He'd been the officer in charge of investigating the aborted robbery at the

Eagle's Nest the week before his first telephone encounter with Giff. Nothing about that caper had added up, either.

He'd tested Giff with a couple of questions only a cop—or an ex-cop—would know the answers to, and he'd been able to make him somewhat that way. Then the guy had mentioned Tucson and Burke had become more curious. Finally, he'd driven down there and talked with Captain Williams. He'd learned quite a bit without revealing a lot.

Burke, like Jake Garrison, or Giff as he was calling himself these days, had also been a maverick undercover cop in his day. At fifty-five, Burke had moved to desk work a while back. But he remembered those days with fondness. And he remembered that he hadn't run things by the book, either.

He'd gone to the Tucson newspaper files and read the account of what had happened to put Giff in jail. He'd learned about Phil Weston's involvement and recalled that that ex-cop had been found dead in a Phoenix alley recently. Then Burke had come back home and looked into Neil Kingston's life.

What he'd discovered was what had him sitting in his office at two a.m. instead of at home in his king-size bed snuggled against his wife of thirty years. If there was one thing Burke hated, it was a crooked cop. There was plenty rotten in Denmark in all of this, though he wasn't able to sort it all out. Yet.

Was Giff on the level with him? He sure as hell hoped so. Was he in danger? The man was cautious to the point of paranoia, but Burke could hardly blame him after what he'd learned about Kingston and Weston. Giff probably didn't trust his own mother about now. But he'd trusted Burke with some of it, at least.

Giff hadn't told him where the meet was to take place, and that worried the veteran cop. Of course, he hadn't been able to promise Giff a heavy backup. How could he with so little to go on? He could just picture himself going to the captain and requesting a couple of uniforms to accompany him to... well, he didn't know where and the time was set for two, but might be later, and the bust was illegal cocaine from Mexico, he thought. The men involved may or may not show and the informant was an ex-cop who also happened to be an ex-con.

He'd have been laughed right out of the captain's office.

Burke lovingly toyed with a wrapped cigar, wishing he could light up. One a day the doctor had restricted him to just last month. It was killing him faster than the heart that seemed to be beating a bit irregularly these days. Couldn't go on stakeouts any longer, couldn't smoke much, held to two ounces of liquor a day. Damn doctors want to take away everything just so you'll live a few years longer. Why, when it wasn't really living?

Burke checked his watch. Five after two. He'd give up tomorrow's cigar to know what was happening. And where. He got up and restlessly strolled among the empty desks in the bullpen. The desk sergeant was out front and the switchboard operator in back. Two officers had just dragged in a DUI and another had just left on a robbery in progress. A slow night, even for suburban Scottsdale.

Another five minutes, and Burke had had it. He ripped off the cellophane and lit up his cigar, being careful not to inhale. Grabbing his cellular phone, he headed for the door, stopping in front of the sergeant on duty. "Transfer all my calls to this phone, Charley, will you?"

The balding man looked up. "You expecting something at this hour?"

"Yeah, and it's important."

"Will do."

Burke headed for his car, needing to be on the move, to do something other than sit and wait.

If only he knew exactly where in Scottsdale he should be driving. However, he had a hunch. Getting behind the wheel, he headed north on Hayden.

Leaning over, Roxie towel-dried her hair, rubbing gently. Straightening, she looked into the steam-clouded mirror.

She wiped it dry, then stared at her image. She didn't really look better, but she felt cleaner.

On the back of the door hung Giff's blue terry-cloth robe. It was thin and cheaply made, but she didn't care. She needed something of his next to her skin, to feel close to him. Wrapping herself in its generous folds, she inhaled his special fragrance. She'd give all she owned if only he would walk through the door, safe and sound, smiling and in love with her.

Hanging up the towel, she pushed open the bathroom door and went to get her comb from the open case on the bed. In front of the mirror, she combed out her long hair and decided to let it air-dry. If Giff called and needed her right away, she could dress in moments, wrapping her head in a scarf if she needed to go out. She took a minute to straighten the bathroom, then snapped off the light.

It felt as if hours had passed, yet the clock on the nightstand read two-fifteen. She sighed with frustration.

A cup of tea might taste good and ward off the chill that was rapidly returning. Roxie bent to pick up the phone and was carrying it back into the living room when she heard a sound from behind her.

Whirling about, she found herself looking into the unsmiling face of a total stranger who was holding a gun aimed at her heart.

A damn mouse! Giff stared at the quivering gray rodent cowering among an assortment of pot lids he'd scurried through while scavenging for food, and almost laughed out loud. Sheepishly, he replaced his gun.

How the animal had gotten into the kitchen Giff couldn't even guess. Patrick, the head chef, who was fanatical about cleanliness, would have a fit. However, Giff didn't have time to catch the mouse right now. Clicking off his flashlight, he hastily returned to his place behind the bar.

He didn't have long to wait. Minutes later, he heard the sound of a key turning in the back door. Weapon in hand, he sat behind the bar waiting, deep in the shadows. Footsteps, one set heavy, the other lighter. Adrenaline pumping, he listened.

Breathing deeply, Giff recognized Sam's cologne moments before the man himself appeared in the bar doorway, the hulking big man right behind him as the perimeter lights flicked on. They both held guns.

"Forget about the mirror behind the bar, Giff?" Sam asked with a nasty laugh. "I saw you from the hallway."

He hadn't forgotten, had in fact intended Sam to find him just so. Sam was wearing a black-and-white-striped shirt, black pleated trousers and a white tennis sweater with its sleeves tied around his narrow waist. His dark eyes behind his wire-rimmed glasses shimmered with impatience as Giff said not a word.

"All right," Sam said, his smile slipping, "I haven't got all night. Where's the stuff?"

"Where's your boss?" Giff asked, his voice low, calm.

"Me, I'm the head honcho, Johnny Prince," the big man said, stepping forward. He wore a blue pin-striped double-breasted suit with the jacket buttons straining over a paunch. "You deal with me."

Giff's eyes flicked to Johnny, then back to Sam. "Don't make me laugh. Even Sam wouldn't be dumb enough to take orders from you."

Johnny's face grew red and ugly as he raised his gun hand. "Now, listen here, you punk, I'll—"

Sam laid a hand on Johnny's arm. "Take it easy." He decided to bluff a bit more. "Just tell us where the stuff is and once we look it over and make sure it's all there, the boss will be here."

Slowly, Giff shook his head. "No dice. He shows or I call in the cops. It's as simple as that."

Johnny was a bumbler, not very bright and impatient to boot. He looked around as if expecting the boxes to have been left out in plain view. "We saw him walk in so we know he didn't bring the boxes with him. Maybe he was here earlier, right after the bar closed, and stashed them somewhere," Jonny said.

"Were you, Giff?" Sam asked, his voice shifting to silky smooth, persuasive.

"You'll find out when you produce the top guy," Giff answered.

"We know the stuff's not in his Bug," Johnny went on. "I went through that car myself." He took a step closer to the bar. "Where is it, you little creep?"

With effort, Giff kept his features even. He'd parked his Volkswagen several doors from his apartment and around the corner. Yet they'd managed to find it. What else had they found? Roxie's Mustang was in Clarence's locked garage. Surely they hadn't searched every yard of every street near the restaurant. "Don't get anxious, buddy," he told Johnny. "You want the goods, you deliver your head man. And do it now. I didn't come here to play games."

"We gonna let this punk push us around, Sam? Just give me two minutes alone with him. He'll talk, gladly." Johnny's meaty hand curled around the gun in anticipation.

Sam's eyes narrowed, assessing his opponent. The cop was as tough as they came. He doubted Giff would talk. Probably die before he'd tell them where the stuff was. Damn. He'd bragged to the boss that he could handle Giff, but he hadn't counted on the man's single-mindedness. They'd have to adjust their plans. Unless . . .

Sam straightened, aiming his gun at Giff's heart. "In case you haven't figured it out, you're outnumbered here. You'd better talk or start saying your prayers."

A muscle in Giff's jaw twitched but otherwise he didn't move. "Go ahead and shoot. I've been shot before. It isn't going to get you the merchandise."

He'd been told to bring back the stuff or not bother returning, Sam recalled. Things were tightening up all over. They needed those cartons to tide them over until the wind shifted. With his gun, he motioned Johnny closer to the bar as he stepped nearer also. "We can make you wish we'd finish you off. Johnny here has a way of breaking bones with his bare hands that'll have you begging to talk. Hand over the gun, Giff. It's two against one.''

"Not exactly," said a well-modulated English voice from behind them.

Shock had both men swiveling and looking into the barrel of a 12-gauge Winchester shotgun in the steady hands of Trevor Ames.

"Drop your weapons, gentlemen," Trevor ordered.

Too stunned and suddenly too frightened to do otherwise, they both did. Sam recovered first. "What the hell is this, Trevor? I . . . I thought we were friends."

"Did you, now?" Trevor asked, the shotgun still aimed carefully at both men. "I thought so, too. Until I learned what you did to the Lowells. Henry was like a brother to me and Roxie, the daughter I never had."

"You believe this pansy knows how to use that shotgun?" Johnny asked Sam.

Sam nervously cleared his throat. "He's a member of the National Rifle Association and has a big gun collection. Showed me a couple once." His mind racing, he changed tactics. "Don't believe what he told you, Trevor," Sam pleaded as Giff quietly picked up the guns they'd dropped, put them behind the bar and then proceeded to carefully pat down both men.

"Are you saying you weren't here when Henry died?" Trevor asked.

"I didn't kill him, if that's what you mean. He had a heart attack. We were just talking and he...he got so agitated and suddenly, he fell to the floor. I never laid a hand on him."

"No, not even to call for help." The disgust in Trevor's voice was almost palpable. He hadn't believed Giff a hundred percent when he'd come to see him earlier that day at his home. But he'd gone along with Giff's plan, deciding he'd make up his mind at the scene. Now he knew. It was one of the few times in life he'd badly misjudged two men. "What shall we do with them, Giff?"

Giff removed a small .38 strapped to Sam's ankle before walking back behind the bar. "Sam, walk over to that wall phone and call your boss. If he's not here in fifteen minutes, I'm phoning the cops and turning the stuff and you two over to them. That's the deal."

Sweating profusely, Sam wiped his forehead with the back of his hand and went to the phone.

"And don't give anything away about how it's going here, pal," Giff warned. "Just tell him to walk in, nice and easy. I don't have a whole lot to lose by putting a hole in you."

His back to the room, Sam punched out the numbers. Ten rings and no answer. He reached in his pocket for a piece of paper, checked it, then punched out a new set of numbers. It was picked up on the second ring. "I need you over here now," he said, keeping his voice low, but aware that everyone in the small, quiet room could probably hear.

He listened, shuffling his feet anxiously. "No, they're not here." He needed to give a warning, but he was too scared. Giff looked like a man who'd calmly kill them all, step over the bodies and walk away. As for Trevor, well, Sam had seen the kind of damage a Winchester could do to a man at close range. "I don't know where the stuff is, okay?" Nerves were making him tense. "Have you found anything?"

Giff's head went up. Who was he calling? What were they looking for, and where were they looking for it? They couldn't have traced him to Roxie. He'd taken such round-about routes, doubling back, walking here. No, he was just getting paranoid. He checked his watch. Only two-thirty. He'd love to call Burke now, but he couldn't risk it until the main man showed, or nothing would be gained. They'd waited too long to get impatient and blow it now.

"Okay, but you'd better bring proof," Sam snarled into the phone, then quickly hung up. Turning, he eyed the two men who'd managed to disarm them both, wondering if the call he'd made would change the tide.

"Keep the shotgun on them, Trevor," Giff said as he reached for a roll of heavy twine. Quickly, he shoved two chairs against the wall. "Sit down, boys. It may be a long wait." Moving swiftly, he tied their arms behind their backs and then fastened their feet together.

Finishing, Giff moved behind the bar. "Roxie's going to be real interested to hear how you watched her father die, Sam," he said, his voice cold. "And the police are going to want to investigate that so-called loan you made to the Lowells, the one that enabled you to take over the restaurant. Funny, how their copy of the agreement was never found."

Sam's flinty eyes blazed. "I knew we should have finished you off the second time."

Giff's smile was malevolent. "Hindsight. Ain't it grand?" His gun in hand, he leaned on the bar. "Is that what happened to Phil? He knew too much, got out of hand and you had to get rid of him? Or was it because he was here that night and he couldn't quite bring himself to finish me off?"

Sam made a disdainful sound. "Phil. He was a dangerous drag on all of us. Constantly whining, complaining, never satisfied. He took off for a while and should have stayed. I don't know why in hell he came back."

Johnny looked over at him with surprise. "Sure you do. Because of Carla. He had the hots for Carla."

Giff felt his blood run cold and his vision blur. "What did you say?"

Trevor, across the room, shifted the shotgun into a steadier hold, becoming concerned at the way this conversation was going. Giff looked as if he'd suddenly come face-to-face with the devil.

"Nothing," Sam said, wishing he were close enough to poke his elbow into Johnny's fat belly. "He didn't say anything."

"I asked you a question," Giff said, biting off each word. "What does Carla have to do with any of this?"

"Everything," said a low, husky voice from the back archway.

All heads swiveled to look at the small person clad in black from neck to boots, head covered in a red-and-black ski mask. In one hand was a .57 magnum. Slowly, the other hand reached up and removed the ski mask. Thick jet black hair tumbled free to frame an oval face with dark eyes and bright red smiling lips.

"You wanted to meet the head man, the boss, the one in charge?" she asked Giff. "Here I am, in the flesh." She smiled at his stunned expression.

"You?" Giff managed to say, his voice barely audible.

"*Sí*, my darling," she purred, her flashing eyes taking in her two men tied to chairs and the portly man holding the heavy-gauge shotgun. "Let the party begin."

Chapter 13

"I'm running out of patience, honey," the man with the gun said to Roxie. "As I said earlier, we know you've been away with Giff for several days and we know he took the cartons with him. I strongly suggest that you tell me where they are. I'd hate like hell to mess up that pretty little face of yours."

Roxie sunk deeper into the corner of the couch where she'd been thrown shortly after finding the man in the living room. She clutched the folds of the robe more closely around her body, willing her hands to stop shaking. She was frightened half out of her mind, but to let him see just how scared she was would only goad him on. Her face still stung. Who was that dark-haired woman who had slapped her, then run out after taking the phone call? Roxie wondered. She raised her chin a fraction as she stared at her captor.

"I told you over and over, I don't know where he put the cartons." Her voice wasn't as steady as she'd have liked, but it wasn't pleading, either.

Neil Kingston stuck his gun into the belt of his trousers, sat down in the lone easy chair to chew on the stem of his pipe. He had to take a minute to think.

Carla wasn't happy with the way things were going, but then, neither was he. However, Carla unhappy wasn't a pleasant scene to witness.

She'd left to go to the restaurant after Sam's call, cursing at her brother's inability to control the situation there. Neil knew that she tolerated Sam's weaknesses because he'd been there for her when they'd both been abandoned kids growing up on the streets of a dusty Mexican town. But she was running out of patience on this last shipment.

They needed the merchandise in those boxes badly. It was time to lie low for a while, move the stuff to the dealers, take the money and integrate themselves into a sleepy little Mexican community along the western coast until the heat died down. They'd have enough cash to wait out the current crackdown by the local authorities and then later, scout out a new point of entry. They'd about exhausted the Arizona border towns and might need to look to Texas as another possibility.

It had been good for so long that they'd gotten complacent. Which was why this last operation had gone wrong twice now. He was tired of the whole police scene and was more than ready to blow that cover. It was too tight a rope to walk. He'd stashed away quite a bit of money, but Neil knew it wouldn't last all that long. Carla's wants and needs were many and expensive.

He glanced over at the woman on the couch. Sam had told him that she was tight with Giff, something Neil found difficult to swallow. Roxie Lowell was too fair, too fragile-looking, not Giff's type. Roxie after Carla was like eating a rice cake after a diet of hot tamales. He remembered all too well when Giff had been hung up on the spice that Carla had brought into his life.

Giff had been so nuts for Carla when they'd all been down in Tucson, he'd have walked on broken glass for her.

The poor stiff hadn't even realized that she'd always been Neil's girl. Of course, they'd been real careful to keep their relationship under wraps. They'd had to be to keep his job safe, and that had included playing the family man with Lisa and a marriage that should never have been. If he'd have met Carla first, Lisa wouldn't have warranted a second glance.

Neil did regret the boys, children Lisa had insisted on having. However, he wasn't the fatherly type any more than he was husband material. He needed to be free, to be with Carla. She was all he needed, all he'd ever need.

Even that dumb Phil had thought Carla was interested in him, which was why they'd so easily won his cooperation. He'd been a handy cop to have in their corner, making sure the police arrived just a tad too late each time or diverting them elsewhere. But then the big jerk had wanted more and more of Carla, going off the deep end over her. He'd quit the force, followed her down to Mexico and made a fool of himself chasing after her. When he'd finally returned, he'd been a mess. Carla had been right; they'd had to put him out of his misery. He'd become a big liability.

Men everywhere fell for Carla. She was just that kind of woman. But Neil knew she was his. They were a team and a damn good one. Carla was handling things at the Eagle's Nest, and he was sure she'd take care of Giff despite Sam's sniveling on the phone about problems. And she was relying on him to get Roxie Lowell talking.

Rising, Neil walked over to her and saw her brown eyes study him with that hint of fear that always turned him on. He reached down and curled his strong fingers around the material of her robe at her neck. "Tell me where those boxes are, or I'm going to have to hurt you."

"I don't know. I honestly don't. Why would I lie to you? If I knew, I'd tell you so you'd leave me alone." She hoped her logic got through to him because it was the truth. She hadn't seen Giff bring the boxes inside so she assumed they were still in the trunk of the Mustang in the garage. But she wasn't about to make it easy for him since she wasn't certain. Giff obviously had his reasons for not revealing the whereabout of the cartons.

"We've searched this place, upstairs and down, and your car and the garage. We've even gone through his Volkswagen. He walked to the restaurant so they're not with him." Twisting the robe, he yanked her closer. "Tell me, damn it."

"I don't know. I—" The slap was backhanded and hard enough to cause her ears to ring. An involuntary groan escaped from her as he jerked her to her feet. The man wasn't big, but he was wiry and strong.

Her eyes were more defiant than cowed. That infuriated him. "That's for openers, lady. You ready to talk yet?"

"I can't tell you what I don't know."

Damn, but she was stubborn. Or stupid. Maybe both. Neil reached for his gun, held it by the barrel and slammed the butt end into her jaw. He heard her cry out before he smashed it into her other side. She fell back onto the couch like a limp doll.

The bitch would damn well talk before Carla returned or there'd be hell to pay. He watched her struggle to hold back the tears, to not pass out. He didn't want her out cold where she couldn't talk. One or two punches and she'd sing a different tune. And he'd enjoy delivering them.

Neil raised his arm.

As an Americanized citizen, Trevor Ames had served in the Korean War. He'd seen many a man in shock and he couldn't help thinking as he watched Giff stare at the woman in the archway that he looked as stunned as any war casualty Trevor had seen.

"Drop the gun, miss," Trevor ordered, his words precise but filled with calm authority.

Carla did, so nonchalantly that Trevor wondered at her easy cooperation. Was it because she had other weapons hidden on her person? He shot a glance at the two men still tied to the chairs, then leveled his gaze at the woman who by her own admission was the kingpin of the smuggling operation Giff had been trying to capture. Even he, who trusted few, found that hard to believe.

"Surprised, darling?" she asked, moving closer to the bar where Giff was still staring at her.

"Stay put," Trevor ordered.

She swung wide brown eyes at him. "You've disarmed me. What harm can I do now?"

Trevor didn't trust her, didn't trust any woman with such a silky smooth way about her. Fleetingly, he wondered what she'd been to Giff who was finally getting some of his color back, slowly.

Giff tightened his grip on the gun he held, his jaw clenching as he regained control. "Why?" he asked her. "Just tell me why."

She inched over to one of the bar stools and gave him a feline smile. "For the money, darling. The money you could never give me. Did you really think I'd be happy as the wife of a small-town cop? I make more in one run than you do in ten years."

Giff shook his head in angry disbelief that he could have once been so stupid, so easily fooled. "I trusted you. I—"

"You always were too trusting, darling." Her eyes became cool and hard. "Now you know. Now you saw me. Where are the cartons?"

"Someplace you'll never find," Giff told her, finding a dull pleasure in the telling. "It's over, Carla."

"Don't be too sure, darling." Quickly, her right hand snaked into the pocket of her slim black pants and she pulled out a piece of jewelry that she held out toward Giff. "Recognize this? It's from your girlfriend. Your pretty blond girlfriend."

Giff's eyes narrowed as he recognized the silver ring that Roxie always wore, the one her father had given her. Realization slammed into him. "If you've hurt her—"

"Not yet, baby. But if I don't make a phone call real soon, your little sweetie's going to have her soft skin all carved up. Neil gets off on hurting women, or didn't you know?"

Carla and Neil. Why hadn't he figured it out sooner? That's why Sam had phoned two different numbers. The second place had to have been Giff's apartment. But how had they discovered where he lived, and how had they gotten in? Surely Roxie wouldn't have opened the door. Of course, no one knew better than a cop that no lock could keep out someone determined to get in. *Word is Neil baby gets turned on by inflicting pain, you know,* Alexandro had said. Giff's hands itched to get to Neil before the traitor could touch Roxie.

He had to concentrate, he reminded himself. Someone worth far more than either Carla or Neil was suddenly in danger. Because of him. He had to outsmart them. "All right, I'll take you to the boxes." He would buy some time, get a call in to Burke somehow, get up the stairs to check on Roxie. He couldn't let anything happen to Roxie. Giff moved to the end of the bar, about to leave.

"Not so fast," Carla said. "How do I know you haven't got the police set up and waiting for your signal?"

She certainly wasn't half as trusting as he'd been. "You don't know. You'll have to take my word."

Carla made a derogatory sound low in her throat. "You should know me better than that. Call off Pops with the shotgun and untie my guys. Then I'll go with you."

"No deal," Giff said, poised behind the bar once more. Time was racing along, precious time that might be costing Roxie. He had to gain her cooperation. "You and I go and they stay. For insurance, honey."

Her dark eyes flashed as she considered that. Apparently, she didn't like the odds, for suddenly she crouched down, pulled a small revolver from her boot and swiveled in Trevor's direction, getting off a quick shot that whizzed past alarmingly close to his head. It all happened so fast that both men were caught off guard.

But not for long. "Now, Trevor!" Giff yelled, and grabbed a knife from under the counter. Swiftly, he cut the one remaining strand of rope left on his side holding up the overhead fishnet. Across the room, Trevor took two steps backward and cut loose the end anchored there, according to the plan they'd put together at his home.

In a split second, before Carla could straighten, the heavy netting fell on her, the thick cactus plants within crashing down and sending her face forward onto the floor, her gun skittering across the room. The two men in the chairs went pitching forward under the weight of the collapsed burden, Sam's glasses flying off. Their cries of surprise, then pain from the sharp needles of the plants, could be heard mingling with ripe curses.

"Good man," Giff yelled as he picked up the phone to call Burke.

But Burke was racing in the back door, having had a hunch this was where Giff had arranged his meet and having arrived in time to hear a heavy crash as he stood out in the parking lot. Gun drawn, he stopped at the doorway, staring at the three people struggling with heavy netting and screaming with pain as the more they tried to push away the prickly plants, the deeper the needles sunk into their flesh.

"Looks like you didn't need me, after all," Burke said as Giff hurried out from behind the bar. "You want to explain who's who in this mess?"

"All three are responsible for tons of cocaine smuggling, but I haven't got time right now to go into it all. Trevor will fill you in. I need to see about something." He headed for the door, then turned back. "Can I borrow your car?"

Burke tossed him the keys. "You want me to go with you?"

"No, thanks. I've got a score to settle and I need to do it myself."

Racing out the back door, Giff prayed he'd be on time.

* * *

She was drifting in and out of consciousness, or so it seemed to Roxie. The lower half of her face felt swollen and hurt so badly she could scarcely breathe. He'd shoved her onto a kitchen chair and tied her arms behind her back with a thin wire he'd found in a drawer. The cable bit into the flesh of her wrists and she could feel warm blood trickling onto her fingers. Her shoulders were numb from the tight restrictions. Struggling to keep from going under, afraid he'd finish her off if she passed out, she slowly lifted her head a fraction.

Through the curtain of her hair hanging down, she could see he had resumed his restless pacing, muttering to himself all the while. He was deranged, she was certain. She'd watched his face as he'd delivered the blows, and seen enjoyment there and a kind of sick excitement. Oh, God, where was Giff?

She wanted to moan aloud but was afraid to call attention to herself. He marched past her, intent on his own agenda. He was sweating and had removed his suede jacket. Damp circles beneath the armpits of his shirt and beads of moisture on his face told of his agitated state. It was the woman who'd arrived shortly after he had, Roxie decided, who was worrying him.

He'd called her Carla. Surely, it wasn't a coincidence. The name wasn't that common. She had to be the Carla who'd hurt Giff so badly. Yet this sadistic man pacing before her seemed to take his orders from the small, dark woman with the fiery eyes, the one who'd slapped her before leaving. Could it be that Carla was the one in charge of the smuggling operation, the one who'd set Giff up twice, had him shot, left him to either bleed to death or be branded a bad cop? Had she also been involved in Giff's partner's death, the one who'd been found in the alley? Why had this man Carla had called Neil, obviously the friend Giff had counted on, turned from the side of the law and jumped the fence? And how were all their lives so intertwined?

Roxie fought the tears that threatened to fall. Her breathing was labored. She wasn't able to get enough oxygen, so she risked taking in a large gulp of air. He heard her and swiveled, moving closer to her. She closed her eyes, wondering if he was about to kill her as she recognized the savage look on his face.

"All right, I've had it with you," Neil snarled. "Carla's going to be back any second. I've got to have that stuff." He grabbed her bruised chin and forced her face upward, watching her eyes pop open. "Tell me now or you'll soon be drawing in your last breath."

"I don't know," she managed to say around a mouth so swollen the sounds coming forth were mere guttural utterances.

Infuriated, Neil grabbed at the belt of her robe and untied it. He parted the folds, exposing her to his dark gaze. He saw the fear move into her face and smiled. "There might be a way to make you talk yet, little lady." From his pocket, he withdrew his lighter and flicked it on. "Where shall I begin?"

Roxie began to pray silently. There were worse things than death, she knew. Giff would be here if he could, she was certain. But it would be too late now. This maniac was going to maim her, perhaps rape her if his suddenly hot eyes were an indication. Oh, God, she didn't want to die, not this way.

Neil leaned toward her, taunting her with the flame hovering just over her breasts. "Open your eyes, bitch. I want you to watch your flesh burn."

She couldn't, wouldn't listen to him. She kept her eyes tightly closed and thought of Giff, of his beautiful face and of the wonder she'd found in his arms. She had to keep herself focused on...

Thundering footsteps sounded, running up the stairs.

"Damn," Neil muttered. Carla was back and she'd be mad as hell that he hadn't been able to make the bitch talk. He straightened as the door burst open.

Roxie's eyes flew open and her heart flipped with revitalized hope. Giff stood there like a dark avenger, clothed from head to foot in black, his fists clenched at his sides as his angry eyes took in the scene, his face like a storm brewing.

"Get away from her, Neil," Giff ordered.

Neil scrambled back, dropping his lighter to the floor as his hand groped toward his gun. "Wait a minute, buddy. It's not what you think."

Giff was past listening, past reason. He hurled himself at Neil, sending the gun flying. On the floor, he straddled the smaller man and his hard, heavy fists went to work on Neil's face.

Roxie watched, the entire scene happening as if in slow motion. She saw Neil trying to dislodge Giff, trying to avoid the pummeling blows, his legs flexing helplessly as his heels dug into the carpet.

But it was watching Giff that frightened her. His blue eyes were cold as a wintry sea, his expression hard as granite. He was like a man possessed, delivering savage blows long after Neil had stopped fighting back. She had to make him stop.

"Giff, please," she begged, the words pitifully low and shaky. "That's enough."

As if recovering from a daze, he glanced up at her, and his heart twisted. Her jaw was black-and-blue and hung slack, as if broken. The robe she wore—his robe—was torn and hanging open, indicating the bastard had touched the sweet flesh beneath. Her eyes were puffy and red, filled with a frightening mixture of fear and pain. There was a cut at the corner of her mouth where blood still dripped down, trailing onto her throat.

Renewed fury at the sight of her surged through him and he grabbed a handful of Neil's hair, raising his head so he could hit him again. He'd done things to her, things Giff had never even wanted Roxie to know of, much less experience. White, blinding rage filled him as he landed another blow and heard the satisfying crunch of Neil's nose breaking.

"No more, Giff," Roxie pleaded, suddenly deathly afraid he'd kill the man. She was sure he deserved to die, but his punishment should be through the courts, not through Giff's hands. They'd lock Giff up, too, if he kept on this way. "He's not worth it, Giff. I'm all right. Stop, please."

As if from a faraway place, Giff heard her. He looked up again and saw her beautiful eyes swimming in tears, saw the naked fear on her poor, battered face. "He was going to kill you, Roxie," he said in a voice he hardly recognized. "He's already hurt you."

She was desperate to get through to him. "My wounds will heal. But yours never will if you kill him. Please. I love you. Let him be."

Beneath him, Neil moaned, too badly beaten to move, but still alive. A part of Giff wanted to finish the job, to put him out of commission forever. He could feel his control teetering, the need for revenge like a living, breathing thing within him.

But Roxie's soft voice pulled him back. "You saved me, Giff. You're free now. You've vindicated yourself. Don't ruin it all. He's not worth it."

His chest heaving with the effort to regain control, Giff sat back on his haunches, then lifted himself from the man lying very still. Taking a deep, cleansing breath, he looked at his hands and saw they were bloody. It didn't matter. He was oblivious to the pain, his inner turmoil far more troubling.

He moved to Roxie, going around behind her. Cursing anew at the sight of her wrists bleeding and raw from the wire that bound them, he undid them as carefully as possible. She began to pitch forward and he caught her just in time. She collapsed into his waiting arms.

"Thank you," she whispered.

Tears he hadn't believed he'd ever shed again gathered in his eyes as he held her, cradling her against him. "Nothing's ever going to hurt you again. I swear it," he promised.

"I love you." But the words she uttered so painfully soft took her last bit of energy. She sagged in his arms, passing out at last.

Giff heard footsteps coming up and decided the marines had landed in the person of Burke and his men. When the veteran cop appeared in the doorway followed by a worried Trevor, he looked up with angry eyes. "Call an ambulance, will you?"

Burke glanced down at the prone figure alongside them and barely recognized the badly beaten face of Detective Neil Kingston. "I'd better make it two," he said as he went to the phone.

It wasn't easy for a man who'd forgotten how to pray to begin again. And he wouldn't have attempted to communicate with the Man Upstairs for himself. But for Roxie, he tried.

Head bowed as he sat at her bedside, he prayed as he hadn't since he'd been a child asking God to please bring his mother back. His prayers hadn't been answered then, and it had taken him years to realize why. But this was different. This was Roxie lying in the bed, her complexion nearly as white as the sheet covering her too-still form.

Someone had to hear his prayers for Roxie. She didn't deserve all that had happened to her because of him.

A serious concussion caused by a heavy blow to the head. A broken jaw wired together making her look like some surrealistic painting. Deeply gashed wrists heavily bandaged. A terrible loss of blood that was slowing her recovery despite the plasma they'd pumped into her. Her throat lined with dark fingerprints where Neil had tried to choke the life from her in his insane frenzy.

Giff swallowed hard as he gazed at her fighting to come back. They'd ruined her life the way they'd ruined his. It didn't help knowing that Neil was in a prison hospital under guard while Sam, Carla and Johnny were behind bars and would be for a long while. He'd thought once he caught the people responsible, he'd feel better.

He didn't.

What would make him feel better would be to see Roxie open those lovely brown eyes and be able to smile at him. She hadn't wanted much from life. A marriage to someone who'd love her without question, as she'd told him. Children, a home. Ordinary things. Things she had a right to expect from life.

He wasn't the man who could give them to her. Not ever.

He knew that now even more than he'd known it then. He'd brought her nothing but pain and chaos, and put her on the brink of death. She'd been catapulted from her safe, orderly world to the lunacy of his.

She thought she loved him. Those three little words had been the last ones she'd whispered before she'd lost consciousness. She'd been in surgery for hours after he'd brought her in. Except for the time she'd been in the operating room, he'd been with her, afraid to walk away for fear she'd leave for good if he wasn't there to watch over her. Though God only knew he hadn't watched over her very well up to now.

Carefully, gently, he picked up her delicate hand and held it between his large warm ones. Her skin was cool to the touch and she didn't respond to the light pressure of his fingers. Everyone seemed to believe that people in this particular state could hear though they couldn't respond from that place they'd gone to to escape the pain. Giff wasn't sure he believed that, but he felt it was worth a try.

He stared down at her hand, unable to bear looking at that bruised and battered face. "Come back to us, Roxie," he pleaded in a voice thick with emotion. "We need you in this world. We need your goodness and your faith in people. You make this a better place."

He cleared his throat, his thoughts a jumble. "I made your life a living hell, and I'm deeply sorry. I'd trade all the rest of my days if only you'd awaken and be all right again. I just need to know you're all right, Rox."

With great care, he lay her hand back down and ran trembling, swollen fingers over his unshaven face. "God, please let Roxie be all right," he murmured as he bent his head and closed his eyes.

"She's out of danger, Detective," the white-frocked doctor told him. "It's been twenty-four hours and her vital signs are good."

Too concerned with Roxie's condition to notice that the doctor had addressed him as detective, Giff moved closer to the bed. "Are you sure? She's still not awake."

"She will be, very soon." The young doctor took in the man's disheveled appearance, his bruised hands, his gaunt face with eyes desperately in need of rest. "Why don't you go on home and come back later? She'll be coming around in a couple of hours."

Giff shook his head and pulled the chair over to Roxie's bedside. "No, not until I see for myself."

Stubborn, the doctor thought, like so many cops. "The nurses will be checking her regularly, and I'll be back later." He started to leave, then glanced back. "You need to have those hands attended to, you know."

"I'm fine, Doctor. Thanks." Giff's eyes and thoughts were on Roxie as he sat down and took up his vigil.

She felt as if she were fighting her way up through black cobwebs. Roxie struggled to break through, a soft moan escaping her throat.

"Rox, I'm right here," a deep voice close by said.

She struggled harder, finally managing to open eyes that felt heavy and weighted down. Her vision was hazy at first, then slowly cleared.

Giff. He was there, looking right at her, looking wonderful. She tried to smile, but her mouth felt stiff and numb, like after a visit to the dentist. She began to raise her hand, but he held it fast in his.

"Don't try to talk. You're going to be okay."

His voice sounded odd, husky. She saw him, but she needed to know if he was truly all right. "You," she finally managed to get out. Then a second later, "Okay?"

He squeezed her fingers and nodded. "I'm just fine. You rest now."

She had little choice, the drug they'd apparently given her pulling her back down. "Stay," she whispered, then fell back into the dark tunnel of oblivion.

He watched her sleep with a grateful heart. He finally believed she was back, that she'd make it.

"No, sweetheart, I can't stay," he whispered back. "It's so much better for you if I go away." Replacing her hand on the sheet, he rose and leaned down to kiss her forehead, then took the chair back across the room.

He needed to get out before he lost his resolve. He'd talk to Trevor still out in the waiting room. And he'd call Nikki. Then he'd take off.

It was better this way, Giff thought, closing the door softly behind him.

Chapter 14

The main Tucson police station was located on the corner of Cushing and Stone in one of the older sections of town. A block away was the fire station and beyond that, the community center with its sprawling parking lot. It was there that Nikki Kendall parked her green Fiat on a windy day in mid-January.

Stepping out, she zipped up her suede jacket, grateful to have her slim shape back once more. Adam Kendall, Jr., had been born the first of December and was already a chubby, thriving six-week-old. She'd hated to leave him with his father and sister, but she had an errand that couldn't be put off. Locking the door, she turned and walked with purposeful strides down Cushing toward the police station.

It was a four-hour drive from Sedona to Tucson, but she'd broken the trip with a stop in Scottsdale to visit her father and brother. She'd deliberately avoided dropping in on her friend Roxie. She knew if she did, they'd tangle again as they had the last few times they'd spoken, something they'd rarely done in the many years they'd been friends.

But they had differing opinions on a subject near and dear to Nikki's heart: Roxie's future happiness.

Nikki turned and hurried along the wide walkway leading to the main door of the police department. She knew that Adam wasn't crazy about what she was about to do, but being the understanding husband he was, he hadn't tried to stop her. She'd never been the interfering type, managing to stay out of people's affairs, allowing them to solve their own problems.

But not this time.

The uniformed officer at the front desk smiled as she approached him. "Hello. I'm looking for Detective Jake Garrison. I called earlier and they said he'd be in after lunch."

"Just a minute." The sergeant checked the sign-in sheet. "Yup. Second floor, Homicide. Want me to ring him for you?"

Nikki smiled back. "No, thanks. I'll just go on up." She wasn't sure Giff would want to see her, so she wasn't going to take the chance that he'd tell the desk sergeant to tell her he was too busy to speak with her. She walked to the bank of elevators and entered the first available, pressing the button.

She'd read all the newspaper accounts of how Jake Garrison, more recently known as Giff Jacobs, was the hero of the day, having broken a smuggling operation that had been flooding the Arizona community with illegal substances for approximately five years. She'd heard Roxie's version of what had happened after the two of them had driven away from the Kendall house that day.

Nikki had found it all hard to believe. The phone call that next night from Giff telling her how badly injured Roxie was but that she'd be all right had been another shock. Due to her late-stage pregnancy, Nikki hadn't been able to make the trip, but Adam had driven down. And told her later what a dreadful state he'd found Roxie in.

Her injuries were bad enough, but having to cope with Giff's leaving her had taken all the fight out of Roxie.

They'd insisted she stay with them after the hospital released her to recuperate and, for once, she hadn't argued. But recovery had been slow mostly because Roxie didn't seem to care if she ever got well again. She'd loved and lost and inside her, something had died.

Not even the birth of Adam, Jr., had cheered her much. As a matter of fact, watching the four of them—Adam, Nikki, Lindsay and the baby—so happy together had saddened Roxie, though she would have denied it. Nikki could see as the days then weeks dragged on with no word from Giff that Roxie was grieving deeply.

Christmas had come and gone, but the holiday that Roxie had always loved hadn't brought her out of the doldrums. She'd moved back to her condo after the New Year and they talked on the phone regularly, but still, Nikki worried. The ownership of the restaurant had been cleared up and returned to the Lowell family. During Roxie's recovery, her mother had come back to help run the place along with Trevor Ames. Roxie kept saying she'd go back to work one day soon, but so far, she hadn't. Despite the fact that she was once more physically fine and even had something to look forward to, she wasn't snapping out of it quickly enough.

Roxie's malaise had forced Nikki to take action. She wasn't about to sit by and watch her closest friend pine away. Not if there was the slightest chance that Giff cared about Roxie as much as she did for him. Which, after seeing them together in Sedona, Nikki was sure was the case.

Stepping out of the elevator, she checked the signs on the wall and saw that Homicide was to the left. She headed toward the door at the far end.

The glass door to Homicide was ajar. Nikki stepped into the large room bustling with activity. There were at least a dozen desks scattered about facing every which way, some occupied while others were empty. Phones were ringing and two men at desks were typing as they questioned people seated facing them. Three separate glassed-in cubicles were along the back wall. She spotted Giff bent over a cluttered desk closest to the window, reading a file spread out before him.

She headed for him only to be intercepted by an officer wearing a shoulder holster who wanted to know who she needed to see. At the mention of his name, Giff looked up. Recognition softened his face for but a moment, then his features evened out again. He rose as she stepped over to him.

"Hello, Giff," Nikki said, looking at him. "I hope I'm not interrupting something important."

He hesitated a fraction of a moment, then shook his head and indicated the chair alongside his desk. He folded his long frame into his swivel chair, his every movement reluctant. "What brings you to Tucson, Nikki?" he asked, as if he couldn't guess.

"I think you know why I'm here," she said without preamble as she settled herself in the chair and unzipped her jacket.

He needed time to formulate the reasons he suspected she wanted to hear. His glance slid over her. "I see you've had your baby. Did you have a boy or a girl?"

"A boy, almost nine pounds. Adam, Jr."

"That's great." He smiled, but the wariness didn't leave his eyes. "You must be very happy."

"I would be, if Roxie wasn't so unhappy."

Giff shifted in his chair, looking away. "Look, Nikki, she's better off, believe me. I brought her nothing but grief and pain. I . . . I have nothing to offer her." Even with his name cleared and his job reinstated, he had mountains of debt and fellow officers who still were hesitant to work with him. It took time for men whose lives were on the line when they went out on the streets to trust you again. "I can barely handle my own life these days."

A small redhead in a wrinkled raincoat was talking animatedly to a uniformed officer at the next desk. Nikki leaned closer. "She's in a bad way, Giff."

His head shot up. "What do you mean? I called every day until she was released from the hospital and I've spoken with her doctor since. I keep in touch with Trevor and he keeps tabs on her. They told me she's fully recovered from her injuries. If someone's been lying to me, I'll..."

Nikki shook her head, realizing she'd been right. His calls and concern told her far more than his own words did. He was in love with Roxie. "No, they're right. Her wounds have healed. On the outside. But inside, she's hurting badly."

As he was, Giff thought, running a hand over his beard. He'd decided to keep it because...because Roxie had said she liked him in a beard. It was a small thing, but important. Yeah, he hurt. Daily, hourly. He thought of her when he lay down at night and woke up wishing she were in his arms, in his bed. He longed to hold her, to talk with her, to hear that laugh that warmed him like nothing else could.

But he'd stayed away for her own good.

"She'll get over it," he said, deliberately hardening his voice. "She'll meet somebody one day. Someone who can give her the world. Like Adam gave you. A nine-to-five guy with a safe job, a house in the suburbs, and all that. That's what Roxie needs, what she wants. Me, I can't give her that." He waved a hand, indicating the busy room, the weapon-carrying officers, the balding, handcuffed man two cops were hauling off toward lockup. "This is my life. Violence, killings, drug busts." He opened his tweed coat to reveal his piece lodged in his holster. "Guns, weapons, danger. What kind of a life would that be for someone like Roxie?"

"I knew it," Nikki said. "You didn't *drop* Roxie. You gave her up—for her own good."

"Same thing."

"Oh, my, no. *Big* difference."

He shook his head, frowning. "Either way, it would never work. She'll forget me."

He'd said enough to convince her he was hurting, too. Nikki lowered her voice. "It might not be so easy come next summer."

He swung his gaze to her as he leaned back. "What about next summer?"

"That's when she's going to have your baby."

The chair zapped forward with a bang and Giff's hands hit the desk's edge. Two officers at nearby desks swiveled toward him, but no one said a word. Nikki waited.

"Say that again," Giff said slowly.

The redhead was weeping now and the officer watching her looked cool and detached. "I said she's going to have your baby next summer," Nikki said evenly. "Of course, if you don't care about her, if you're so certain things would never work out between you, then I don't imagine you want anything to do with your child, either." Rising, she met his eyes. "Sorry I bothered you." She was about to turn away, but his voice stopped her.

"Just a minute." He waited until she faced him once more. "Are you sure? I mean, did she tell you or—"

"She didn't have to. As I said, she stayed with us while she was recovering. She kept getting nauseated, couldn't hold anything down. My doctor came to see her and told us both the news."

Like a man in a daze, Giff ran trembling fingers through his hair. "I'll be damned. A baby." He glanced up at her again. "Is . . . is she upset about it?"

Nikki eased back down onto the chair. "No, she's wonderfully happy about the baby. I believe her exact words were, 'If I can't have Giff, at least I'll have his child.' Her only sadness is that you don't love her."

His forehead furrowed. "Who said I don't? It's because I love her that I've stayed away. Don't you see? She deserves better."

"She deserves what every woman does, a man who loves her unconditionally. And your baby deserves a father. I understand you lost your parents when you were young. Is that how you want your child to be raised, without you?"

His mouth became a grim line. "You don't quit, do you? And you sure don't pull any punches."

"Not when I know I'm right." Nikki reached out and touched his arm. "If you love her, go to her, Giff. She needs you so much."

No one had ever needed him, not him alone. He'd always been the one in the way, the one tossed about. Could it be true, that Roxie wanted him back? "You really think she wants me?"

Nikki's smile was bright. "I *know* she does."

She needed color in her yard, in her life, Roxie decided as she carried the large pink rhododendron out into the backyard of her condo. She'd already planted an azalea and several geraniums. This last addition should do nicely until the warmer weather when her roses would bloom again.

Placing the heavy plant in front of the brick-edged flower bed, she straightened, then rubbed the small of her back. Amazing how quickly she tired these days. The doctor had told her to take it easy, to sleep when she felt sleepy, and she had been. Way too much, as a matter of fact.

She needed to get on with things, to make plans, to begin to live again. Nikki had been right to scold her last week. This was no way for a woman about to bring a child into the world to act. So today, she'd decided to make some changes.

She'd called Trevor and had a long talk with him. He'd been positively wonderful since the whole mess at the restaurant had happened. Kind, supportive, considerate. She didn't know what she'd have done without him now that her mother had returned to Florida. She told Trevor that beginning next week, she'd go in a couple of days and help out until they found a buyer for the Eagle's Nest. She no longer wanted to keep the family restaurant, filled as it was with too many haunting memories. Her mother had agreed to the sale. Trevor had made a suggestion, which she was considering.

In the meantime, she'd gone back to the doctor and gotten a slew of vitamin pills and begun a daily walking program, hoping to regain her strength and lose the lassitude that had lingered since her hospital stay. Thank goodness the morning sickness had abated and she was feeling fit again. She'd decided to brighten her surroundings to cheer herself up, beginning with the flower bed just outside her kitchen window.

Next, she wanted to plan how she'd decorate the nursery.

Removing her gardening gloves, Roxie found herself smiling, something she didn't do often lately. All right, so she'd been left by her baby's father. She certainly wasn't the first or the last woman who'd have to raise a child alone. Giff cared, she felt, but not enough. How was it that she attracted men like that? Roxie wondered.

She still loved him, but she wouldn't rope him into marrying her by telling him about the baby, as Nikki kept insisting she do. That was no foundation for a marriage. She wanted Giff to want her for herself alone, not because he felt obligated to make an honest woman of her, using her mother's old-fashioned expression. Since she couldn't have that, she could at least conduct her life with dignity and stop sitting around sniveling because things hadn't worked out as she'd hoped.

Looking down, she patted her still-flat stomach, awestruck anew that a tiny life was growing inside her. Because of her love for Giff. It was too bad he didn't want to share all the love she and his child had to offer, but they'd manage. Once the restaurant sold, she'd be all right financially since her mother was splitting the proceeds with her. Later, when the baby was older, she'd find work, though just what kind she wasn't yet certain. Something that would allow her to be with the baby when she was needed.

She wouldn't allow the child to be raised like Giff had been, shoved from pillar to post, left with a feeling of being unwanted at every turn. Those kinds of beginnings shaped a person's life and left indelible imprints. It wasn't what she wanted for her son or daughter.

A gust of wind blew her hair around her face. She shivered. It was chilly out today. A cup of coffee would warm her, she decided as she left her gardening things and went inside. She'd just plugged in the pot when she heard the doorbell. Probably Trevor, she thought, wiping her hands on a towel as she walked to the front door. He'd fallen into the habit of dropping in to check on her every few days on his way to work.

She swung open the door and the welcoming smile she'd had on slipped a bit.

Giff stood there wearing an oxford button-down shirt and a brown tweed jacket over jeans, his beard neatly trimmed. His black hair was longer, just touching his collar, the front falling forward onto his forehead. Those incredibly blue eyes were filled with an uncharacteristic hesitancy that had her relaxing somewhat.

"Giff, I... come in." She sounded inane and felt awkward.

He didn't seem to notice. "If I'm not keeping you from anything..."

"No." She swung wide the door. "I just put on a pot of coffee. It's cold out. Maybe you'd like a cup." Trivial small talk. She knew he hated it, but since she had no idea why he was here, she'd have to let him take the lead.

He sat down on the couch, remembering the last time he'd been here, the night he'd found her still damp and fragrant from her shower, wrapped in her robe. He'd almost taken her right here and the memory was enough to harden his body. He looked around while she disappeared into the kitchen for the coffee.

Social amenities, he thought. What would we do without them? Both of their lives were in turmoil, and she was serving coffee so formally, like they were strangers who'd just met. He ground his teeth as he sat forward, his elbows on his knees. He had no one to blame but himself for her guarded approach to him.

Roxie returned with a tray and his eyes drank in the sight of her. She had on a yellow turtleneck and slim black slacks. There wasn't a hint of roundness nor any other telltale sign of pregnancy about her, yet he couldn't seem to keep his eyes from centering on her middle where she carried their child.

He'd been a basket case since talking with Nikki yesterday and had lain awake most of the night. He was taking a hell of a chance believing Roxie's friend. What if Nikki was wrong and Roxie didn't want him back? What if they couldn't make it, if he'd be a rotten husband and an even worse father?

But around six in the morning, when the sun wasn't quite up yet, he'd decided he had to find out. Some things were worth sacrificing for, making changes for.

Roxie sat down at the opposite end of the couch, took a sip of her coffee, then set the cup down, pleased to see her hands were quite steady. She could handle this, she decided. After all, he didn't know about her little secret, so whatever he'd come to say, she would hear him out. Since she'd already resigned herself to living without him, how could he upset her further?

Looking at him, she cleared her throat, waiting.

Giff took a hot gulp. "Good coffee."

"Thank you."

This was stupid. He angled his body toward her. "How are you? Any aftereffects from . . . from your injuries?" He had to hear it with his own ears.

"I'm fine." She raised a hand to touch her face. "Jaw's a little tight now and then, but otherwise, I'm okay." She looked at his hands, saw the new scars. "And you're all right?"

"Yeah, sure. I'm back on the force in Tucson."

"I read about your reinstatement in the paper. I'm so glad for you." She looked into his haunted eyes and wondered what he was thinking, feeling. "I'm so sorry it turned out to be Carla. That must have hurt most of all."

He ran a hand over his face, searching for the right words. "I should have guessed, but I was blinded by her for a while there. Trevor told you that Sam is her half brother?" He saw her nod. "It's hard to imagine the way they grew up. Mother a prostitute, fathers unknown. Doing everything and anything to survive, and they were just kids. When this drug dealer found them and the money started rolling in, who could blame them for grabbing what they thought was the brass ring?"

"So you've forgiven her." It was more statement than question.

He wondered if he could make her see. "Cops who get emotionally involved with either perpetrators or victims don't last. You have to detach yourself, not let it get to you, or you're useless. Now, I can stand back and look at Carla and Sam and feel sorry for the hard life they endured that made them into criminals. But the cop in me says they have to be punished. They've killed and, almost worse, they've shipped God-only-knows how much of that poison into our country and sold it to adults, kids, anyone with the money. If I were the judge, I'd lock them up and throw away the key."

She nodded, wondering if it was all that simple. "Trevor surprised you, didn't he?"

For the first time, Giff's features lost that tight look. "Yeah, he sure came through. I took a chance and went to him that day, but I worried that I'd tapped the wrong guy. After the way I've been calling things, I didn't trust my judgment anymore." He met her eyes. "I misjudged you, too."

"Did you? How?"

"I figured you were one of the soft, pretty ones, raised with the proverbial silver spoon in her mouth, well-educated, well-traveled. Somewhat shallow." He shook his head. "Man, was I wrong. When I found out that you go the distance for the people you care about, come hell or high water, I began to see you differently. Maybe that's when I fell in love with you.''

Her eyes widened, but she didn't say anything as he shifted closer to her on the couch.

"Or maybe it was the way you are with people, treating everyone with equal respect. The way you stayed on at the Eagle's Nest to pay off your father's debt, even though you weren't obligated and you had to work with that slime ball Sam. Or it could have happened that first time I kissed you out in the parking lot. Do you remember?''

She wasn't sure she could speak past the lump in her throat. "I remember,'' she said softly.

He moved closer, daring to reach up and touch the ends of her silken hair. "Roxie, in all my life, no one ever truly cared about me for me alone, you know? My mother left, my father had to work twelve, fourteen hours a day to take care of us. My brother helped me because . . . well, because I'm his brother and he's a good guy. Then there was Carla, who used me. But nobody ever stuck their neck out for me or wanted me just because I was who I am.'' He paused, his hand settling on her neck beneath her heavy hair. "And then I met you.''

She stared at him and he could see the moisture gathering in her eyes. "For the first time in my life, I wanted to kill a man when I found Neil with you. I probably would have, too, if you hadn't stopped me. I would gladly have taken every blow he gave you, gladly have endured your pain, if I could have. I felt so damn guilty knowing I was responsible for you being hurt.''

Roxie took his other hand in hers and intertwined their fingers. "It wasn't your fault. Things just happened, got out of control. I went with you willingly. I'm an adult, and I make my own decisions. You aren't to blame for any of it. You're the one who saved me.''

"No, *you're* the one who saved *me.*'' He blinked, struggling with more emotion than he was accustomed to.

"Roxie, I've stayed away because I felt you'd be better off without me."

"I'm *not* better off without you. I'm only half-alive without you." She couldn't prevent one lone tear from trailing down her cheek.

With his thumb, he smoothed it away. "I don't deserve you or your love."

"Yes, you do. You're a wonderful man, strong and caring, honest, dependable. Don't you talk against yourself. Not around me. You're everything I've ever wanted."

"I love you more than I ever dreamed it was possible to love another person."

"Oh, Giff." She shifted until she was in his arms, held tightly, exactly where she'd been wanting to be during the long, lonely weeks since they'd parted. "I love you so much."

He kissed her, gently, thoroughly. "I don't have anything to offer you. I've got a mountain of debts and this job you hate."

"I don't care. The bills will get paid. You love your work, and you're good at it. I can live with that. As long as we're together."

His hand caressed her hair almost reverently, wondering if this was really happening. "I don't know what kind of a husband I'll make . . ."

She smiled at him through damp eyes. "You'll make a wonderful husband."

"Or what kind of father." He moved his hand down and pressed it to her belly. "Were you not going to tell me?"

Surprise jumped into her eyes, followed by suspicion. "Nikki. It had to be Nikki. She had no right to—"

His hands on her tightened. "She had every right. She loves you and she wants you to be happy."

Roxie's shoulders drooped. "If you came back because of the baby, you can leave again. We can manage just fine without you."

He wouldn't let her pull away. "I came back because Nikki convinced me that *you* loved me. I still can't believe it."

Warily, she looked at him, wanting to believe.

"Well, do you, really?" he asked. "For all time, unconditionally?"

"Yes."

"That's how I love you, too. And our baby." Giff pulled her close, feeling as if he held the world in his arms. "Oh, Roxie, you can't know how much I've always wanted a family of my own. I . . . I was just afraid to say it out loud, afraid it would never come true."

She burrowed into his neck, then her mouth sought his. Lord, how she'd missed this, missed kissing him, holding him. "You're all right about the baby then? I want you to know I didn't plan this, but I want this baby with all my heart."

"So do I." He smiled into her eyes. "No more tears. Let's get married. Tomorrow. Wait. How about today?"

"This seems a little sudden, Mr. Jacobs. Oh, I guess I have to get used to calling you Jake Garrison."

"You can call me anything, just don't leave me."

"You can count on that."

He sighed as a few questions begged for answers. "What about the Eagle's Nest? And where we'll live? I don't know if I could get a transfer to the Scottsdale Police Department."

"You don't have to. I don't mind moving to Tucson. And as for the restaurant, Trevor's offered to buy it."

"Hey," he said, grinning. "Old Trev's coming through again."

"It looks that way. Maybe we could get married at Nikki and Adam's place. And we could ask Trevor and my mother. Of course, your brother and his family, and—"

"Whoa! How about we elope? I don't like crowds."

Roxie sighed as she nuzzled her cheek along his beard, loving the feel of him. "Actually, I don't care where or when. As long as it's soon.'' And she raised her face for his kiss.

After all the years of loneliness, at last she had her family, Roxie thought as she gave herself up to the wonder of Giff's kiss.

* * * * *

COMING NEXT MONTH

#607 LOVING EVANGELINE—Linda Howard

No one had ever dared to cross American Hero Robert Cannon, until someone began stealing classified information from his company—a situation that Robert intended to remedy himself. But when the trail led to beautiful Evie Shaw, Robert found both his resolve—and his heart—melting fast.

#608 A VERY CONVENIENT MARRIAGE—
Dallas Schulze *Family Ties*

Sam Walker and Nikki Beauvisage got along like water and oil. So neither was too happy about having to get married! But though their vows were just a charade, they quickly found their roles as husband and wife a little too easy to play....

#609 REGARDING REMY—Marilyn Pappano
Southern Knights

Wounded Special Agent Remy Sinclair needed some down-home TLC, and nurse Susannah Duncan seemed like the perfect candidate. Almost *too* perfect. And before long, Remy had to wonder if his tantalizing angel of mercy had come to help—or harm.

#610 SURROGATE DAD—Marion Smith Collins

Luke Quinlan had noticed sexy next-door neighbor Alexandra Prescott long before her son urged him into action. But she considered him too straitlaced for her tastes—until trouble visited her door. Then Alexandra experienced firsthand Luke's fierce protectiveness—and unquenchable desire.

#611 NOT HIS WIFE—Sally Tyler Hayes

She'd loved him forever, but Shelly Wilkerson knew Brian Sandelle would never be hers. To him, she would always be just a friend. But when someone began threatening Shelly, Brian became a man impassioned, both in his pursuit to save her life—and his desire to claim her heart.

#612 GEORGIA ON MY MIND—Clara Wimberly

He'd sworn he would never return home, but Cord Jamison had to find his sister's killer. Soon, solving the small-town scandal became the least of his worries when Cord came face-to-face with ex-love Georgia Ashley, the woman whose memory still haunted his dreams.

MILLION DOLLAR SWEEPSTAKES (III)

No purchase necessary. To enter, follow the directions published. Method of entry may vary. For eligibility, entries must be received no later than March 31, 1996. No liability is assumed for printing errors, lost, late or misdirected entries. Odds of winning are determined by the number of eligible entries distributed and received. Prizewinners will be determined no later than June 30, 1996.

Sweepstakes open to residents of the U.S. (except Puerto Rico), Canada, Europe and Taiwan who are 18 years of age or older. All applicable laws and regulations apply. Sweepstakes offer void wherever prohibited by law. Values of all prizes are in U.S. currency. This sweepstakes is presented by Torstar Corp., its subsidiaries and affiliates, in conjunction with book, merchandise and/or product offerings. For a copy of the Official Rules send a self-addressed, stamped envelope (WA residents need not affix return postage) to: MILLION DOLLAR SWEEPSTAKES (III) Rules, P.O. Box 4573, Blair, NE 68009, USA.

EXTRA BONUS PRIZE DRAWING

No purchase necessary. The Extra Bonus Prize will be awarded in a random drawing to be conducted no later than 5/30/96 from among all entries received. To qualify, entries must be received by 3/31/96 and comply with published directions. Drawing open to residents of the U.S. (except Puerto Rico), Canada, Europe and Taiwan who are 18 years of age or older. All applicable laws and regulations apply; offer void wherever prohibited by law. Odds of winning are dependent upon number of eligibile entries received. Prize is valued in U.S. currency. The offer is presented by Torstar Corp., its subsidiaries and affiliates in conjunction with book, merchandise and/or product offering. For a copy of the Official Rules governing this sweepstakes, send a self-addressed, stamped envelope (WA residents need not affix return postage) to: Extra Bonus Prize Drawing Rules, P.O. Box 4590, Blair, NE 68009, USA.

SWP-S1194

JINGLE BELLS, WEDDING BELLS:
Silhouette's Christmas Collection for 1994

Christmas Wish List

*To beat the crowds at the malls and get the perfect present for *everyone,* even that snoopy Mrs. Smith next door!

*To get through the holiday parties without running my panty hose.

*To bake cookies, decorate the house and serve the perfect Christmas dinner—just like the women in all those magazines.

*To sit down, curl up and read my Silhouette Christmas stories!

Join *New York Times* bestselling author Nora Roberts, along with popular writers Barbara Boswell, Myrna Temte and Elizabeth August, as we celebrate the joys of Christmas—and the magic of marriage—with

JINGLE BELLS, WEDDING BELLS

Silhouette's Christmas Collection for 1994.

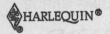 HARLEQUIN®

The movie event of the season can be the reading event of the year!

Lights... The lights go on in October when CBS presents Harlequin/Silhouette Sunday Matinee Movies. These four movies are based on bestselling Harlequin and Silhouette novels.

Camera... As the cameras roll, be the first to read the original novels the movies are based on!

Action... Through this offer, you can have these books sent directly to you! Just fill in the order form below and you could be reading the books...before the movie!

48288-4	Treacherous Beauties by Cheryl Emerson	
	$3.99 U.S./$4.50 CAN.	☐
83305-9	Fantasy Man by Sharon Green	
	$3.99 U.S./$4.50 CAN.	☐
48289-2	A Change of Place by Tracy Sinclair	
	$3.99 U.S./$4.50CAN.	☐
83306-7	Another Woman by Margot Dalton	
	$3.99 U.S./$4.50 CAN.	☐

TOTAL AMOUNT $ _____
POSTAGE & HANDLING $ _____
($1.00 for one book, 50¢ for each additional)
APPLICABLE TAXES* $ _____
<u>**TOTAL PAYABLE**</u> $ _____
(check or money order—please do not send cash)

To order, complete this form and send it, along with a check or money order for the total above, payable to Harlequin Books, to: In the U.S.: 3010 Walden Avenue, P.O. Box 9047, Buffalo, NY 14269-9047; In Canada: P.O. Box 613, Fort Erie, Ontario, L2A 5X3.

Name: _____

Address: _____ City: _____

State/Prov.: _____ Zip/Postal Code: _____

*New York residents remit applicable sales taxes.
 Canadian residents remit applicable GST and provincial taxes.

CBSPR

"HOORAY FOR HOLLYWOOD" SWEEPSTAKES

HERE'S HOW THE SWEEPSTAKES WORKS

OFFICIAL RULES — NO PURCHASE NECESSARY

To enter, complete an Official Entry Form or hand print on a 3" x 5" card the words "HOORAY FOR HOLLYWOOD", your name and address and mail your entry in the pre-addressed envelope (if provided) or to: "Hooray for Hollywood" Sweepstakes, P.O. Box 9076, Buffalo, NY 14269-9076 or "Hooray for Hollywood" Sweepstakes, P.O. Box 637, Fort Erie, Ontario L2A 5X3. Entries must be sent via First Class Mail and be received no later than 12/31/94. No liability is assumed for lost, late or misdirected mail.

Winners will be selected in random drawings to be conducted no later than January 31, 1995 from all eligible entries received.

Grand Prize: A 7-day/6-night trip for 2 to Los Angeles, CA including round trip air transportation from commercial airport nearest winner's residence, accommodations at the Regent Beverly Wilshire Hotel, free rental car, and $1,000 spending money. (Approximate prize value which will vary dependent upon winner's residence: $5,400.00 U.S.); 500 Second Prizes: A pair of "Hollywood Star" sunglasses (prize value: $9.95 U.S. each). Winner selection is under the supervision of D.L. Blair, Inc., an independent judging organization, whose decisions are final. Grand Prize travelers must sign and return a release of liability prior to traveling. Trip must be taken by 2/1/96 and is subject to airline schedules and accommodations availability.

Sweepstakes offer is open to residents of the U.S. (except Puerto Rico) and Canada who are 18 years of age or older, except employees and immediate family members of Harlequin Enterprises, Ltd., its affiliates, subsidiaries, and all agencies, entities or persons connected with the use, marketing or conduct of this sweepstakes. All federal, state, provincial, municipal and local laws apply. Offer void wherever prohibited by law. Taxes and/or duties are the sole responsibility of the winners. Any litigation within the province of Quebec respecting the conduct and awarding of prizes may be submitted to the Regie des loteries et courses du Quebec. All prizes will be awarded; winners will be notified by mail. No substitution of prizes are permitted. Odds of winning are dependent upon the number of eligible entries received.

Potential grand prize winner must sign and return an Affidavit of Eligibility within 30 days of notification. In the event of non-compliance within this time period, prize may be awarded to an alternate winner. Prize notification returned as undeliverable may result in the awarding of prize to an alternate winner. By acceptance of their prize, winners consent to use of their names, photographs, or likenesses for purpose of advertising, trade and promotion on behalf of Harlequin Enterprises, Ltd., without further compensation unless prohibited by law. A Canadian winner must correctly answer an arithmetical skill-testing question in order to be awarded the prize.

For a list of winners (available after 2/28/95), send a separate stamped, self-addressed envelope to: Hooray for Hollywood Sweepstakes 3252 Winners, P.O. Box 4200, Blair, NE 68009.

CBSRLS

OFFICIAL ENTRY COUPON

"Hooray for Hollywood"
SWEEPSTAKES!

Yes, I'd love to win the Grand Prize — a vacation in Hollywood —
or one of 500 pairs of "sunglasses of the stars"! Please enter me
in the sweepstakes!

This entry must be received by December 31, 1994.
Winners will be notified by January 31, 1995.

Name _____

Address _____ Apt. _____

City _____

State/Prov. _____ Zip/Postal Code _____

Daytime phone number _____
(area code)

Mail all entries to: Hooray for Hollywood Sweepstakes,
P.O. Box 9076, Buffalo, NY 14269-9076.
In Canada, mail to: Hooray for Hollywood Sweepstakes,
P.O. Box 637, Fort Erie, ON L2A 5X3.

KCH

OFFICIAL ENTRY COUPON

"Hooray for Hollywood"
SWEEPSTAKES!

Yes, I'd love to win the Grand Prize — a vacation in Hollywood —
or one of 500 pairs of "sunglasses of the stars"! Please enter me
in the sweepstakes!

This entry must be received by December 31, 1994.
Winners will be notified by January 31, 1995.

Name _____

Address _____ Apt. _____

City _____

State/Prov. _____ Zip/Postal Code _____

Daytime phone number _____
(area code)

Mail all entries to: Hooray for Hollywood Sweepstakes,
P.O. Box 9076, Buffalo, NY 14269-9076.
In Canada, mail to: Hooray for Hollywood Sweepstakes,
P.O. Box 637, Fort Erie, ON L2A 5X3.

KCH